Henry Hamlet's Heart

Henry Hamlet's Heart

Rhiannon Wilde

Charlesbridge
TEEN

Published by Charlesbridge Teen,
an imprint of Charlesbridge Publishing
9 Galen Street
Watertown, MA 02472
(617) 926-0329
www.charlesbridge.com

First published by University of Queensland Press, 2021;
excerpts from *Letters to a Young Poet* by Rainer Maria Rilke,
translated by Stephen Mitchell, translation copyright © 1984 by Stephen Mitchell.
Used by permission of Random House, an imprint and division of
Penguin Random House LLC. All rights reserved.

Library of Congress Cataloging-in-Publication Data
Names: Wilde, Rhiannon, author.
Title: Henry Hamlet's heart / by Rhiannon Wilde.
Description: Watertown, MA: Charlesbridge Publishing, 2022. | "First published 2021 by
    University of Queensland Press." | Audience: Ages 14 and up. | Audience: Grades 10–12. |
Summary: Despite their differences, soon to be eighteen-year-olds Henry Hamlet and Lennon
    Crane have been best friends for most of their lives, but in their senior year at Northolm
    Grammar School for Boys in Brisbane, Australia, Henry realizes he is in love with Len.
Identifiers: LCCN 2021053531 (print) | LCCN 2021053532 (ebook) | ISBN 9781623543693
    (hardcover) | ISBN 9781632893475 (ebook)
Subjects: LCSH: Gay teenagers—Juvenile fiction. | Best friends—Juvenile fiction. | Interpersonal
    relations—Juvenile fiction. | High schools—Australia—Brisbane (Qld.)—Juvenile fiction.
    | Brisbane (Qld.)—Juvenile fiction. | CYAC: Gays—Fiction. | Best friends—Fiction.
    | Friendship—Fiction. | Interpersonal relations—Fiction. | High schools—Fiction. |
    Schools—Fiction. | LCGFT: Gay fiction. | Psychological fiction. | Romance fiction.
Classification: LCC PZ7.1.W5335 He 2022 (print) | LCC PZ7.1.W5335 (ebook) |
    DDC 823.92 [Fic]—dc23/eng/20211129 LC record available at https://lccn.loc.
    gov/2021053531 LC ebook record available at https://lccn.loc.gov/2021053532

Printed in the United States of America
(hc) 10 9 8 7 6 5 4 3 2 1

Jacket illustrations done in digital media
Display type set in Black Mountage by Sarid Ezra and Uncle Edward by Hanoded
Text type set in Adobe Jensen Pro by Robert Slimbach and Brandon Text by
    Hannes von Döhren
Printed by Berryville Graphics in Berryville, Virginia, USA
Production supervision by Jennifer Most Delaney
Typeset by Sarah Richards Taylor
Designed by Jon Simeon

For James

You were always there. There was a time, remember, that we even insisted on combining our names. What's the word for that? Memories that aren't just yours—glittering, gone.

Maybe it started then, soft and secret. Maybe it was later, after lying dormant like the flu. Or maybe it never started. They say time isn't linear, right? There's not always a clear beginning, especially for the things that end us.

I

Maybe we were always two pieces of the same thing, but cut in half. Or with a bridge across them.

never

Maybe it started because of your face, so much more carefully made than other faces. Obliviously fine-boned beautiful. The cheekbones. The Cupid's bow on your lips. Your *lips*—it might have been them.

meant

It could have been my mother, because she said that when you smiled it was like the sun. Or the time you fell and broke a tooth, and I felt something—watching you cry—and thought, *it's the worst idea in the world, this.*

to

The way you speak may have played its part. Uptalking confidence that so quickly bleeds to fear, the kick at the end of your sentences.

want

Maybe it happened because you think nothing scares me, when really it's nothing but

you.

Part I

Ultimately, and precisely in the deepest and most important matters, we are unspeakably alone; and many things must happen, many things must go right, a whole constellation of events must be fulfilled, for one human being to successfully advise or help another.

—Rainer Maria Rilke

1

"Gran, are you a lespian?" my brother asks at Sunday brunch. Hamish is twelve years younger than me, more Tasmanian devil than boy.

Mum and I exchange glances, but Gran just chucks him under the chin.

We're sitting in the winter sun at the café that's been at the end of our street since forever. I look over Mum's right shoulder and our house stares back at me, bright yellow with mismatched flowery leadlight windows.

"Not quite, darling one," Gran says to Ham in her lilting Irish accent. "The term is 'bisexual.' Right, Henry?"

I feel my cheeks redden. I love Gran, and I'm thrilled for her and Marigold, but there are some images you don't want in your head just as the waiter delivers your eggs benny.

"I think so, yeah."

"What does that mean?" Ham touches her cheek with his fat little palm.

"That I loved your pa, and now I love Marigold."

"I love Goldie too," Ham says. His little face lights up; Marigold has put in some serious brain-eating-children's-television time. "Does that mean I'm a bike?"

Mum laughs softly.

I look at my dad; he's staring intently into space with a latte half-raised to his lips, probably painting in his head.

"Bi," Gran corrects. She never loses her patience with Ham, which is more than any of the rest of us can say for ourselves.

"You might be," Gran continues, wiping a bit of cake off his temple, "but you'll figure all that out later on."

Ham digests this for a moment, brushing his hair out of his eyes. He's the only one to have inherited Gran's vivid red. "Will I get to live with you and Goldie if I am?"

Sensing that Gran's about to go off on one of her I'm-not-long-for-this-world tangents (she's sixty-eight, just a realist), Mum interrupts by pushing Ham's hot chocolate toward him. "Look, Hambam, three marshmallows!"

He beams and picks one up, distracted by the sugar.

"Mollycoddler," Gran whispers under her breath.

Mum ignores her. "Henry, tell Gran again about your subject award."

At the mention of school, I feel a prickle of anxiety about the impending first day back for term three, which is only a week away.

"Feels a bit grandiose to brag on myself," I tell her. "I'd much rather watch you do it."

Dad grins suddenly, and says, "Oh, don't try for humble now. We've got too many years of contradictory evidence!"

Dad is an artist who hated school, so every time I get even a participation award, he's ridiculously excited.

"Fine." I put my drink down. "I topped my class for English."

"Out of *everyone*," Dad emphasizes, tapping the hinge on his glasses as if to demonstrate intelligence.

My school, Northolm Grammar School for Boys, isn't exactly top tier, more upper-mid. It is still an accomplishment, I suppose. There's pressure that comes with topping a subject though. An expectation that I have my shit together; that I know what I'm doing. I guess it does kind of look like that from the outside. Now that it's the last semester of year twelve, the pressure's only going to get worse.

I don't mention any of this at brunch; the fact I have no idea what I want to do with my life is my sweaty secret to carry around.

"That's lovely, darling," Gran says distractedly, punching out a text (probably to Marigold) on her ancient Nokia.

"Mum!" my own mother admonishes. "No mobiles at family brunch—you know the rules."

Dad slowly slides his phone off the table and into his pocket.

"I am sorry, *Sybilla*," Gran enunciates the dreaded full name with knife-like precision. "I didn't realize somebody had died and made you the warden."

"Oh, pl—"

"Let her text," I placate. "She's in love."

Mum shakes her head; Gran continues texting with one hand and eating her bagel with the other.

Ham suddenly drops the marshmallow he's been licking and jumps up. "Len! Len! Len!"

"Hey, little man," says a smooth voice.

I turn to see my best friend, Lennon Cane, gold-topped head caught in the sun and film camera looped around his neck.

Ham launches himself at Len, who catches him neatly. Len waves at the rest of the table. "Everyone."

"John Lennon!" Dad beams.

"Christ," I say in mock-indignation. "They'll let anyone in here."

"Obviously," Len returns, gesturing to me.

I wind up my middle finger at him.

Len's been my best friend so long neither of us can remember why; it just is. He snaps a picture of Ham's marshmallow massacre.

"Lovely to see you, Lennon darling," Gran says. Evidently, Len is more motivation to break from the Marigold bubble than I am. "I hope you're keeping well. How is your sister?"

"She's good." Len runs a hand through his hair where it's longer and slicked back at the top. "Freaking out a bit because she's starting uni mid-year."

"I'll bet," says Gran, sipping her cappuccino noisily.

"Lacey's too good for a formal education," Dad laments. "You can't teach creativity."

"She wants to be a *politician*, Dad." I huff. "Some stuff can be taught."

"You look snazzy!" Mum compliments Len as a distraction.

He's wearing a green printed shirt that Gran would call "zany" and black suit pants rolled up over paisley socks and Doc Martens Oxfords. Let us simply say that of the two of us, Len is the one you would classify as having style. Our friend Emilia says he's like an eighties song—"pretty but with dark themes."

"Not as snazzy as you, Billie," he teases.

"Suck-up," I cough.

Mum swats my arm.

My own style roughly translates to sweeping my untidy brown hair across my forehead and throwing on whatever's clean. Song-wise, I am the 2000s. Know thyself, etc.

"You staying to eat with us?" I ask.

Len shakes his head. "I'm helping Lacey pack. Just needed a coffee break."

I look around the table: Mum's glaring at Gran, who's still texting; Dad's lost in the distance again, painting another imaginary scene; and Ham's pulled apart his last marshmallow, which he's now spreading on the tabletop.

"Need any help?" I ask meaningfully.

"N—" Len notices my pleading look and arranges his face into an expression of exaggerated gratitude. "Yeah. We actually—desperately—do."

His coffee order is called.

"Mum," I ask quickly, "can I go help Lacey pack for uni?"

She looks slightly miffed at being left alone with Gran, but she can't say no to Len. No one can. "Oh, all right. I'll see you later."

"How come he's allowed to leave?" Gran demands.

"Oh, you're listening now, are you?" Mum returns. "I thought you only communicated in smiley faces these days."

"You know what, dear? Whenever I wonder what purgatory must be like, I think of you screeching 'family time!' at me on a loop until I saw off both my ears."

"Mum! That's a horrible thing to say."

Len muffles a laugh and we leave them to it, ruffling Ham's hair on the way out until he squeals happily.

We weave the familiar streets between our houses quickly, Brisbane suburbia, blurred blue sky, and bald jacaranda trees around us. It's pretty, but there's a sameness to the neat rows of Queenslanders that sometimes feels as close as the constant humidity.

Len's house is an immaculate white colonial that's set back off the main road by a heavy concrete fence. He enters the security code and the gate swings open into the tree-lined yard. We clatter up the steps to the latticed veranda that hugs the house front, the only original feature besides the gnarled wooden floors.

Len's mum, Sarah, inherited this place. There's a pool and a tennis court, and a beaten brass plaque by the door that reads "Scott's Corner."

Sarah died, suddenly, two years ago. Cancer. It was quick and aggressive, and I didn't understand how it could happen. I didn't get how she could be here, Sarah Scott with her Len-eyes and gold tumble of hair, and then just *end* in an awful unwilling goodbye that took just a few weeks and also everything.

"Scotland Yard," Len says sarcastically now, pushing the door open.

When we step inside, it's white on white, save for a giant black chandelier and a framed photo: Len's dad, John, in his high school football uniform glory days.

The man himself is sitting directly underneath it, drinking coffee from a glass cup and reading the paper. His pale eyes flick up to meet mine briefly.

Visually, John is nothing like Len. He's all sharp cheeks and slicked chocolate-and-gray hair—kind of Byronic hero-ish. Dark and intense. A lot.

I look back to Len, who's already at the top of the giant staircase, his gold brow furrowed. He motions for me to follow.

Lacey pops her head around the door to her room, eyes bright. She's only eighteen months older than us, but she could be thirty with her severe bob and endlessly superior expression.

"What are you doing here, Henri Antoinette? Don't you have anything better to do?"

"It would appear not."

"I saved him from family brunch," Len explains, handing Lacey her coffee.

"Oh lord, the Billie and Iris variety show." She takes a sip of her drink and tilts her head back. "I'm going to miss this. Apparently all the coffee in Victoria tastes like a burnt shoe."

Len looks at her sardonically. "Where did you hear that?"

"I read it somewhere."

"Isn't Melbourne meant to be, like, the coffee capital of the country?" I ask.

Lacey glares at us. "Just because I'm moving to another city doesn't mean I accept its supremacy, okay? I'm in mourning."

"You're only going there to study politics and become prime minister," Len reminds her. "Not relocate for good. That I won't accept."

She laughs briefly and then flicks her eyes (the same shape and sunstruck steel color as Len's) over to me. "Right. Hamlet, you're useless at heavy lifting, yes?"

"Yes."

"And Lennon, you are similarly afflicted."

He looks affronted. "I can lift."

She ignores him. "I'm thinking, the two of you can pack this stuff"—she gestures vaguely to the haphazard piles of possessions strewn across the room—"into bags, and I'll start putting the big stuff into boxes."

"Whatever you say, Sarge," Len says under his breath.

———

It's past five by the time we finish. Lacey surveys our handiwork and, sufficiently impressed, asks if we fancy attending a party.

"Whose party?" I ask.

"Not whose party. The Party."

"The Party as in *the* Party?"

"The Party" is the honorary title given to the back-to-school event someone usually throws at the start of each term. It's generally held a full week before the holidays actually end to ensure maximum recovery time. (Last year, the entire football team got suspended for streaking down Queen Street and posting it online.)

Naturally, as school captain, I'm above such things. And, naturally, I wasn't invited.

"I don't know. I wasn't gonna go," Len says.

I turn to him in outrage. "You got an invite?"

He tips his head to one side semi-guiltily.

"Only because Sean Heathcote's little brother is hosting," Lacey puts in.

I guess Henry Hamlet isn't exactly someone who screams "party." He's more the type to be seen screaming while running *away* from a party, but still.

(Did I not get an invite because I speak in third person too much? Do people *know*?)

"We can go, if you want," Len offers.

"Yeah!" Lacey says. "You can be my plus-one. As long as you expressly state it's a pity date to anyone you speak to."

"What an offer."

She laughs. "I'm kidding. You're cute enough, since you stopped being an acne factory. Too uptight for my liking, but defs a solid seven." Lacey pats me on the back.

I shake my head. "My life's ambition is complete—I'm a solid seven. I may as well just check out now."

Len watches our exchange with amusement.

Then Lacey stands up, batting dust off the knees of her jeans. "I'm leaving in twenty minutes if you guys want a ride."

I look at Len helplessly.

He shrugs. "It could be fun."

He would say that. He who slips in and out of social situations like jumpers, without lying awake half the night afterwards obsessing over everything he said.

"Fun like last time?" I ask.

Len smirks, remembering. "Touché. Not many people can say they've vomited into a container holding somebody's dog's ashes."

"It was the only available vessel!" I cry. "God, I'm definitely going to hell for that, aren't I?"

"Yep."

"You're the one who said tequila wouldn't make me sick, and helped clean up Lucky's entire top layer. We're going to hell together."

He rolls his eyes. "So are we going tonight, or what?"

I want to say no, but something stops me. It *is* the last semester of our misspent youth. The last clump of weeks before we leave high school's sweaty bosom behind and enter the World.

"Fine. Let's go."

"You sure?"

"Yeah."

Len eyes me cautiously. "No tequila."

We make our way back down the ornate staircase. His dad's gone out.

It's beautiful, don't get me wrong, but there's something about the Cane house that reminds me of Queensland summer. Too-bright light and then showers that flood you before you notice it was even raining.

———

The Party is in full swing by the time we pull up outside the sprawling Hamilton house in Lacey's car. Laughter and music twist together on the wind and panic rises in my chest. Len puts his hand on my shoulder, more to force me forward than anything.

Sam Heathcote greets us in the doorway. "Lacey Cane!" he cheers. "Little Cane! And . . ."

He looks me up and down. I wait for him to add "and friend" or something, but he floats away instead. We stare after him.

"Off to a roaring start, then," I grumble.

"At least he didn't kick you out!" Lacey says, hoisting a six-pack of beer, as well as one of something stronger, inside.

Len looks like he's trying not to laugh. I elbow him in the ribs.

Lacey disappears into a group of squealing St. Adele's girls. She's got a silk dress on that I remember Sarah wearing. Len watches her and chews his lip.

We stand in the foyer for a bit, searching for people we know among the dozens of teenagers clustered around clutching bottles. It's an impressive house—all high ceilings and polished concrete. I can see a deck out the back with views across the river to tall tea-light buildings beyond.

"Dude, you're sweating," Len says. "Calm your farm."

"I'm just excited to be here," I respond, with affected cheer.

"You look high."

"High on *life*."

"You are so not drinking tonight, if this is what you're like now."

"I most certainly will be," I protest. History of being the biggest lightweight to ever live aside, there is no way I'm going to get through tonight without some assistance. I tell him as much.

Len rolls his eyes. "You'll be fine, Hamlet. Relax. Try to mingle a bit."

Most of the guys at North call me by my surname, especially since we studied the play last year. Apparently I'm tragic enough that the moniker suits me better than my actual name.

"Mingle." I say it like it's a dirty word.

"Yeah. Meet people. It's a party."

I glance around; several girls are milling nearby, eyeing Len in his tweed jacket and black suit pants and avoiding me in my T-shirt and jeans.

Willa Stacy is hovering with them, staring intently through her curtain of strawberry hair. Len was seeing her for a couple of months, but they split up before the holidays. He eyes her back.

I purse my lips. "Is that what *you're* gonna do?"

"Hmm?"

I wave a hand in front of his face. "Hello? It's me, your sister's invisible plus-one."

"Shut up. I'm gonna go get us a drink, if only so I can monitor what goes into yours. Lacey'll kill you if you get sick in her car before a three-day drive."

"Fine. I'll just be here, looking for cats to befriend." I'm only half joking.

"Mingle," he commands, and he disappears into the crowd.

Willa follows him in a blur of thigh boots, so I know not to expect his speedy return.

Needing to do something with my hands, I text Emilia.

@ The Party. Torture. Tell me ur not busy.

She replies instantly. **WHAT? Take mental snapshots, pls! Studying, sorry! There with u in spirit.**

Ems is the only person I know who could possibly find something to study during the holidays. We went to primary school together, and I don't think I've seen her without a book in her hand since the day we met, on the playground in year two.

I snap my phone shut. Emilia hates school parties even more than I do, but I feel deflated nonetheless. Why did I agree to this? There aren't even any cats.

I make my way into the living room toward a high-backed armchair beside the window. I sit down to wait for Len, but then I realize I don't know if that's something people do at these things, so I spring up again. (I also don't know *anyone*.)

"Henry?"

I spin around on my heel to see Lily Bassett from debating last year. I grin wide, grateful for the friendly face. "Hiya! How are you?"

(*Hiya?!*)

"I'm well, since we haven't versed you guys yet this year." She smiles too.

I laugh awkwardly. "Glad to be of service."

She looks different out of her uniform. She's wearing a sparkly top/dress thing, and red-red lipstick.

"What brings you here?" Lily looks around at the crowd, who are badly dancing while Fall Out Boy asks through the speakers if this is more than I bargained for. (*Yes.*)

"Oh, you know," I say airily. "Last semester of school and all that jazz."

"I'm so jealous you're almost finished. I don't know how I'll do another year."

(I don't know how I'll *leave*.)

I spread my arms, gesturing around us. "Yep. I'll soon be sitting drinking wine in a courtyard somewhere, far too worldly for things like this. So I thought I'd put in an appearance last minute."

Lily makes a knowing face. "Did you not get invited?"

I drop my arms. "That obvious?"

We laugh.

"I didn't either," she confesses. "My sister dragged me along." She points to one of the girls in Lacey's group.

Len comes back with our drinks: one of the clear drinks Lacey brought for him, and half a beer in a cup for me.

He glances at Lily and smiles slowly with recognition. "Hey."

Lily's cheeks go pink. Great. The Len Effect. I take my drink from him angrily.

"I'm just gonna . . ." He gestures to where Willa is waiting by the French doors that lead to the deck.

"I haven't seen outside," Lily says.

"You guys should come," Len responds easily.

"I'm fine here," I say.

"Okay," Lily says, and follows after Len.

I glare at them both. Neither seems to notice.

I flop back into the chair and go through the five stages of the Len Effect—jealousy, rage, irritation, resignation, and acceptance—in quick succession. He's always been good with the ladies; I've always been . . . not. It's been that way for so long that I barely register it anymore, but tonight I feel particularly needled.

A few people look at me, briefly, as they walk past. I think about striking up a conversation, but for some reason I just . . . can't. Crowds always make me feel even more alone than I do by myself.

I brood for a bit about the general state of my life, before I get tired of myself and down my drink in one.

At first I don't think it's worked, but then a few songs later the brick wall in my chest starts to lift. I even manage to wave at a few strangers.

I decide to go in search of more.

I walk into the kitchen, where there are intimidating bottles of spirits lined up along the bench. I steer clear of those in favor of the smaller bottles in a cooler against the wall. I try to find Lacey's drinks but give up and grab two at random—blue fizzy vodka something or other. They look sugary enough. I unscrew the cap of one and take an exploratory sip.

Not bad. A bit like cordial, spliced with battery acid. I drink some more. By the time I finish the first bottle, I don't even notice the aftertaste.

A little later, after making small talk with two guys from my drama class, I've drunk three vodka concoctions. I bump into Ged, and I'm so relieved Len and I aren't the only ones from our group here tonight I nearly hug him.

"Henry Hamlet, as I live and breathe!"

Ged looks like a pro wrestler, and we have next to nothing in common, but he's a strangely solid friend. He forced the entire football team to vote for me for school captain.

"Hey, man," I slur, buzzed enough not to see looping my

arm around his neck as the invasion of personal space it one hundred percent is.

Ged untangles my arm, sniffing my sugar-blue breath. "Whoa there, my little tiger-peach. Is that alcohol I smell?"

I nod suavely. "I'm being a bright young thing for one night only. They call me Cool Hand Henry."

"Do they really?" He looks at the bottle I'm holding. "My mum drinks those."

I try to scowl at him. He's blurry. "They're fun. I'm being fun."

"Fun Hamlet—I'm here for that. You do look a bit less stick-up-the-arse."

"Thanksh."

"Shall we find some of the real stuff, fun Hamlet?"

Ged grabs a bottle off the table and pours two glasses of sticky amber liquid. "Bottom's up."

I knock back what tastes like congealed bleach. "Shots!" somebody behind us calls.

A group forms and it escalates before I have a chance to think about it. Ged turns it into a game that he calls "scull." I throw myself into it and manage to keep up, drinking several tiny glasses, the burn swirling through my chest like smoke. I inwardly congratulate myself—what was I even worried about? I am a champion at this. A hero among men. A—

I suddenly, desperately, need the bathroom. I farewell Ged and make my way upstairs.

When I'm washing my hands afterwards, they don't feel like my hands. I dry them on my jeans and look in the mirror.

My face is different too. It warps and bends. The walls seem to be moving closer to me—I blink my eyes, trying to clear them, which only makes it worse.

I stumble out of the door and down the stairs into the living room. I can just make out Len's familiar shoes dangling off the end of the couch: black vintage Converse he got from a second-hand shop for $5.99.

"Hamlet!" he calls, then pauses. "Why do you look weird?"

"Nobody panic, but I think I may be drunk," I announce, right before I projectile the entire contents of my stomach onto the floor. It splashes onto Willa's thigh boots. Not all the way up, but it's a close call.

"Oh my god!" she screeches. "What is your *problem?*"

"I'b thorry," I splutter weakly.

"Geez, Henry," Lily says. "You good?"

I wipe my mouth with the back of my hand. The girls rush away. I feel so terrible I don't even care that everyone's staring.

Len sits up, eyes narrowing with concern. "What'd you have? Not tequila again, surely?"

I shake my head weakly. "Vodka. And something else, I think. They were pretty."

"Hamlet." He looks angry.

"They didn't feel like anything at first!"

"Yeah, well, vodka's a cruel mistress. Come on, we'll go."

"I just . . . need to lie down for a second."

He frowns, but obediently kicks off the couple kissing at the other end of the couch.

When I'm sure my stomach is settled (for now) I lie down, shifting uncomfortably on the too-short couch. Why do rich people always buy such impractical furniture? I adjust my pillow, pushing it up against Len's leg.

"Are you all right?" He wriggles underneath me. "You smell like blueberry-flavored manure. Let me up."

My vision is starting to fuzz at the edges. I close my eyes against the pounding in my ears.

"God, your head is heavy," Len says. "No wonder—it's full of rocks."

I ignore him. It's warm here, and the room can't spin if I can't see it.

"What am I meant to do, then?"

"Watch for opportunistic people who might be dick-on-the-face drawers," I mumble.

He huffs in reply.

"I'm sorry I ruined your night." My words slur together.

"You're a public menace." Len shifts again.

"Joke's on you, then." I yawn. "That I'm your number-one friend."

"More like a compulsory full-time job, at this point."

I know he's trying to irritate me into moving. I start to think of a snarky reply, but everything goes dark.

We'd never say it, but we look out for one another—especially since Sarah. Except for right now, apparently, because in my half-asleep state I can feel him using Lacey's kohl pencil to draw a meticulously detailed dick and balls down the right side of my face.

2

When I come to in the morning I'm in my own bed, looking over at Len's addition to the decor of my room. Collaged newspaper letters shellacked and stuck to the far wall that spell out: DON'T STAY IN BED.

(Don't tell me what to do.)

My room is my favorite part of the house. It's in the attic and is painted a dark blue color Dad mixed when I was nine. The window takes up one wall and makes a postcard picture of Brisbane if you stare at it and squint.

The wall directly next to my bed houses all my books. *The Old Man and the Sea* from my Hemingway phase, weird crime thrillers, obscure artist biographies from Dad, Gran's old *Selected Poems of Keats*, well-loved books from childhood with their worn rainbow spines, Emilia's *Twilight* I keep forgetting to give back: a tomb of past Henrys, stacked together in no real organized order. I kind of read everything.

I sit up slowly because my head feels like it's inside a nutcracker. Someone's been in under the cover of darkness and replaced all my blood with sand. My stomach roils, and I run to the bathroom, but nothing comes up.

Everything in there must have deposited onto . . . Willa.

Shame trickles down my back. Shame and sweat—that would be the name of my eau de toilette.

I stumble back to bed and throw a hand over my face. Sunlight streams through the window, baking my face insistently. Brisbane's great and everything, but sometimes I wouldn't mind more mornings without chipper lemony warmth shining in and judging me. A bleak sky would be more fitting today.

I check my phone. Two texts from Emilia asking what happened last night. Then a photo of me passed out in my driveway from Len, and another from Lacey of them rolling me to the door. There's definitely balls on my face. She's captioned it: **best going away present x**

I groan and cover my face.

There's a knock on my door, and I groan again.

"My son, the drunkard," my mum sings, as she swings the door open.

I part my fingers sheepishly. "Am I grounded?"

Mum snorts. "Today will be punishment enough. Plus, I lived through the eighties. Grounding you for pretty much anything would be hypocritical. Though, I do think you need to work on your concept of moderation."

I wince.

She sits on the edge of my bed. "I was worried for a minute that I'd have to take you into work to pump your stomach, but Len said you'd already taken care of that."

Mum's an obstetrician at the local hospital. I screw up my face at the thought of her having to explain that one to her boss.

She laughs and pats me on the leg. "Hungry? Dad made pancakes."

I consider the state of my stomach: tolerable—mostly sick

in an empty way. It's my head that's killing me; it feels like it might fall off.

"Yeah. Just need some Tylenol first."

Mum stands up. "I'll get it." She pauses in the doorway and looks back at me.

"What?" I ask.

"I'm just making sure I remember how you look right now, so I can think of it next time you try to claim the moral high ground with me."

I throw my pillow after her.

Once I'm dressed and medicated, I make my way downstairs, squinting against the daylight like a vampire. Dad's standing at the stove completely covered in green paint; he cracks up as soon as he sees me. Big, loud guffaws.

He keeps doing it as he dishes up two pancakes with butter and maple syrup. Ham is sitting on a stool at the island and joins in laughing, confused but committed. I ignore them and start regally assembling a bite with optimum pancake to syrup ratio. It slides down my throat with sickening slowness. *Ergh.* I stop for a second, hand over my mouth.

Dad claps me on the back. "Welcome to adulthood, kiddo."

"So, it starts, not with a bang or a whimper, but with projectile vomit?"

"Pretty much, yeah."

———

I meet Emilia at the café down my street just after eleven for emergency affogato. Len's already inside in his work uniform: white T-shirt and black pants rolled up over his Oxfords and yellow geometric-y printed socks. He managed to persuade the café to keep him on part-time after doing work experience with them in year ten. Another example of the Len Effect.

"You look almost as much of a disgrace as I do," Ems says by way of greeting. She gestures to her outfit: leggings and a faded Killers T-shirt with her hair pushed back by her glasses.

Emilia looks like a young Kate Middleton, all heart-shaped nose, big blue eyes, and billows of dark hair, but soft round the edges. The fact that she's beautiful is something I've always thought of as just a part of her. It's never changed things between us—I mean, I love her madly, but not *that way*. She'd kill me if it were *that way*.

She sits down and steals my newspaper. A waitress Len dated briefly before breaking up with her in record time (even for him) reluctantly takes our order. I get Len's specialty, dubbed the Lethal Weapon (three espresso shots poured over a vanilla pod and a bed of ice cream). Ems gets a chai latte, which I immediately mock.

She holds up a hand. "You don't get to make fun of my beverage today, my friend. Not with your own life choices in such turmoil."

My eyes still feel like someone's rubbed the backs of them with a toupee. "It was hardly a life choice."

"I beg to differ. You chose, and you chose wrong. And you, a pillar of the school community." Her face is mock-stern.

"Har har."

She imitates our old head of primary. "You think doing the alcohol is cool, do you?"

"No, Miss." I put my hand on my heart.

21

"I knew a boy once, about your age, good prospects—he did the alcohol. Thought it would be fun, he said. Just a little sippy time with some mates, he said. Well, would you believe it, once turned into twice, then thrice—*thrice*! Before he knew it, he was addicted."

"To the alcohol." I try to keep a straight face.

It's rare we just act stupid like this anymore, but it used to be our thing.

"The next time I saw him," Ems intones, "I'm sorry to say that he was even engaging in *sins of the flesh.*"

"Surely not, Miss!" I pipe up. "That's us boys' worst nightmare."

We're still laughing when Len comes out with our drinks.

"What are you doing hanging around with this mess?" he asks Ems.

She waves a hand dismissively. "Oh, you know—charity work. Gotta give back, and all that."

I glower at them both over my soupy coffee.

"What even happened?" Emilia asks curiously. "Henry won't tell me."

"Because it's a boring story," I insist.

Len leans against an empty table behind him. He tilts his chin at me, amused. "You look deservedly rough."

I rub my bloodshot right eye. The world is too bright. "Don't know what you mean."

"I turned my back on him for five minutes," he starts, looking at Ems.

"It was longer than that!"

"Five minutes," he continues, "and this prize fool you see before you managed to drink all of Sam Heathcote's *sister's* drinks and be stupid enough to do shots with Ged."

Emilia giggles but pats me on the arm sympathetically. "Oh, Hen."

"He then proceeded to dramatically announce that he was drunk—no shit, Sherlock—and aim his vomplosion all over Willa Stacy's boots."

Ems claps a hand over her mouth, barely muffling peals of laughter.

"I didn't *aim* at her!" I burst out indignantly. "She was just, very regretfully, in the . . . projectile trajectory."

Len chuckles. "She called me this morning to ask where you live so she can send a bill to replace her boots. Sounded very unimpressed."

"Understatement of the year," Emilia says. "She posted something on Facebook last night about the two of you needing to be institutionalized. There was a photo too."

I blanch.

"Don't worry," she assures me. "You can't really tell it's you."

"*Can't really* or *can't?*"

"Relax," Len says. "It's not like the teachers even know what social media is."

"Wait. Did you give her the address?" I ask.

He nods.

"Len!" Ems chides.

"For that place that sells all-weather boots," he says. "She did not find it funny."

I put my face in my hands. "I'll be a social pariah now, won't I?'"

"I think that ship has sailed and crashed already," Len says.

Ems's mouth twists to the side. "Willa's calling you Spew Grant."

"Oh *excellent*. Everyone's gonna think I'm a loser!"

"Nobody at school really cares what Willa thinks, apart

from her minions," Ems says. "Plus, everyone already *knows* you're a loser."

Len chokes back a laugh. Traitors.

"Chin up." Len pats the back of my chair, and heads inside.

I sip my lethal affogato broodingly. It's good, damn him. We watch for a minute as Len serves people, then scoots over to the retro coffee machine.

"It'll blow over," Emilia says.

"Mmm."

I wish I didn't care what people thought as much as I do. I try to put last night out of my mind. Ems is right—each of our schools have upwards of nine hundred students, so there's always a fresh story, and the news cycle is fairly quick.

"I am so not emotionally ready for this term," she says in an obvious attempt to distract me.

"I know. Me either."

"Have you thought more about what you want to do next year?" she asks tentatively. If a subject can still be called "tentative" when it comes up every time you talk to someone.

I press my fingers to my forehead. "I don't know. I still think maybe journalism. Gran's pushing hard for arts."

"Just because that's what she lectures in doesn't mean it's all there is to study," Ems points out.

"Telling her that only makes the pushing more aggressive."

Ems leans her chin on the heel of her hand. "I'm actually shitting it a bit. I have do well on all my assignments if I'm going to get the end of year grades I need. This term feels impossible."

She's wanted to study law forever. She'll get in, no question. I tell her so.

"Your faith in me is unfounded."

"What do you mean? I found it in the primary playground."

"Corny to the level of actual corn."

I stick around after Emilia leaves, pleasantly caffeinated. I watch Len as he works, one lip tucked as he steams milk and swirls it into mugs, each movement careful and precise.

I stay until it's almost closing time, customers tapering off down the gold-licked street until I'm alone, pretending to read the paper. The other staff don't comment; they're used to cleaning up around me.

Len shuts the till and comes over with a takeaway cup in hand.

"Reserve?" he asks. "I don't wanna go home yet."

"Yeah. Okay."

The Reserve is a bush track in the back of the next suburb over. It's a bit Tarzan for me, but it is kind of peaceful.

We walk down my street and to the main road, crossing at the lights. The weather's indecisive, sun spilling on my face, but cutting wind pulling at my jacket.

When we get to the top of the big hill, we stop and look at the rows of pastel-colored Queenslander houses map-spread below. Beyond them the skyline's clear enough to see the whole city dotted on it like an outstretched hand, poking skyscraper fingers up into blue.

Once the path turns to dirt Len walks several meters ahead as usual, stopping to snap pictures and—occasionally—wait for me. The traffic noise is swallowed by gum trees and birds.

The path overlaps with the trees' exposed roots, and I concentrate on my Vans to keep them from twisting out underneath me.

"I've texted her that you had a preexisting, severe stomach issue," Len says when I catch up with him.

I squint at him in slanting green light. "What?"

"Willa. You were worried about your cred, right? So, sorted."

"Not sure 'guy with vom disorder' is that much of an improvement on being a lightweight," I point out.

His eyes crinkle. "Probably not. But at least she's not as pissed off."

"Great. Life's never looked better for me." Len gets a picture of swaying leaves above us.

"You," he pronounces, "need to loosen up a bit."

"Says *you*. I've got fourteen weeks of trying to milk B-pluses into A's coming up, and a low-budget dance to organize. Plus, camp. My soul's probably gonna fragment by the end of it."

"Have actual experiences," Len continues. "Not just in your head all the time."

"*Experiences?*" I raise an eyebrow suggestively.

He shoves my shoulder and walks ahead again before I can get him back. "*Life* experiences, douchebag. Experiences with a capital E."

"I don't really think—"

The toe of my shoe snags on a rogue stick. I throw my arms out and wobble sideways, before crashing down hard and skidding into a ditch.

I lie on my back for a minute, stunned-blinking at clouds I can't fully see.

Len's shoes crunch across dry rocks and appear next to my head. "Genuinely cannot take you anywhere." He holds out my glasses.

"Shut up." I snatch them off him and scrub dirt off my cheek. "Who the hell put that there? It's a hazard! Nature is a hazard."

Len leans down toward me and wraps his fingers around my

forearm. He pulls until I'm upright, with my dust-covered legs scrambling like Bambi.

"I think you'll survive."

"*Barely*. I definitely tasted death for a second."

"That, Hamlet," he grins, the sun hitting his teeth, "is how you know you're alive."

3

The first day back at school arrives too quickly. I snooze my alarm twice, have a shaving-related mishap, and end up leaving twenty minutes late.

My car's still full of holiday takeaway containers when I barrel into the driver's seat at 8:10. It's a fourth-hand and ancient Pulsar Dad got for me to learn in, because the paintwork hides all manner of sins.

I have to say a prayer to the car gods whenever I hit the ignition. She grumbles to reluctant life straightaway, but I stall, and then nick the curb.

Our school motto is emblazoned on the stone fence I park in front of. *Qui conatur amittere no potest*: He who tries cannot lose.

Or: *underdogs*.

North doesn't have a social hierarchy, as such, but people tend to cluster in patchwork groups. Mine consists of Len, Ged, Harrison, and Vince—otherwise known as the Boiyss, because our New Zealander PE teacher shouted "Boiyss!" with a hard "s" at us so much in year eight that it stuck.

"What happened to your face?" Ged asks when I meet them at the gate, his too-small school shirt straining across his shoulders. "I told you, don't shave if you've only got three facial hairs."

"It's not that bad, is it?" I pat my raw, bald cheeks.

"What did you use, a hunting knife?" Harrison Ford adds. Harrison is Ged's cousin, hence that nickname having been spread through the entire school, even though his real surname is Fehr.

I hold up my phone, trying to use the blank screen as a mirror. The tissue I shoved onto the (deeper than I realized) cut is bloody and half-slipping down my face. I try unsuccessfully to pick it off, almost dropping my phone in the process.

"For god's sake," Len mutters, reaching across to pull it from my jaw. He tosses it into the bin behind him.

"Mummy got it for you," Ged teases.

My cheeks flame. "Shut up, *Gerrard*."

"Oi. That's not funny."

Vince sidles up to us even later than I am, with no blazer and the wrong-colored socks.

"Morning, gents," he drawls in his cockney accent. We head toward the year twelve homerooms.

North is a collection of redbrick buildings spread out across several manicured acres someone donated after the war. The senior classrooms are at the top of the only hill, so we join the steady stream of gray-and-red pinstriped blazers making the climb.

"We still on for tonight?" Vince asks.

It's been a tradition for the past year or so that we go down to the coast on the night of the first day of term. There's a tiny headland beach, since dubbed the Place We Go because we are wordsmiths. We sit, eat, drink beer, and build a shitty bonfire.

"Yeah, I got off work. Whose car are we going to take?" Harrison says.

"I'm good with any except the Pissar," Ged puts in hastily.

"Don't call it that!" I snap, stung on my steed's behalf. "It's a perfectly reliable Nissan *Pulsar*. Just because the air con's a bit—"

"Nonexistent?"

"Touchy. And it doesn't always—"

"Turn on?"

"Corner all that smoothly, doesn't mean it—"

"Is the actual color of piss. A Nissan Pissar."

"It's *gold*," I protest. "Surely, it'd have to be yellow for that insult to even make sense."

"We can take mine," Len offers. He has his dad's old Land Cruiser which, admittedly, does put my steed to great shame.

"Coolio! Catch ya later." Ged waves, and he and Harrison line up outside 12A. Len, Vince, and I take our place at the door to 12C.

"I'm picking the music," Vince stipulates.

"Not 'Amity Affliction,'" I beg. "I swear during that one song actual blood comes out of my ears."

"There's actual blood coming out of your face, mate," Vince says.

"What?" I rub it frantically. There are rules about sloppy shaving. As respectable young men representing NGS to the public, having a face like a dropped pie isn't an option.

"He's just winding you up," says Len, laughing.

I pull out my phone again for a closer look.

"Vincent Hastings!" a voice booms from behind us. "What do you call this look? Dickensian orphan mugs schoolboy and assumes his identity? Do up your tie properly!"

Mr. Schiffer approaches us, nose raised high. He looks like

Kevin Rudd but taller, and his face is much less jolly. He's been principal here for the last twenty years. People call him the Sniffer because he can smell misconduct from within a ten-kilometer radius.

"I'll take that." He snatches my phone out of my hand and tucks it into his shirt pocket before I have time to protest. He raises his nose even further into the air and sniffs. "I expect more from our captain."

Vince and Len disguise their sniggers as coughs.

One of my duties as school captain is hosting the whole school assembly, alongside the vice-captain, Martin Finch. Martin lost to me by ten votes and they gave him vice as a consolation prize. He's not over it.

"Have a good holiday, Henry?" he asks when I enter the auditorium through the side door after homeroom.

"Er, yeah," I say, surprised by the cordiality. "What about you?"

"Oh, you know." Martin sniffs like the Sniffer's apprentice he is. "Not so good that I was late to school."

I make a face at him when he turns around to plug in the microphone.

Hundreds of guys are already filing in through the front and back entrances and spreading out across the tiered seating. I rub my hands on the thighs of my gray trousers, waiting.

"Try to remember to greet the guest," Martin snips, referring to the one time a member of the school board was present and I forgot to formally introduce him.

"Will do."

We fake smile at each other. Martin's got something in his teeth; I decide not to tell him.

Once everyone's seated, Mr. Schiffer gives me the signal to start. Martin hands the mic over reluctantly. I tap it three times, and the noise slowly dies down.

"Good morning honored guests, parents, staff, and students," I say clearly.

Martin hisses out a breath. He's probably disappointed that I got it right.

"Welcome to term three. I hope you all had a wonderful holiday. I know I did. What about you, Martin?"

"Wonderful, Hamlet. Wonderful." He smiles tightly.

"But not so wonderful that we aren't glad to be back for another term of living and learning at NGS," I say.

The audience titters sarcastically.

"I, for one, am just so happy to be back standing next to *you*, Finch. The Fincharoo." I put my arm around Martin for extra effect.

"Oh, *ditto*, Hamlet," he says, clasping my shoulder in return so hard it's really more of a smack. "So, tell us—what do we have in store this term?"

"Well, it's a big one all round, but especially for us twelves. Let's have a big cheer for the class of 2008!"

After a half-hearted *wooo*, I move on to rambling about study habits (three hours a night, boys) and this year's spirit theme ("we're all mates") before giving the day's notices and handing it over to Mr. Schiffer so he can berate us (again) for losing the athletics cup to St. Sebastian's.

"See you next time, eh?" I wave to Martin once we're dismissed.

"Can't wait," he deadpans.

I wait for the guys by the side entrance.

"Was that necessary?" Harrison asks, gesturing toward Martin. "He's not a bad guy."

(Harrison is a rules person. It's mostly endearing, except when he calls you out.)

"He requested I be *impeached* last term, when I allegedly swore in front of a year seven," I remind him.

"Oh, bloody hell, that's right," Vince says. "Git."

We start walking toward the lockers.

"Did you do it?" Ged asks curiously.

"Yeah, but I'd just dropped my last two bucks down the drain near the cafeteria!"

Harrison looks unimpressed.

"It wasn't full-on swearing," I defend myself.

"You said 'fuck a duck,'" Len puts in helpfully.

"Yes, thank you, Lennon," I snap. "Good to know you're on my side."

"We're all on your side, mate," Ged says, flicking me on the back of the head. "Giving you shit is part of the deal."

———

Classes tick by slowly. We're given assignments for two subjects the moment we walk in: modern history and English— which I don't mind—we're doing *The Great Gatsby*. I already read it during my classics phase.

Mandatory PE still sits like a stain on my timetable. It's particularly abhorrent this year, now that there's so many other things I could/should be doing.

I sleepwalk through our first basics of basketball lesson. It's probably my least favorite of all sports—people always assume my height somehow equals hand-eye coordination.

Coach Jamieson marks notoriously hard on participation, so whenever he looks over at our group, I half-heartedly chase the ball and throw him a thumbs-up like a wasted Wiggle.

"Cane!" Coach barks twenty minutes later. "Go help Hamlet, for the love of god. Hopeless."

Len jogs over obediently.

After a shared look, we manage to craft an elaborate pantomime wherein I knock the ball out of his hands while he's dribbling it.

"You got me," Len shouts when I swat the ball away. "Wow. I'm a fool."

"Tone it down," I hiss, bouncing the ball against the gym floor so hard it nearly whacks my favorite Atticus Finch–esque glasses off my face. I bounce it some more.

Coach looks over and grunts approvingly. "Better!" he shouts. "But still not good."

"Title of your autobiography," Len says in an undertone, and I peg the ball at him.

———

When the bell finally rings, we all pile into Len's car. He stops at a service station just outside the city for coffees and food supplies, and we hastily shuck off the itch of ties, jumpers, and blazers.

We wind our way along the highway, Ged sticking out of the sunroof until Harrison drags him down. I lean against my open window, chin on folded arms, listening to the familiar squabbling and watching trees spin past. Salt air kicks my hair all around.

Len drives well, if a bit fast, so we beat the traffic and arrive before the sun slips.

We park on the grass near the headland and unload musty old camp chairs and a cooler full of trans fats. The sky is starting to turn the vein-blue of a dying afternoon, the sea flat underneath it.

Since we started doing this, several traditions have evolved:

What happens at the Place We Go stays at the Place We Go (e.g., the time Ged told us he hooked up with Harrison's sister, Casey—yes, first cousin as in *first cousin*).

Everyone is responsible for bringing one item of junk food. Vince is always in charge of beverages, because he never gets carded. (*I* always do. I'll probably be thirty and still get asked for my ID.)

Skinny-dipping is optional.

We scratch stuff down on paper—goals, thoughts, etc.—and feed it to the fire. (Ged swears if we ever tell anyone he participates in something so lame, he'll kill us and sell us on eBay as free-range mince.)

We dump our stuff down far enough from the rising tide that it won't get washed away, and Ged and Vince walk off to collect firewood. I set the chairs in a semicircle while Len and Harrison fan out the snacks on the lid of the cooler. Gummy worms, Cheezels, Tim Tams, potato chips.

Lastly, Harrison holds up a sad-looking, crushed packet of Arrowroot biscuits. Not even the good kind—the no-name brand.

"Ugh. Seriously, Ged?" He tosses them aside.

"Isn't this like the third time he's done that?" Len smirks.

"Ah well," I say indulgently. "At least he remembered."

Vince and Ged return with armfuls of driftwood.

"Chuck us the matches, then," Vince grunts, dropping the logs down.

I clear my throat guiltily. I knew I'd forgotten something this morning, besides how to shave like a regular human. "Er, about that . . ."

Vince looks up sharply. "Chrissake."

"Relax. I've got this," Ged says, bending down over the stack of wood and whacking two rocks together. Nothing happens.

"Nice try, First Man." Harrison laughs.

Ged tries again, with no luck. The light is starting to fade by the time Len steps in and puts him out of his misery. He squats down and leans back on his knees for a couple of seconds before a flame catches.

Ged folds his arms across his chest. "What are you, a Scouts leader?"

"He was, actually," I say. "He was a total Mussolini. Power went to his head."

"It's not my fault you couldn't pass the bushcraft badge," Len says calmly, standing up and brushing the sand off his knees. The fire makes a satisfying crackling noise as it starts to lick the wood.

"*Bush*craft badge. That sounds intriguing," Ged says.

"Literal bush, you knob," I say. "You had to pitch a tent and stuff."

"Which Hamlet—despite his best efforts—failed at, dismally," Len adds.

"I pitched that thing fifteen times. You couldn't have given me the badge out of pity?"

"Where's the fun in that?" Len's mouth twitches. "Those pictures of you sulking in a mess of tarp are some of the most treasured from my childhood."

"Enough camping talk," Vince commands. "Being this far out in nature is effort enough for me; don't make me vom with your wholesome young escapades."

(Vince can't even cut someone off at a roundabout, but we respect his right to a brooding emo facade.)

Once the fire is established, we sit and rip open the various packets of food. Len and I select soft drinks, and the others crack the caps off ciders.

Vince's got one of those portable speakers, which he plugs into his bulky iPod classic. The soft keening of Dashboard Confessional ekes out across the sand.

Night comes over us slowly, and there's a lengthy pink-striped sunset to ponder before the fire builds enough for the Ritual. I pull my notebook out of my bag and tear pieces of paper for everyone.

"Can't believe you guys still do this," Vince says, but when I look over he's filling the page with looping sentences.

I read somewhere that the ancients thought there was power in writing something down then burning it, and the idea kind of stuck.

We usually write our goals for the term. Last year, I wrote a bunch of crap about better grades and getting school captain, spending more time with my family, etc. The last two terms I've kept it similar and also (rather optimistically) added the postscript *lose virginity?*

Needless to say, not even the flames of intention have that kind of power.

I hesitate over what to write this time. Family—check. My grades are okay, even if I don't entirely know what I'm going to do with them. "Figure out life direction" feels too broad, and also vaguely terrifying.

I peek at Len's for inspiration. He's only written two words, underlined in thick black strokes: *Tell him.*

I look from the page to his face, which is taut with concentration. He covers it when he's done, hunching his shoulders like it's a proper secret.

We've never had secrets. Sometimes I wish we did, especially when he reminds me about my childhood crush on Howl Jenkins Pendragon (the *book* version, because I thought his magic was cool).

So.

Tell who what?

Ged interrupts my train of thought by triumphantly tossing his page into the fire. He hasn't bothered to fold it—I can see the words *Hilton* and *formal* and *Jess.*

Jessica Fitzpatrick is the uncontested Most Beautiful Girl at St. Adele's. His goal for this term is even more far-fetched than mine last term.

Vince throws his in next, looking proportionately bored.

I quickly write *keep looking for "it"* and toss it in after Harrison's. The great "it" feels as noble a pursuit as any, even if it means nothing as a concrete goal.

Len goes last, folding the paper over and over until it's a speck in his hand. He chews his lip, the way he does when he's nervous, which he almost never is. I watch the fire swallow the folded paper in one breath.

Vince pretends to cast a spell. "So mote it be."

"Dude," Ged says. "Do not mock the Ritual. The Ritual gave me my first kiss, my first B-minus in biology, my car."

"The Ritual didn't do that," Vince scoffs. "That's chance."

"Shh," Ged hisses. He gestures to the flames. "She'll hear you."

Harrison scrunches his face. "Stop bringing up your first kiss already."

"*Why?*" Ged demands, spreading his arms out. "I'm not ashamed of it."

"Well, Casey is—" Harrison starts.

"Look. Your sister and I had a beautiful moment of comfort and discovery together, and if that threatens you—"

"Oh my *god*, no," Harrison begs, covering his ears.

For a while the sky's almost big enough to cancel out everything else. But then it starts to get cold, and it's a school night, so we head back to the car.

I sit up front again, thinking and watching Len carefully. "You good?"

His gray eyes flick over to me, irritated. "Why wouldn't I be?"

But he's weird all the way home, quiet and distant.

Tell who what?

4

The familiar routine of school, study, sleep, repeat settles over me like an old jumper.

Ems isn't wrong about this term being intense. There are only ninety boys in our graduating class, so they push us pretty hard academically. Labels are assigned in year eight, and once you've been given your role, there's really no choice but to perform.

For English this term, our task is to turn a key scene from *Gatsby* into a play script. I try not to be too dispirited when Ms. Hartnett pairs me with Vince, who I know for a fact hasn't read the book. Or any book that isn't a graphic novel.

"I want you to challenge yourselves," Ms. H. says, clasping her hands together. She's my favorite teacher—she talks about books in a way that makes even Ged listen. Mostly.

(She's also a massive improvement on the teacher we had last year—an ancient ex-alum who wrote "Henry's imagination is almost as big as his boots" on my report card.)

"Find something in Fitzgerald's writing that speaks to *you*," Ms. H. continues. "The real you, not just the one that other people see. Tap into that and use it to transform the scene into something new."

Vince catches my eye and mimes dry-retching. We pair off

to brainstorm. Ged is texting under the desk; I watch, wistfully, as Len draws up an intricate mind map for their group.

"I don't know why we even study classics anymore," Vince says, chipping black polish off his thumbnail and looking disinterested. "They're so tired and overdone."

"Because they're *classic*," I say patiently. "They tell us something about the broader human experience."

"I still don't see why we can't just watch the film."

"We did. It was the black and white one."

He looks up, disgusted. "That was it? No wonder the ruddy book's so unpopular."

"It's Fitzgerald's *seminal work*."

Vince tilts back in his blue plastic chair. "Ooh, lookit—we've got the dictionary out."

"I can't help it if you've only got the vocab of a cat's arse," I hiss.

"Having some deep intellectual debates over there, boys?" Ms. Hartnett calls.

"Er, yeah!" I reply.

Vince snorts. "No, we're not, you tosser."

"We would be, if you'd drop your dark-prince persona for five seconds and actually do some schoolwork!"

"Whoa." He holds up a pale hand. "That's Night King to you, mate. And, no, d'you know what? I don't think I will. It's not as if you're gonna let me anywhere near this assignment anyway."

"What's that supposed to mean?"

"Just that you tend to micromanage in group situations."

"*Micromanage?*"

He tilts his head. "Well, it's kind of like how you've got a micropenis, only—"

I punch his arm.

"Henry!" Ms. Hartnett chides from across the room. "Violence is never the answer."

———

Friday afternoon is debating club. Len's a member too, despite being apathetic toward it at best. We meet by the lockers after sixth period to grab bulk Violet Crumbles and salt and vinegar chips from the vending machine.

Our headquarters is the senior drama room in S block at the back of campus, nicknamed "shit block" because neither the structure nor the decor have been updated since it was built in the seventies—it's all yellow walls, brown carpet, and musty blackboards.

We drag the desks into a semicircle facing the front of the room. I love debating—the structure, the passive aggression, the chance to use words that'd make my friends kick me in the groin if I dropped them in conversation.

Mum made me start when I was in primary school to combat a fear of public speaking, and it's like clockwork to me now. We won the cup last year; I think that's part of why the Sniffer voted for me to be school captain.

The team trickles in slowly: Harrison, Martin, Eamon Matthews, and Ben Cunningham. Our numbers have severely dwindled since the hockey team moved their training to the same day and time in retaliation against Eamon for quitting last season.

I position myself on the stage and pull on a powdered Shakespearean wig I found in the prop closet. Len watches me but says nothing, this being well within the realm of things I do.

"So, I thought we could start off with our practice topic from over the holidays: did Henry the Eighth love any of his wives?"

"Nobody's-interested-in-that-except-you," Ben coughs.

(Ben doesn't actually debate; he's here at the request of the faculty because he's failing English. And not bitter at all.)

"So we're all delivering an argument in one sentence. Want to start us off, Ben?" I eye him meaningfully.

He blanches. "Er—nah. You're right."

"Go on, man," Len says. "You seem to have a lot of *thoughts*."

"Uh," Ben starts, scratching his head. "Well. The first one— Cath whoever."

"Catherine of Aragon," I supply.

"Yeah," Ben says. "Her. She was kind of like wife-goals. He totally screwed her over cause he was mad he couldn't make a son."

I tap my chin. "Hmm. Anyone else have any thoughts?"

"I read a great paper on that recently!" Martin says.

I stare hard at the popcorn ceiling to avoid throwing my Violet Crumble at him.

"Apparently he had some sort of disease that made him unable to beget male offspring."

"Snooze," Ben says. "Let's talk about the hot one."

"Her name was Anne Boleyn," Martin snaps.

"I think she was a badass," Eamon pipes up suddenly. "That's why he fell for her, or whatever."

Eamon dated Emilia briefly, earlier in the year. She won't tell me why they broke up, but looking at him now, I'm thinking maybe it wasn't entirely mutual.

"Couldn't you also say Anne just wanted power?" I point out.

"But she waited for him for ages," Eamon argues.

"Does waiting so long kind of negate how much she could have loved him?" I counter.

It's Len who answers. "Maybe she waited *because* she loved him."

I look over at him. "What d'you mean?"

His cheeks fizz with color. "Just, like . . . if you look at the early letters—they were connected, on a personal intellectual level, even when they weren't together romantically. Isn't that what loving someone is?"

Len never really says much in these meetings. We all stare at him for a moment in shock.

Ben finally speaks. "He fully chopped off her head though, so it's kind of irrelevant."

Len rubs his hair in silence, leaning back in his seat.

"To be fair," I back him up, "that last part was probably due to the syphilis."

We speed through the remaining wives, and then it's almost time to go.

"Okay, we didn't really do a proper mock today," I finish. "So let's try to be a bit more organized next time. And just before you go—"

"Hamlet, you do realize you're not our mother. We can leave whenever we want."

"Yes, thank you, Harrison. My cervix and I thank the good lord for that fact every day. But we do need to talk about finals coming up, so can the team stay back, please?"

Once it's just Martin, Harrison, Len, and me left, I announce dramatically, "We have been given our topic."

"For finals? Is it bad?" Harrison tries to read my face.

"Not . . . exactly," I say, and look down at the sheet I printed out over the holidays. "It's: spouses should have to testify against each other in court."

"Ooh!" Martin sits up excitedly. "I like it. Spousal privilege is ridiculous."

Len's watching me. "What side are we though?"

"That's kind of the thing."

Harrison grimaces. "We're on negative again, aren't we?"

"Indeed."

"Oh, *fantastic*," Martin spits. "How the hell do we argue a moral negative for that?"

"Look, I get that it's a bit—"

"Shit," Harrison finishes. "Yeah."

"But we can still win—we just have to rally and find our angle! So, um . . . thinking hats on for next week, okay?"

Martin and Harrison grumble away.

I pull off the wig and put it back where I found it, trying not to think about the colony of head lice I've no doubt invited into my life. Len helps me put the desks back where they belong, and we lock up behind us.

Amber light spills into our eyes when we step outside. This far up the back of campus, we're surrounded by scrub. Ancient gum trees that look like they've seen some serious shit over the years are silhouetted gray against the cornflower sky.

The walk to our cars is too quiet for me. I say the first thing that pops into my head. "Who were you talking about?"

Len looks up—there's sun all over him. "Huh?"

"Back there."

"What about it?"

"Just kind of sounded like you were—"

"A better debater than Ben Cunningham?"

I snort, grabbing my keys from my pocket as the Pissar comes into view. "Yeah. That's exactly it."

Len hoists his bag over his shoulder, blinking under scattered light to look at me. "Empty words, captain."

"I'm full of those. Just ask Martin."

"You're full of something."

I clutch my side theatrically. "*Et tu, Brute?*"

"*Et* me." He rolls his eyes. "And my car's this way." He walks down to the other end of the parking lot, pulling his tie off as he goes.

———

When I get home, Mum is sitting at the kitchen table in a work outfit with the phone clutched to her ear. I can tell from the stiffness in her spine and the wheel of cheese she's contemplating (she's lactose intolerant) that it's somebody she hates.

"Of course. I understand," she says, voice clipped. "I will. Thank you." She hangs up the phone and reaches out to squeeze me around the waist. "How was your day?"

"Fine. Who was that?"

Mum cuts off a giant slab of brie. "Ham's school."

Ham goes to the alternative primary school two suburbs over, where the kids sit on beanbags and engage in soft play rather than bullying.

"He's got an in-school suspension."

My eyes widen. "They do that?"

She shrugs around her mouthful of cracker and cheese, and says, "Apparently."

I sit down across from her and let my bag slip to the floor. "What happened?"

She pulls her hair back into a ponytail. "His teacher doesn't like him. She wants him to repeat a year. He lashed out when she mentioned it."

I've heard a lot about the oddly dictatorial Ms. Scarfe. Dad calls her "Ms. Arse" because she had a go at Mum at the parent-teacher conference about her not being involved enough in school life.

"Well," I say to Mum. "You *did* name him Hamish Hamlet. That's kind of asking for him to be at least a little screwed up, isn't it?"

It's a cheap shot, but it works.

Her face crumples into an almost-laugh and she swats my arm. "It sounded poetic at the time! I didn't realize he'd be—"

"Ham Ham?"

She shakes her head. "I ruined his life, didn't I? That witch is right. I should be around more."

"Mum, no. She hasn't got a clue."

"I don't know. Your dad and I have been talking about this. I think it might be time for me to take a step back for a bit, to be here more. While Ham's still young."

My brow knits. "What does Dad say?"

Mum smiles, but it's faint. "That he's happy being a kept man, and he won't stand for it."

"I can help with Ham," I tell her.

"No, Hen, I don't want you worrying about anything. Year twelve is enough to worry about. I'm just venting."

"I want to help, though."

Mum pinches my cheek. "I know, love. But sometimes shit

just happens." She stands up and takes her plate to the sink to rinse off the evidence, then turns around. "Actually, there is one thing—can you help me draft an email to Ms. Arse?"

"Yes! What tone are we going for?"

Mum pretends to deliberate. "Hmm. I think passive-aggressive but with the barest hint of a real threat."

"Consider it done."

Two hours later, we've crafted a response with enough bite to chew through plaster. Mum proofreads over my shoulder, bending down occasionally to squeeze me hard.

Emails are one of my specialties—writing and rewriting, backspacing and switching out words until they're shiny-perfect. You don't get redos like that in real time.

5

The weekend starts with the big football game. St. Sebastian's has stolen our honor, apparently, and it's the team's job to get it back by brute force.

I've never understood what it is that makes people's eyes light up when they see a ball flying through the air. Our school is huge on football though, and so I dutifully gather with the two hundred other students and parents at nine on Saturday morning.

It's so cold, a thick cover of gray blocking the sun. The air hangs with anticipation—of rain, of winning, of going home early enough to get a decent coffee (but maybe that's just me).

Len and Ged are both jittery. Ged has only two sausage sandwiches and a Sprite from the cafeteria, a sure sign the pre-match nerves are intensifying.

"Australia is such a sports-obsessed culture," I complain, gesturing around me with my bacon and egg roll. "Why is it necessary for guys to validate themselves by kicking a ball around a field?"

"You're only saying that because you can't catch, throw, kick, or walk without falling A over T," Ged says.

I look at him, stung—mostly because he's right. "I'm just *saying*," I argue, while Len rapidly pulls apart a piece of plain toast, "you shouldn't have to stress this much in the biggest term of your lives."

"We won't be stressed when we win!" Ged says through his teeth, chucking his half-chewed sandwich away and taking savage sips from his drink.

When it's time for the game, Len and Ged jog down to the field while I go to sit on the bleachers with Harrison and Vince, who never gets up this early on a weekend and is so sour about it that I almost laugh.

"All right?" Vince asks.

I bump fists with him. "I never know the correct response to that. Do I tell you how I am, or just say it back?"

"In your case, the response is 'I'm a wanker.'" He scowls into his cup of tea. "Tastes like piss."

The teams are assembling on the field. The North boys stand out in their bright red jerseys while St. Sebastian's are flat gray, yet more reason to dislike them.

I don't know much about footy positions, but Ged is something important that involves pulling St. Seb's boys to the ground every few minutes, and he's super competitive. Ten minutes into the game he holds a guy down for a moment too long, shoving his face into the grass, and has to be yelled at by the ref.

"He's going to get carded again," Harrison predicts.

"Cousin telepathy?" I ask.

"Just the knowledge that he's a dickhead."

Len, from what I've observed over the years, mostly runs long distances with the ball. It's rare that anyone catches him.

The first half passes without further Ged-related incidents, with North in the lead.

Len's dad, John, makes a rare appearance, probably because

it's the first game of term. He's in a white polo shirt and white sneakers, starkly clean and beardless compared to most of the other dads.

He strides along the fence line at the edge of the field, staring intently and cupping long hands around his mouth to shout play advice.

"Pick it *up!*"

"Just throw the ball!"

"Stay on him, Lennon! On him!"

A few seconds before halftime, Len kicks the ball in a giant arc across almost the entire field. I join in with the raucous cheering and follow the crowd down to where the team is gathering near the fence.

"Good job, *boiyss!*" Coach Jamieson says.

"Yeah, boiyss," Harrison mimics softly.

Ged's dad comes over and flicks Harrison on the back of the head, then greets Vince and me warmly.

"Little bloody rascal," he reprimands Ged, grinning. "What've I told you about holding people down?"

Ged rolls his eyes. "Don't—" he gulps water "—be an animal." His dad laughs and clasps Ged's shoulder to steer him toward the towel station.

"You're definitely my son, but you don't want to hand them easy points."

Len's jogging over, sweaty and red-faced. John heads toward him at the same time as me—he's carrying a water bottle.

When I'm a few meters from them, John puts the bottle behind his back, holding it with both hands.

"Guess which hand, or you can't have any," he jokes, juggling the water back and forth. At least, I think he's joking.

Len shakes out his sticky hair and rubs his eyes.

"Not that you deserve it, really," John continues. "Relying on flukes like that. Luck isn't skill—anyone could've done it."

John's voice is so suddenly sharp that I look around to see if anyone else heard him, but it's just me, hovering uncertainly.

"Whatever," Len says tonelessly.

John pulls the water out from behind his back and tosses it without warning. It hits Len in the chest, but he still catches it.

"It's not all kicking and running away like a pussy. You can't just coast forever—you've got to take control. Be a man. Coasting's for no-hopers."

Len looks like he's about to say something. Then another dad calls, "Mad-dog Cane! How are you, mate?" and John spins away.

Len's eyes find mine. He stares at me brightly for a second, then unscrews the top of the water bottle with his teeth. He tilts his head back and tips the water over his face. Rivulets snake down his eyebrows and over his collarbones, staining his NGS jersey a darker blood red.

The buzzer sounds the end of half-time.

"Come on, boiyss!" Coach Jamieson shouts, and the guys jog back onto the field. "Hustle! We've almost got 'em!"

We do have them, until fifteen minutes into the second half, when Len gets smashed to the ground. It's a straightforward tackle—the kind he usually sees coming and dodges a mile off.

"What the hell?" Vince says.

Len rolls onto his side. I lurch forward, squinting down at the field. Coach blows his whistle and a circle of suddenly compassionate burly football players gathers around, blocking him from view.

Eventually he stands up slowly, the sight of his gold head

reassuring. Ged's beside him and loops one of Len's arms around his shoulder. Together they limp to the bench.

I try to catch Len's eye, but his gaze is fixed on his boots. He stays that way until the end of the game.

I'm jittery waiting for the horn to finally sound. North wins, 12–3. The Sniffer looks like he might cry real tears.

Len's still weird when we meet up after.

"Slashed 'em! Nice game, Canester," Ged says in an obvious attempt to lighten the mood, cuffing Len's shoulder. "You absolute menace."

"Hardly," Len says flatly, shaking him off. "I was sitting for most of it."

Silence blows over us, an icy wind. Harrison and I exchange glances.

"Do you wanna do something now?" I ask. "Vince said he needs real tea or he'll die."

"No."

"But—"

"Leave it, Hamlet," he snaps. "I'm gonna go home and crash."

Even Ged looks unconvinced. There's no arguing with Len, though. No choice but to watch him limp away.

———

Gran summons us all to New Farm Park the next day with a text marked **URGENT**. Dad tries to get permission to shower first, but Mum just blearily bundles us all into the car without even stopping for coffee on the way.

It's one of those perfect winter Brisbane days—wind on the river and proper bright, blue-sky cold—of which we get only about three each year. Gran's sitting on a giant picnic blanket at the far end of the park, beside rose bushes that match her hair.

Ham immediately runs off to chase a bird.

"Hamish, don't lick . . ." Mum trails off, and Dad rushes after him.

"Family!" Gran calls when we reach her blanket. She stands up to hug us. "My beloved family."

"What's up?" I ask. "You said it was urgent."

"I have *news*."

"Oh, lord," Mum says, pushing her sun visor back tiredly. "You can't come out twice, Mum. You know that, right?"

"Yes, dear. Thank you. However, Marigold and I . . ." Gran takes a deep breath. "Have decided to get married."

Mum blinks at her for a second, searching for the least inflammatory protest. "But . . . you said you'd never get married again."

"Did I?" Gran says airily. "When?"

"My entire life." Mum grits her teeth. "You always said your first wedding was such a headache that you'd never bother doing it again. You tried to talk me out of my wedding, the morning of. Remember?"

Gran waves a hand. "Well anyway, obviously it won't be legal," she continues. "But we love each other, and we're going to throw a tremendous party to celebrate."

"That's great, Gran," I tell her.

She winks at me. "Thank you, my sweet. You, at least, appear to have remembered your manners." She shifts her eyes pointedly toward Mum.

"Of course I'm happy for you!" Mum snaps. "It's just a change of tack, that's all."

"Billie, if nobody ever changed tack in their lives, the world would be boring indeed."

"I guess you're right."

Gran smiles self-satisfactorily.

"It just would have been nice if you'd had this change of heart on the subject of matrimony *before* you almost convinced me to leave Reuben at the altar," Mum says.

"Speaking of altars!" Gran hijacks. "We're going to have it at that old church, St. Andrews. You know the one . . . "

My mind starts to wander for a bit and I stare at the mansions across the water while Gran outlines her vision for the day (including a three-course reception meal at a posh restaurant on the river).

When I come back, Mum's widening her eyes at me.

Caffeine, she mouths.

"Right!" I stand up. "On it."

I walk along the path to a coffee van, order three cappuccinos, and wait.

Then I see him.

Len is crouched by a yellow rose bush, taking pictures with his long lens. He looks blank. Whether it's just the photo-taking kind or not, I can't tell.

I think about yesterday, him crashing down onto the muddy field, and then I'm walking over.

He looks up, shielding his eyes from the sun. "What're you doing here?"

I inspect his face. There's still something off.

"Family time," I explain. "How come you're not at work?"

"Took the day off."

I think again about the football game. About that guy smashing into him. About John. But directly bringing it up isn't going to get me anywhere.

"Guess what? Gran's getting married."

Len's face animates a little, eyebrows raising.

"To Marigold?"

"No, to her plumber—yes, to Marigold. They want to have some sort of commitment ceremony, at St. Andrews."

"Will the church even do that?"

"Apparently Gran has dirt on the priest. He owes her one."

He laughs softly. "She's a force of nature, I'll give her that. How's Billie taking it?"

"*So* well."

"She'll come around."

"You should come say hey," I suggest, turning back toward the river side of the park. "Actually, you don't have a choice— they've seen us."

I collect my drinks from the cart and drag him to Gran's mat. Dad's back and looking exactly like he spent the night with his sculptures, paint all over his face and clay clumped in his hair. I give him my coffee.

Ham launches himself at Len with a muted shriek. "Len! I failed my math test this week!"

"Really, darling?" Gran coos. "That's marvelous. Stick it to the man."

Mum makes a sound like a cat hissing.

Ham swivels around to stare into Len's eyes. "Did *you* fail math in year one?"

Len looks back at him seriously. "I don't remember, mate. But Henry's failed every year of mandatory PE."

I mouth a very not-Ham-appropriate word at him.

Ham giggles. "You're too old to fail, Henry!"

"Never too old for that!" Dad booms, patting my shoulder with his clay-stained hand.

"Can we leave off my failures, please?" I interject. "We're meant to be celebrating."

"Yes!" Gran claps her hands together. "Let's eat! Help me with this, Henry."

"Help you with what?"

She flips open the lid of her picnic basket to reveal that the inside is taken up, almost entirely, by one thing.

"Cut it up for me, will you, love? We can have it with crackers."

"But . . . it's a monster!"

"It's an eggplant."

"That is the Hulk of eggplants. Where did you even get it from?"

"My fruit man!" Gran says testily. "Stop being so dramatic and get it out."

Len perks up. "Yeah, go on. Get it out."

I heave my best put-upon sigh and slide my hands under its mushy wine-colored skin uncertainly. Then I drop it, and Gran screams.

"Oh, honestly!" Mum grabs Gran's picnic knife and neatly divides up the Hulk.

We dine on coffee and warm eggplant for a while, until Dad starts staring into space, and Ham stands up, Hamlet-bored with the silence.

"Guess which movie I'm acting out!" he demands with his mouth full.

I sigh again.

He commences flapping his arms wildly; Mum and Dad

look at him blankly. Then he claps both hands together above his head and squawks.

"Ooh!" Gran shouts suddenly, and several other families look up in alarm. "I know, darling! It's that Harry Potter and the phoenix . . . the order . . . The phoenix he ordered!"

Len tips his head slowly toward me behind Mum's back. "I love *Harry Potter and the Phoenix He Ordered*," he murmurs, deadpan.

I bite down on my lip. "Why *did* he order it, in the end?" I whisper back.

"No one knows."

Gran's face darkens. She flicks gooey eggplant seeds in our direction.

"Mum!" Mum says. "You can't throw food in a public space!"

"Seeds aren't food, Billie."

"Hey, Hamlet," Len says. "Do you think you could maybe help me take some more photos this afternoon?"

(Thank god.)

"Yes!" I say, a bit too enthusiastically. "Absolutely. And we should probably leave soon too, because the . . . sun."

"Oh, bugger off, then," says Gran. "Search for the muse."

"Congrats again!" I tell her. "Mean it."

We escape quickly, Len leading the way to where his car's parked, toward the silvery towering buildings of the Valley in the distance.

"Where are we going? Please say far."

"I was gonna head to Sandgate."

"Perfect."

He winds northward through redbricked Teneriffe.

I watch him drive for a while before I crack. "So."

58

"So, what?"

"So . . . how are you?"

"How *am* I?" He rolls his eyes but keeps them on the road. "Who are you, Doctor Phil?"

"You know," I drop my voice, "after yesterday."

His face hardens and he rubs his forehead. "How many times do I have to say I was fine?"

"You weren't, though," I press quickly as we fly past factory buildings. "You were down. You never go down."

"That's not true; I do it all the time. Ask anyone."

"Be serious, please."

"Why? I got tackled. It happens."

"Not to you."

"Well, maybe I was having an off day. I'm entitled to at least one of those in my lifetime, surely?"

I picture John. Polo shirts and *pussy*. My mouth opens and closes again.

Len's eyes go harder still, as if he's reading my mind.

———

When we get to Sandgate, we walk along the seafront (if you can call it that—compared to the Place We Go it's decidedly suburban, the water churlish and brown).

I'm always the designated companion on these expeditions — it's just sort of happened that way, over the years. I guess because I'm used to it, having grown up with Dad. I know a tiny bit about composition, so am *somewhat* useful (in a technical sense).

Len has both his film and digital cameras, so I settle in for the long haul, tight-roping along the edge of the promenade while he takes shot after shot. There's seagulls swooping lazily overhead, but other than that we're completely alone.

"I can't believe your gran's getting married," he says finally, eye pressed to the viewfinder.

I smile slightly. "I know, right? It's mental."

"Don't know if I'd bother a second time. Or a first, come to think of it."

I know what he means. "Yeah. I can't imagine signing something that'd stick me with just one person forever."

Len clicks the shutter. "Mmm."

"But then," I say, wobbling a bit and narrowly avoiding falling into the spitting sea, "*I'm* not the one dating the most popular girl in our year."

"We aren't dating."

Of course not; they never are. Len's been with lots of people, but none of them last long.

"Does *she* know that?"'

Click. Click. Click.

"You're terrible."

He lifts his head. "I feel like you're in a bit of a poor position to be doling out relationship advice."

"True. It is increasingly looking as though my destiny is to become a lonely cat lady by twenty-one."

He doesn't disagree.

"*You'll* get married, for sure," I continue, swinging my legs out over the water. "You're all free spirit now, but then you'll be thirty with six kids and a wife who looks like Keira Knightley. I'll just be . . ." I scrunch up my face. "I don't know—breastfeeding cat number six, or something."

He looks down at his camera. "Let's just get through the rest of this year first. That's enough of a head fuck."

He's not wrong. In year eleven I barely studied at all, and things just kind of sorted themselves out. Mostly. This year's more like being on a hamster wheel, running toward a future I can't see.

I used to have this idea of us, a vague outline like when you're dreaming about strangers and your brain can't come up with the face. I even wrote it out—I'd be a journalist, and he'd be a current-affairs photographer, and we'd be living in some amazing apartment we couldn't really afford. Len's got the opposite kind of pressure to mine, though; Dad and Gran want me to light the arts landscape on fire, but everyone reckons *his* cleverness should go to something sturdy, like medicine.

I watch the water move for a bit. Then sunset finally comes, so quickly that we almost miss it.

Len switches to film, adjusting the lens so that it picks up the pinks and burnt orange.

"Hamlet," he calls. "Come stand here."

He gets bored with landscapes sometimes. He likes there to be a figure to break it up.

"Seriously? I look like shit."

"Doesn't matter." He's got his concentration face on. "Hurry up."

I walk slowly into the frame, making sure I look harassed.

I know from similar shots, though, that I'll probably just be a silhouette.

He snaps a few times, tilting and kneeling down, capturing every angle. The sun falls, beaming its last rays of the day straight into my eyes. I hold up a hand but Len makes a noise of protest, so I reluctantly lower it again, squinting into the light as it washes over my face.

"Just because it's in the name of art doesn't make this any less abusive," I say, trying not to move my face.

"Shut up. I'm almost done." He gets closer, and the lens adjusts again. He switches back to digital after a beat.

"I take it back," I say. "You'll definitely die alone."

Len's lip quirks up. His mouth is wide and kind of uneven, so it's always halfway balanced on a smile when he talks. "Noted."

"Are you done already? I'm hungry."

He checks the last frame in the display, cupping his hand around the screen. "Yes, you child. I'm done."

I relax my posture gratefully.

"Pizza?" he asks.

"Obviously. Your treat, though."

We start walking back to the car.

"How d'you figure that?"

"For services rendered. Plus, you're the one with a job, and I spent my last ten bucks on coffee today."

"Did you also drop it and then say 'fuck' in front of a small child?"

"Are you ever gonna stop bringing that up?"

"Nope."

"Prick."

"Dickhead."

"Knob."

"Drama queen."

"Man-whore."

"Spinster."

He unlocks the car.
"Pepperoni, then?"
"Yeah."

6

Over the next few weeks, time starts to feel like a downhill slope toward exams. Our teachers lecture us daily about how These Are the Important Days and we're Deciding Our Lives Right Now.

This is the thing I've thought about since the end of year ten. Getting out. Into the world. But it's as though the closer I get to it—the getting out life part—the less real it seems. I keep getting bursts of a sticky melancholy.

"I hear you've got your period," Ged says in sixth period math on Friday when we're meant to be studying.

I slide further down in my seat, glowering with a confusing fury I can't unwrap. "That joke is so reductive toward the menstruation experience."

"*Reductive*," he sing-songs. "Big word. I bet you learnt it because that's what happened to your dick."

"No, I learn*ed* it because that's what I'm gonna do to yours."

"Ooh. I'm terrified."

"What're we talking about?" Harrison asks, leaning forward in his seat behind us.

"Hamlet's a Grumpelstiltskin," Ged explains.

"Am not," I protest. "I'm having a moment of intense disillusionment. There's a difference. Don't you guys feel freaked out?"

"I am having a *fantastic* term so far," Ged says.

"Why?" Vince asks suspiciously.

"A man never kisses and tells."

"Both Casey and I really wish that were true," Harrison puts in, and I laugh.

"You bastards seriously need to let me live that down already," Ged scowls.

"Unlikely," I say.

"Give us the details, then," Vince says. "You're bound to anyway."

Ged strokes the stubble on his chin. "I have a date."

"Right. With . . . ?"

"Jess, of course! Who else?"

"Jess Fitzpatrick?" Vince asks.

"Yep."

"The same Jess Fitzpatrick whose brother punched your lights out last year for ringing their home phone every day?"

Ged shakes his head. "It's all in the past. We're good mates now."

"And her boyfriend," I remember suddenly. "Didn't he punch you last year as well?"

"*Mates*," Ged repeats tersely. "And anyway, they broke up, so . . ."

"Good luck with that," Vince says.

"Why are you all looking at me like that?" Ged asks. "She's gonna like me! You'll see. Everything's coming up Gedster."

"Sure." Harrison says, as he tries to keep a straight face. "Of course she will."

"I mean it. Stop looking at me like that."

"Like what?" Harrison asks innocently.

"Like I'm being sent off to bloody war! This is a date, with the hottest girl in our year."

"Uh-huh," Vince says. "It's great. Really."

"You'll see," Ged says with slight menace. "All of you. Life is good, my disbelieving friends. Life is g-o-o-d-e good."

The bell rings, which means it's time for debating. This perks me up slightly, but it also means capping an already crap day off with Martin Finch.

Len's leaning against my locker when I get there, one spotted socked ankle crossed over the other.

We start walking across the sun-dipped quad.

"Have you cracked it, then?"

"Mmm?"

"The allegedly shit topic: spouses shouldn't have to testify against each other."

Shit. I started workshopping our argument angle, but . . . it's sitting half-cooked on my desk, at home.

"Yep! Fully cracked."

"Sure it is."

We get to shit block two minutes late. It's just the competing team today, and once everyone's sitting at the sticky desks, I cut right to the point (or at least attempt to).

"All right, everyone—"

"What's everybody thinking?" Martin butts in. "Because I have some ideas."

I breathe in deeply. "*Thank you,* Martin—but I have thought about this extensively." I throw a look at Len, who folds his arms, feigning rapt interest. "*I* think the only thing we can do is

66

redefine the topic a little. Make it fit whatever argument we pick."

"How?" Harrison asks. "It's pretty self-explanatory: married couples *should* have to testify against each other, but we have to argue that they don't."

I did at least get this far in my workshopping. "We probably need to try and prove that spouses don't often commit crimes together. There'd be evidence for that. Some, at least. And it's original."

"But then who *does*, Hamlet?" Martin asks almost before I'm done talking. "You'd have to counterargue."

This is exactly where I got stuck. I shuffle the papers in front of me (my math notes), trying to look like the answer's in there somewhere.

"Friends do it," Len says after a beat.

Martin snaps around to face him. We all do.

He chews the inside of his cheek sheepishly. "Leopold and Loeb? The Manson family?"

"True. Not married," Harrison agrees.

"What," I say. "So we'd do BFF duos? Like Susan Sarandon in that movie where she goes off the cliff at the end?"

Len gives me a leveling look. "Yes, Hamlet—like Susan Sarandon."

Martin clears his throat loudly. "I'm not sure that's—"

"You can use friend examples to argue it's not just married couples who commit crimes together," Len says.

"Hmm . . . like 'partners in crime aren't romantic' or something," I say as I run it through my head. "So, there's no point making spouses testify against each other."

"Yeah. Exactly."

Harrison looks impressed.

"I . . ." Martin sniffs unhappily a minute later. "I actually think that could work quite well."

"Wow, Finch," I say sarcastically. "Don't get too excited. You'll hurt yourself, and I'll have to fill in an incident report."

"We'd have to do research, though," Harrison adds when Martin's eyes flash.

"Yes!" I start moving toward the dusty blackboard. "We need case studies. Let's brainstorm some criminal partnerships to start researching this week."

———

By the time we've exhausted all our existing knowledge of friend-crimes (since when did Bonnie and Clyde *date?*), and loosely decided on some possible argument points, a cotton-candy dusk has settled outside.

Len and I walk out still talking, until his phone lights up with a text mid-conversation. He flips it open and punches in a brief reply. I feel a flicker of my earlier irritation return—this slipping sense that I'm tugging him away from more exciting things.

"Who was that?"

He shrugs.

"Are you gonna take her to formal?" I ask.

Len snaps the phone shut. "Who?"

"Willa. That's her, right?"

"Maybe. Haven't really thought about it."

"Seriously? It's all I've been thinking about. Martin told me a captain hasn't gone stag since the fifties."

Len rolls his eyes.

"I wonder if they'd let me just go with Ged, since there's next to no chance things will actually work out with Jess." I fish for pity.

"You can't take same-sex dates, remember?" Len says.

"Sure, it's frowned upon." I frown upon that. "But I don't think it's technically banned."

"Fucking fascists," Len says with surprising force.

I laugh, even though I'm not sure if I'm supposed to.

"Good to know that in an ideal world you'd choose Ged as your date," he continues when we're passing the spire of the admin building. His voice sounds weird.

"Ged's the only one likely to wind up a loner on the night!" I say. "Besides me, obviously."

Len shakes his head. "You could get a date if you actually tried."

"How? By just approaching some poor unsuspecting St. Ad's girl at the bus stop and saying, 'Hey, I'm Henry, but you might know me as Spew Grant?'"

"You could just ask someone."

I scoff. "Who?"

He looks suddenly irritated. "Dunno. Ged, apparently."

"What's up yours?"

Len's expression smooths back to something closer to normal. "Nothing. I'll ask around, if you want."

"*Thank* you."

———

When I drop my bag in the hallway twenty minutes later, it's chaos in the Hamlet house. Gran's baking something with

Ham—the kitchen counter is covered in flour, ditto the walls. He's propped up on a stool, stirring carefully. I sneak up behind him and pretend to electric shock him in the ribs.

He giggles, falling back into me. "I'm *stirring*."

"Sorry, Hambam." I set him back on the stool.

"You should be," Ham says. "I could have rooned it."

"Ruined, sweetheart," Gran corrects.

Ham thinks for a second. "That's what I said. Rooned. It's like when Dad says, 'I've fucked it,' but you can't say that when you're a kid, can you?" He turns to me. "Hen, can you say 'fuck' when you're a kid?"

I nearly choke on my glass of water. "Uh. No, little man."

"Are *you* allowed to say it?" he asks curiously, licking sugar off the palm of his hand.

"Um."

"Of course, he is!" Gran says. "He's allowed to *do* it, if he wants."

Ham laughs. "Gran, you're silly. You can't do fu—"

"Let's maybe stop saying that word for now," I put in, because Gran's got a dangerous glint in her eye. Just as well too, because Mum comes home a few minutes later.

"Apple pie for dinner?" she questions.

"Just go with it, Billie," Gran says. "You need sugar."

"How was work?" I ask Mum quietly once she's put her bag down and is sitting at the table.

"Oh, good, Hen. Great. Lots of babies being born."

"Boys or girls?" I ask, because she always remembers.

"Two boys." She smiles. "How was school?"

"Eh. Fine, I guess."

I make my way upstairs to rip off my uniform and then I run a blisteringly hot shower.

Afterwards, I lie on my bed listening to Panic! at the Disco for a bit, trying to wind down. When that doesn't work, I log on to my computer and aimlessly update the coding on my Myspace for a while.

I scroll through updates from my friends, guys from school, and St. Adele's girls I know from debating and various musicals over the years.

I look at the profiles of the ones I've actually spoken to (that leaves three), trying to discern through the song/picture on their page whether or not they'd be open to a pity date.

I stare at Lily's the longest while it plays a choppy pop song through my speakers and think about asking her.

It'd be fun. We were getting on, I think, during the section of the Party I actually remember. But would a dance be a friend thing? Or too close to a Move? (A Bonnie-and-Clyde type of friends thing.)

I click back to the home page.

Ged's put up a photo of his toe after footy training. It's scrunched in on itself at an unnatural angle and looks like an angry toad.

Broken? I comment.

Absolutely fucked XD, he replies immediately. I shake my head.

Len's just posted a bulletin.

I click on it and scroll through the questions, reading his brief response to each one. As confirmed Desperate and Dateless, I'm pathetically pleased to be the last person he spoke to, called, and hugged.

7

On Friday the week after, Len and Vince are home sick with a fever-dream flu that's picking off our whole class. Despite Martin's sniffly indignation, I call it on debate club.

Ged persuades Harrison and me to catch the bus into the city with him after school instead to look for a "date shirt." He's managed several miraculous dates with Jess Fitzpatrick already, and none of us can figure out how.

"It's *different* this time," Ged tells us on the way. "I think she might be the One."

"That's great, man," I say, keeping my eyes on the progression of old brick buildings as we wind through the city.

Harrison snickers beside me. I thump him on the knee, and he turns toward the window too. It's been raining all week, the world outside smudged pearl.

We get off near ANZAC Square, pulling our shirts untucked and making our way down the footpath and then over the pedestrian crossing toward Queen Street. Harrison stops in the Plaza for Starbucks while Len's not here to judge. I get a cream-topped monstrosity too, out of rebellious solidarity.

The dripping city is quiet around us, still holding its breath in the four-thirty light before it exhales commuters for the day.

We duck inside a menswear store, and Ged holds up a Hawaiian shirt that even I know should be an actual crime.

I communicate a hard "no" with my eyes, and he shoves it back on the rack.

"So, anyway," Ged says. "What're you guys doing this weekend?"

Harrison and I shrug.

"Ant's having a bit of a gathering."

"Ant as in Anthony Fitzpatrick, your best mate who punched you?"

Ged gives me a look that could kill a small bird, then picks out a button-up with violent red and purple stripes.

"Yes, Hamlet. My mate. It's a bit of a welcome back thing for him, and Jess wants me to bring friends."

"Welcome back from where?" Harrison asks, replacing the shirt gently with a plain blue one.

"He got kicked out of uni."

"Ah."

"Why d'you want us to go?" I ask as Ged starts toward the changing rooms, already pulling off his NGS blazer.

He sticks his head out from behind the curtain a minute later, annoyed. "Cause she wants to like 'meet my friends' or some shit, and as bad luck would have it, that's you dickheads."

"We're not friends—I'm related to you," Harrison points out.

Ged emerges wearing the blue shirt. It's *quite* tight across the chest, but otherwise not entirely awful.

"Potato, tomato," he says. "I need you to come. The others too."

"But they're sick," I protest.

Ged gives me another look. "As if Cane won't come if you ask. Leave our off-brand Russell Brand to me."

"I really don't think he'll want to," I say.

"It's dress-up," Ged says suddenly, with the finality of "checkmate."

I open my mouth to argue, but then I remember the debacle that was Spew Grant. This is, possibly, my last chance for party redemption.

"Fine. Where and when?"

"The Shack. Seven-thirty."

"You're inviting us to a party at an abandoned house in the outer suburbs with blood on the walls?"

"We don't know for sure that it's blood, do we? And people have parties there all the time!"

"Jesus."

"Sorry, Jesus," Harrison says gleefully. "I'm pretty sure I have work."

———

I ring the Canes' doorbell on Saturday morning. It's sunlit-freezing under a hard blue sky, and I'm wearing the one coat I own—thrifted and camel colored—thrown haphazardly over an old jumper of Dad's with paint all over it. Len's street isn't fully up for the day yet, curtains forming tight-shut eyelids on the houses.

The door is painted black, with the old embossed cherubs underneath. I ring the bell again. There's footsteps inside, and then John swings it open. He's squinting down at his BlackBerry.

I wait for a long minute, before clearing my throat loudly.

"Hello, Henry," he finally says, his voice clipped like a politician's. "How are you?"

"Good!" I reply, too cheerily. "And . . . you?"

"Fine." He picks up a black leather bag from beside the door and slings it over one shoulder. He's wearing a suit and the sort of spicy cologne that has physical weight.

"Going on a trip?" I ask.

"Work," John corrects smoothly.

He does something high up in an advertising firm. Something important involving oozing charm and traveling most weeks out of the year.

"Right! Sorry."

John tilts his head. "What for?"

"Uh."

Conversations with John always feel weirdly as though I'm competing in a sport I don't know the rules of. He looks at me expectantly for a bit, then says, "You're after my son, I'm guessing?"

" . . . Yeah, if he's home?"

"Upstairs."

"Great."

He looks down at the bottom of my jumper where it's caked in yellow paint.

"My dad's got an exhibition coming up," I explain, crumpling it in my hand. "Occupational hazard."

John watches me. His eyes are the same color as the sky looks through the clouds drifting above us. After a beat of awkwardly silent jumper-assessing, he clears his throat even louder than I did.

Apparently, this signals the end of the conversation, because then he sidesteps me so narrowly that I almost trip over, and walks down the wooden steps.

He gets into his Porsche and accelerator-snarls backwards onto the road without checking his mirrors. I stare after him for a minute, then push the dead-cherubs door back open.

When Sarah was here, the house had a smell that was warm—roses maybe, or incense. Now it's gone, and still, save for the chandelier tinkling on a heating-duct breeze.

I jog upstairs and find Len lying upside down on his bed with the PlayStation and The National murmuring on an eighties turntable in the background. There's a photo of his mum hugging her corduroy-covered knees beside it that I haven't seen before. I think it's one he took.

"How's the plague going, then?" I open as brightly as I can, standing in front of him.

He pauses the game and sits up. His eyes are pink-rimmed, and he looks wiped out, but otherwise through the worst of it.

"What're you doing here?"

"I'm your flu tour guide, here to take you on the journey of recovery."

He snorts snottily. "Right. How's school?"

"Boring. Half the class is sick; even Martin's got it, though he refuses to go home. The Sniffer's got extension requests coming out of his eyeballs. I brought your homework."

I pick up the spare controller from his desk and wipe it gingerly with a tissue, then sit down on the floor.

We play for a few hours. I even almost beat him a couple of times. He has to keep stopping to cough up a lung into his sleeve.

I look over at his blotchy, sad face. I don't like it. For some reason, it clogs up my throat.

"It's settled!" I announce, pausing the game again. "You're coming over to mine, and we're doing something."

Len looks confused. "Something?"

"We're going to a party," I say with forced excitement.

"Where?"

"The Shrieking Shack."

"When you said you wanted to do something, I wasn't exactly picturing being willingly sacrificed to the Satanic gods."

"Technically, there aren't Satanic gods."

Len shoots me a dark look.

"What? I'm just saying, I feel like Satan would be a flying solo type of guy."

He doesn't concede me the point. "Still, that place is creepy."

"It's a bunch of private school kids. What's the worst that could happen?"

He sighs.

I grin.

"You said I had to get out and socialize more," I point out. "Experiences, et cetera."

"Did I? I don't recall."

"It's just a party. It'll be fun."

"Need I remind you of what happened last time?"

Low blow—he *is* in a bad mood.

"That's all changed now. I'm a new man."

He rubs his eyes. "Why are you so into the idea?" he asks. "Normally you'd just want to stay in and, like, watch Meryl Streep movies."

"Meryl can wait. Tonight, I'm your party guide."

"I thought you were my flu guide."

"It's a dual role. My range is endless."

Len shakes his head while he swings his legs over the edge of the bed.

We're still bickering about it when we clatter through my front door. I hold up Ged's pleading texts in rebuttal.

HAmLET R U GUYS CUMING

ANSER ME U FUKR

HAMLET PLS

PLS HAMLET

Len sighs forcefully.

"Come on," I plead. "He really wants us to go. You're good at parties!"

Mum's in the living room reading. "Party?" She sits up and looks at us. "What party?"

"We're not going," I tell her.

"Why not?"

"Because he's chicken." I point at Len.

"You have to go!" Dad's disembodied voice calls suddenly through the open casement window. He shakes what sounds like a paint bottle forcefully. "You're the son of *the Reubenator*! Partying's in your blood."

"It's really, really not!" I shout back. "But maybe it *could* be, if only . . ."

Len tosses a cushion at my head. "Dress-up parties are gauche," he says. "And we don't have anything to wear."

"Speak for yourself, Margaret Thatcher. I quite fancy myself with some vintage Chandler Bing hair."

"What's the theme?" Mum asks. "*Friends?*"

Len looks at me warningly, knowing as well as I do that if we tell her, his cause is lost.

I pull my eyes away. "Made in the eighties."

Mum actually screams. "But we have plenty of stuff, Hen! Most of Dad's old clothes are still in the garage."

"Perfect!" I grin at Len. "See? We have to go."

———

A while later we're posing beside the staircase dressed in what closely resembles a tracksuit made of scrunched up, fluorescent raincoats (me), and baggy jeans, white sneakers, black sunglasses, and arm warmers (Len).

"Wait!" Mum says, pulling something bright purple and elastic out of the musty box Dad refuses to throw away.

"Mum, no."

"*Yes*," Len encourages, his eyes lit up vengefully. "Go hard or go home, H-squared."

"I choose home, then."

They both pretend not to have heard me.

I let Mum slide the headband onto my forehead. It does look kind of cool. Plus, it holds my hair back where it's long and unruly at the top.

Len's fixing his own giant hair in the mirror over the mantle-piece. It took enough hairspray to fuel a small car to get it to look like that, but at least he finally got into the whole idea.

"Oh, you two look so *cute* together! Can I get one more to show Gran?"

Reluctantly, I let her take a couple more, indulging Len as he poses with his chin in his hand. And he says I'm dramatic.

We leave soon after, speeding onto the overpass in Len's car. The Shack looks even worse than I remember, rising up in the cold.

Still, I pull him along by his sleeve, enjoying the role reversal for a minute. I'm a good-time Sally, damn it.

The opening strains of "Time After Time" roll down the street toward us as we cross the road. (Cyndi Lauper's a good sign, right?) And at least there's lights on inside.

I follow Len up rickety stairs to the latticed entryway. It's like the one we have at home, except this one looks like someone recently set it on fire.

Blessedly, *everyone* is dressed up—a sea of fluorescent nylon and chiffon dots the chapped floorboards. We're in what was once a living room, with moth-eaten lace curtains billowing against the open windows. The party spills through several other rooms, and there's a makeshift drinks station against a wall in the corner.

"Coke?" Len asks.

"Beer," I correct confidently.

He raises his eyebrows.

"Go hard or go home, right?" I neglect to mention that I plan on nursing the same stale beer for the entire evening.

He grabs one for himself too. "Let's do this, then," he says flatly.

"What is this attitude? You really do need a party guide."

Len looks away from me, toward noises coming from outside. "Nothing. Come on."

We venture through a gutted prewar kitchen to the surprisingly expansive patio. I hang back, watching as Len greets his mates from the footy team. They acknowledge me with a begrudging tip of their chins.

Len comes alive, all at once, until he's the biggest public version of himself. Laughing joking sparring flirting.

More beer appears, but it's like that just narrows his focus. His eyes glint, movements blurring.

"My boiyss!" Ged says, sloppy, when he finds us. He's wearing what looks to be the top half of a *Ghostbusters* costume.

"Harrison Ford actually is working—you'd think Ronald McDonald could give him one night off! Vince cancelled, the bastard. Says he's too sick. Why aren't you sick, Lennon?"

Len snakes a hand around Ged's shoulder. "I am. Just wear it better."

"Where's Jess?" I ask.

"*Drank.*" Ged wrinkles his nose. "Jäger is not pretty, my friends. But she is. Even with spew all over her. Isn't that something?"

"Mmm," we agree.

"I love her," he says solemnly. "I want to have her babies. I should go find her, so we can do that."

"Maybe help her get cleaned up a bit first," I suggest.

Ged's eyes widen like he's just remembered something very important. "Yes! I'm meant to get towels."

"You go do that."

He tries to look serious, chin tucked into his chest. "Aye aye, Cap'n. You guys enjoy, though. Try to catch up with Ant!" He stumbles off.

Len mutters, "Sure. Can't wait not to do that."

"I guess this is a bit of a fizzer," I apologize. "It's fine. Always is with Ged."

Most of the guys from our school are gathered around a fire pit in the backyard, facing the forest reserve.

We join the group, but I hover off to the side. There are only a couple of faces I recognize—Travis Burrell and Jake Clarkson, whom Len beat for his position on the football team.

"Wow. You guys look *awesome*," Jake quips with fake enthusiasm.

"Jealousy is a disease, Clarkson," Len responds. "Get vaccinated."

"Fuck off."

Clarkson and his mates are all wearing flannel shirts and acid-wash jeans. I feel decidedly over-the-top in comparison, but Len seems unfazed. He sprawls on the grass and warms his hands by the fire.

The guys stare at us.

Len takes control of the situation with a force that makes me uneasy. "What are we up to, then?"

"Truth or dare," Clarkson says.

"How avant-garde of you. Deal us in."

Clarkson twists his lips up toward his nose, à la Donald Duck. "Nah."

"What? Afraid I'll win?"

"Is your loser mate even up for it?"

Impulsively, I down the rest of my beer in three gulps. It burns the front, sides, and back of my throat before moving into my stomach.

The other boys look at me like I'm a freak.

Len holds back a laugh. "Guess you have your answer."

And we play.

It goes on for a long time, each dare grosser than the last. I earn some paltry points for licking Vegemite off one of Travis's toes. Len runs through the party stripped down to his underwear.

Eventually, it stops being a game and becomes a pissing contest between Clarkson and Len. The truths taper off and the dares intensify, until we've all opted out except the two of them.

Somebody brings more beers over.

Clarkson cracks one and offers it to me. He watches me, waiting to see if I'll actually drink it. I take a long slug, just to annoy him. Then I drink two more bottles.

Travis declares a while later that the next dare is the last. Winner takes all.

Len leans back nonchalantly, but he has his all-in-nothing-to-lose look that tells me this will be a fight to the death.

"I dare you," Clarkson taps his chin thoughtfully, "to make out with . . ."

"A kissing dare?" Len mutters under his breath, "Original. Who's the lucky girl?"

"Hamlet," Clarkson finishes victoriously.

There's enough alcohol in my system that the words don't fully register for a moment. Everything feels slightly unreal and the sky swirls overhead. Indigo trees and stars. I do note that Len's three faces cloud over.

He sits up. "What? No."

Clarkson folds his arms. "That's the dare."

"It's stupid," Len says. "Give me another one."

"Nope. I'm pretty set on this one, to be honest."

"Forget it."

"Take it, or forfeit."

I'm dimly aware that the gathered crowd, which by this point is rather large, has gone quiet. Len glances at me for a moment. Eyes bright. Calculating.

I nod once. Multiple beers on an empty stomach isn't doing much for my judgment. I want him to win. My world has narrowed in focus to that questionable goal alone. He has to beat Clarkson—our very lives depend on it.

"Go on, then." Clarkson's grin takes over his face, until it's something sicker. "And make it a *show*."

Len still looks conflicted. I feel a bit outraged, in a sleepy kind of way, that dare-kissing me is such a repulsive prospect.

With one last lip-biting scowl, he leans forward slowly on his knees. There's a tense pause. Then his jaw sets, decisive, and he puts cold hands on my cheeks to pull my face toward his.

The crowd whoops, and there's a disjointed beating in my ears that could either be the music or my pulse, and then I'm not aware of any of those things anymore because Len's mouth is on my mouth.

It feels odd, at first. Clinical. A neat sentence with no commas.

Then it happens in a spill like thoughts: the bottom of my stomach drops out, and before I know what I'm doing I start to kiss him back. Hard.

I reach my hand up to grip his shoulder, the other spreading out on his cheek so my thumb holds the cut of his jaw. Len's mouth opens wider; lights switch on under my skin, bursting bruising color. He scrunches a fist in my shirt.

With him kneeling and me sitting we're almost level, but still I pull him in, until our knees touch. He pushes back, his tongue nudging at my teeth, and—

Oh.

I know Len's been with guys before. He just likes whoever he likes. I've heard stories—vague details—and okay, maybe I've *thought about it*, but I didn't think it could be like this. Like being turned inside out and rearranged differently in a tumble of seconds.

I watch, stunned, as he falls back on his heels with one hand still cupped in the shape of my head.

84

Everyone is staring.

The place may be on fire. (I definitely am.)

I have never kissed anybody like that in my life. (I've never kissed anybody, full stop.)

I keep looking at Len, my hampered mental function trying, desperately, to figure out what the hell just happened. He isn't looking at me but at our audience, which has gone mum with shock.

Slowly, he wipes his lips on his sleeve, then bows. If there's one thing Lennon Cane does well, it's *make a show*.

Reluctantly, Clarkson claps once. "Jesus," he says loudly, looking both impressed and a little scared. "You're off the planet, Cane."

"You have no idea," Len says.

"Truly. Completely cooked."

"Told you I'd win." Len's voice sounds off. It feels like we crossed a line, but I don't know which one.

"I need a drink," he announces.

Everybody laughs. It's a testament to his social status that nobody sees this as anything more than a dare, another layer to the ever-shifting enigma that is Len. No big deal.

Because it wasn't.

(Was it?)

A long-fingered hand appears in front of my face.

I let it pull me to my feet, the world seeming to tilt even more than it did before. Suddenly we're face to face, my hazy eyes gripped by the storm in his.

He smiles tightly. "Experiences with a capital E."

I want to ask, *What was that? Did you feel . . . ?*

"Right," I say instead.

We stand for a minute, awkward. So awkward.

"I hope I don't get pregnant," I joke. Weird. So weird.

He laughs gratefully and punches my shoulder. "Yeah. Or sick."

We're back to being normal us, the friends who walked into this party an hour ago. So why do I still feel like my heart just shit itself?

"You coming?" He gestures to where the others are gathering on the creaky balcony to go back inside.

"I actually think I'm gonna head home." I decide on the spot. "I mean, it's late."

(I need to process whatever just happened. I need to *go*.)

Len bites his lip. "Oh. Yeah."

I turn away, trying to put some space between the washing machine in my stomach and the look on his face.

"Hamlet," he calls after me.

"Yeah?"

"Are you . . ."

I spin back around. His face is pained.

"What?"

He takes a breath. "Will you be okay to get home?"

"Mmhmm." My head pounds. "I'll be fine."

"Okay. Guess I'll see you Monday, then."

I'm already moving. "See you."

I push through the people with their voices too loud and find my way to the overgrown front garden. Once I'm sure I'm out of sight, I lean against the battens underneath the house, sliding down until I'm on the ground with my legs stretched out and my elbows on my knees.

I drop my head and let my fringe fall over my face. I lost Dad's headband at some point. I think I saw it get tossed away.

While I was playing seven minutes in public heaven/hell.

With my best friend. My *male* best friend. Whose *lip I think I just bit*. Like I'm Edward frigging Cullen. Except I'm pretty certain he never kissed Emmett.

Shit.

What if this changes every single thing?

It's past midnight, late-night wind grabbing my wrists. I look up, trying to find the moon, but it's too cold or too cloudy or too late.

I have one of those floaty out-of-body moments where I feel like I'm watching myself. Alone on a street corner, completely lost even though I know exactly where I am.

I pull out my phone. "Mum? I need you to come pick me up."

8

I don't get pregnant, but I do get sick. The kind of sick that makes you wonder what terrible things you could have done in a past life to deserve it. I wake up on Sunday morning feeling like I've been hit by a truck, with my phone vibrating in my pocket.

I flip it open and wait for my vision to un-blur.

Missed call from Emilia. I punch the call back button with my thumb.

"Hen!" she answers. "Where are you? I'm at the café, and Len's not here either."

A faint memory floats up about plans to meet today to look at the uni course books she ordered.

"Ems," I groan into the phone. "I forgot. I'm sorry."

"Whoa. Why do you sound like Cher?"

"Sick," I choke out. "Er, Len is too. Sorry again. Raincheck?"

"Don't even worry about it. Keep those germs to yourself. Want me to bring you anything?"

I could kiss her, if not for the fact that that's what got me into this mess in the first place.

"I'll be okay. But thanks."

"Drink fluids," she instructs. "I'll see you soon."

Mum eases my door open just as I'm hanging up the phone,

leaning her cheek against the frame. "Hey, slugger. How're you feeling?"

I flop back on my pillows, wincing as my brain slides around in my skull. "Shid."

She reaches down to feel my forehead. "Hmm. You've got a temperature. That's weird—you were fine yesterday."

"Must have picked something up."

"That's fast, though ..." She thinks for a minute. "Wait! Did you kiss someone last night?"

Last night. Clarkson. Stars spinning. *Len.*

Heat floods my cheeks, doubled by the chills racing over my skin.

"You did!" she guesses, reading my face. "Do I need to be worried? Are we about to repeat the Talk?"

"*Mum*. It's me. As if." I mustn't sound convincing, though, because she purses her lips slyly and squeezes my arm.

I wince again. Everything hurts.

"All right, sweet. I'll get you some Tylenol."

"Don't you have anything heavier?" I beg. "Like, morphine?"

She rubs my fiery cheek. "From what I can tell, you've got a cold. Tylenol will do fine."

"What's the point of having a mother who's a doctor if she won't hook you up with the goods when you've got death flu?"

"I'm happy to hand deliver your babies one day," Mum says brightly. "But beyond that, I've got nothing."

"You do," I accuse. "You just won't give it to me. Your *firstborn*."

"You're right, I'm saving the good stuff for Ham. He just feels more likely to succeed. Got to invest wisely." She winks and leaves.

Thoughts of last night start to settle like a heavy blanket over me. *WhatwillhesaywhatwillotherpeoplesayJesusgodshit.* I shove them to the back of my mind with as much force as I've got.

Mum returns with, god bless her, the heaviest kind of cold tablets—the ones with codeine and angels' tears in them. I gulp two down gratefully and switch on the TV, keeping my mind resolutely on the midday movie. After a while, I switch my phone off too.

———

I'm sick for days, bedridden and bored out of my mind. The wet weather sticks around, blowing an arctic draft under my bones if I dare crack a window. My room ends up an incubated cocoon.

I venture outside only to use the bathroom. Dad and Ham are too scared to come near me, so Mum brings me dinner and treats from the hospital vending machine each night when she takes my temperature. She doesn't complain about me watching *Air Crash Investigations* nonstop for twenty hours, so I know she's at least a little concerned.

It's cleansing, after a while. I slow down for the first time in months—just lying there and looking out at the sky bleeding from pink to blue to black and back again.

I start to come around on the fourth day. I'm able to stand up in the shower and shave for the first time since last week.

By Thursday, I feel pretty much back to normal, but I avoid school anyway, deciding to give it an even seven days before facing the world again.

On Saturday, I switch my phone on for the first time since the morning after the Night That Was. There's a flurry of concerned texts from Emilia, a few random updates from Vince, Harrison, and Ged and . . .

Nothing.

———

"The prodigal nerd returns," Ged cheers outside homeroom on Monday. "How the fuck've you been?"

"Terrible, obviously. Desolate over not seeing your ugly face every day."

"Sorry if I gave it to you, mate," Vince says sincerely. "That shit was no joke."

"Oh, I don't reckon it was you! It was just a bad bug."

"Bad is an understatement. I got so high on cough medicine one night that I sicked in my mum's wellies."

Ged looks at him blankly.

"Gumboots," a voice explains from behind us.

I turn around, but my organs stay put.

"Good to see you're still alive," Len says.

He looks the same as always—morning-pale in the sun wearing against-the-rules purple socks—except he's standing slightly further away than usual, like I'm contagious even though he's already had it.

Inside my head is kaleidoscopic: *lips-tongue-teeth.*

(Normal. Be normal.)

"Ha! Yeah," I near-shout at him. "Um. Only just."

"You must have been destroyed, mate," Vince continues obliviously, steering me toward the classroom. "You look like a POW."

I turn away from Len's forehead, which has creased down the middle.

"Oh my god."

Len sits so far on the opposite side of homeroom that I'm almost looking forward to assembly afterwards, until Martin smells blood in the water.

"Look who decided to show up!" he shouts once I'm at the auditorium door.

"Jeez, Finch." I wince. "Can you just—"

"Can I just what, Hamlet? Not exist?"

"No, just—"

"Because someone has to tell you we missed the deadline for formal in the ballroom."

"What? How?"

Martin rolls his eyes upwards, pretending he has to think about it. "Maybe the fact that the person in charge of it was incommunicado for a week with the Consumption?"

I almost swear out loud, but he's already doing impeachment eyes.

"That," I admit, "is not ideal."

Students are starting to file in. "You reckon?"

"But weren't we just going to do it in the gym anyway, originally?"

Martin kicks the mic stand like it's my face. "We'll still have to hold an emergency year-level meeting to vote on it."

"Okay."

"*Soon.*"

"Yes, I just said okay."

———

The Not Normal actually intensifies after that. I feel like I'm unravelling with everything else, walking around in a daze for the rest of the week, worrying that people will talk about what happened. (They haven't, as far as I can tell.)

Len talks to me, sort of, when we're with the Boiyss, but we bolt if we're ever left alone together. I can't figure out whether that means he's thinking about it too, or that he's decided to forget it, and I'm weirding everything up by being me.

He gets this look on his face sometimes—a frowning echo of his expression when I ran away from the Shack. It's . . . embarrassment (I *think*). It's the same look that's on mine.

I wrote a story once about a first kiss. There was some magical element I can't remember, lips touched, then the girl went to sleep forever because she'd tasted perfection or something equally dramatic. It was full of unnecessary adjectives, and all the things I didn't know.

I want to go back there now: not knowing. Kisslessness. I envy that girl—eternal slumber sounds like a pretty sweet deal.

This . . . isn't like that. It's waking up.

Every time I have to get a book from my locker and he's at his, it's a defibrillator shock.

I can't stop picturing it—every time I see him, even when it's in my mind—his fingers gripped into my shirt. My skin.

I tell myself it must be normal to remember your first kiss. To attach meaning to it, even when there isn't—can't be—any. Anything else is surely just a proximity thing. A phase.

We've been too close for too long and just need some space for a while.

———

I'm thinking about it, the proximity thing, when we're working on our English monologues on Thursday afternoon. We've been looking at the way inciting incidents can bulldoze into everyday life. *Gatsby* wouldn't even have a plot if the two central characters weren't neighbors.

It's stiflingly warm in the period six light, and the air conditioners are all still switched to heat. We're meant to pick our topics today, but Vince is still only a few chapters in and Nick is pissing him off.

"Bloody hell," he complains. "All this guy does is go on and on about how great Gatsby is. Why don't you just marry him?"

I'm half-watching Len and Ged brainstorming outside and am hyper-conscious of every muscle in my face. "Mmm."

Vince snaps his book shut. "How're we gonna spin a whole monologue out of that, then, duck face?"

Len looks up and catches me looking.

Blood explodes in my cheeks and the space between my collarbones.

He does a sort of wave, lifting his hand halfway. I freeze.

It's so awkward I think he actually winces a bit before turning away.

"Hello?" Vince snaps. "What are you looking at?"

"Nothing!" I burst out. "I'm just . . . I'm thinking."

"Oh yeah? Thinking about what?"

"Thinking . . . that's kind of a valid reading."

He pulls a goofy disbelieving face. "What, that it's secretly a bromance?"

(Why is it so hot in here?)

"Er, yeah. I'm pretty sure there's a whole theory that Nick was, like . . . into Gatsby."

Vince digests this for a minute. "Hmm. Bit gay, isn't it?"

(I'm sweating. I can feel it on my top lip.)

"Um, we could link it to the love theme." My brain clicks into gear despite itself. "Gatsby's pretty much the only character Nick actually cares about."

Vince still looks doubtful. "I dunno."

"Think about it," I say, my own thoughts coming faster. I check none of the guys around us are listening. "He's barely interested in Jordan, except to describe her as if she's a horse, but Nick's *obsessed* with Gatsby. It's almost like . . . I don't know. Like he's only made real through Gatsby, or something."

"Interesting ideas, Henry!" Ms. H. exclaims. She was walking around the room, but she stops behind us. "Because of—"

"The elevator scene!" I finish too loud and too fast.

She smiles down at me. "Good to see someone was listening to me talk about subtext."

"Suck-up," Vince hisses under his breath when she leaves.

He slumps back in his seat for a minute, blowing out a breath, then picks up his copy of *Gatsby* again. "Fine. Where's that bit?"

"Here—I bookmarked it."

9

In debating at the end of the week, Martin gives us each a stapled folder of research and a breakdown of our time between now and finals, which are only a few weeks away.

We're up against St. Ad's, so everything is very us versus them and school pride-y.

"Is this necessary?" I flap the thick folder in my hand. "I already found us two case studies."

"*Yes*, Hamlet!" he erupts. "We have to beat the girls if we want the cup again."

I set everyone working on their own arguments so we don't have to talk. We're doing a more complex model than usual, but I can't focus on mine.

Len is sitting right up the back, writing rapidly with one cheek resting on his splayed fingers. I can't help *watching* him—every tiny mannerism.

I pull out my notes just to look busy and don't absorb a word.

I pack up ten minutes early and wave goodbye to everyone (Martin frowns), then bolt out the school gates as quickly as possible.

Mum's working tonight, Gran's got Ham, and Dad's head's

in the clouds, so it's just me and the moon. Proximity may be the enemy, but my imagination is almost as big as my boots, which are size eleven and a half.

As soon as I get up to the safety of my gabled room, I'm a swarm of scenarios for how this could play out long term—none of them good.

Option 1: I sit on whatever this is as hard as I can until it goes away.

Option 2: I try kissing someone else, just to see what happens (unlikely, given Spew Grant).

Option 3: I talk to him.

The last one is the best-worst option because it's exactly what I'd do if things were different. If it was just me worrying that I'd kissed *someone*. Not him.

I try to sleep but can't. My eyes roam the dull dark, until they reach the row of photos on my desk. It's terrifically ironic that the biggest one is of me and Len at the beach last summer.

There's so much history in his face. The square set of his jaw, the golden brows, the way his teeth grip the right side of his bottom lip. I can picture him when we were five, when we were eleven, when we were sixteen.

How can I think of him like this? (How can I *not?*)

———

I make up my date with Emilia in the morning to keep from being alone with myself. It's uni open day season, and trying to focus my runaway brain on the future feels like as sound an avoidance strategy as any.

She picks me up at nine, and I fold my legs into the front seat of her Fiat while she steers us carefully toward the city and we listen to my emo mix CD.

I think about telling her. For four and a half songs.

We find a car park and walk through the campus, coming to a stop under the shade of a tree outside the stoic off-yellow law faculty building. There's a band playing, and the air smells faintly like freedom. I breathe in deep and watch as Emilia disappears inside.

I wait, clutching a shiny course brochure while a sun shower starts up. It's humid—the claustrophobic Brisbane kind that clings wet to your skin even when you're asleep. Baked flower petals hiss across the cement and stick to the bottom of my shoes.

"Okay, I think I'm done," Ems says when she emerges fifteen minutes later. "Are you done?"

"So done."

We get lunch from a stand selling sausages in bread. There's an amphitheatre cut big and gray into the hill directly beside it; we dump our goody bags and sit down.

"What do you think?" Ems asks, taking a bite.

There's a blond guy coming out of the admin building across from us—my heart stops for a second.

(Not him.)

I try to focus on Emilia and not on the chaos that has become my life.

"I could definitely see us here," she prompts, wiping mustard off her cheek.

"Yeah?"

"Mmhmm. Having cute brunches we can't afford when we should be at a nine o'clock class."

I smile through the pain.

"All you have to do is decide what you want to do," she finishes, flicking onion off her sausage.

"Is that all?"

"Preferences are due in a month. Have you picked yet?"

"Working on it," I lie.

Her forehead creases. "Is something going on with you? You can tell me."

Mind reader. I stuff half the slice of bread into my mouth. "No."

She hesitates, watching me chew, then says bluntly, "Because your mum sort of asked me if we've kissed, when I picked you up."

I drop the rest of the bread in my lap, appetite evaporating like a humidity mirage. "She *what?*"

"Actually, she said, 'Are you the flu-tongued assassin?'"

"Oh my god. Oh my *god.*"

"Don't worry." She pats my hand. "I set her straight. My standards aren't that low yet."

"God!" I say again. My mouth is drier than the bread. "What a wishful . . . she's in . . . "

Ems is watching me carefully. "*Did* you kiss someone?"

(Oh god.)

I look away and take a rushed breath, furiously picking petals off the toe of my shoe.

My pulse is so loud I wonder if she can hear it.

How do you even begin this conversation? There's no dry run, no way to be sure of the outcome.

So I stall.

"I mean . . . define 'kissed someone.'"

"Did you put your mouth on someone else's mouth?"

"Um. Technically, they put their mouth on my mouth."

"*Technically?!*" Emilia explodes, then sees the terror on my face and reins herself in. "Wait. At Ged's thing?"

I can taste metal. "Yeah."

"But wasn't Jess the only girl there?"

"Um."

I watch it play out across her face. Agonizingly slowly.

Ems was with me when I sent a ten-page fan letter to Ben McKenzie from *The O.C.* when we were thirteen. It's why I chose her, both this weekend and in year two, but still.

This is maybe the worst wait of my life.

" . . . It was someone from North?" Her voice is soft.

I nod once.

She tucks her hair hard behind both ears. "So then . . . what? Did you . . . do you think . . . ?"

My skin feels too small for body. I can't say it. But I've come this far, and I have to keep this focused on me so she doesn't figure out the rest; Ems is even more protective of Len than I am.

I shrug helplessly.

"*Wow.*" Ems blows out a breath. "Sorry! But wow!"

I can see her mind whirring, analyzing which is the right question to ask first.

"Why didn't you tell me this? We've been together all day!"

"Because I was freaking out about it! *Am* freaking out about it. And I was . . . I don't know. Worried, I guess."

Ems frowns deep and serious. "About what?"

I pull my glasses off and wipe them on my shirt. "Just—that things might be different, with us. Or, I don't know—weird.

Because it's like a . . . *development.*" I have to force myself to keep looking at her.

Her eyes go big and wet. Mine are burning. She takes my hand and holds my fingers tightly, even when I try to pull away.

"Oh, Hen—*no.* You're finally physically interacting with another human being—I'm *excited!*"

Something very heavy lifts off my chest.

"But," she bites her lip. "Do you . . . *like* him, this person who kissed you?"

Panic pours down on my head. I yank my hand away.

"*Henry.*"

"I don't know! It all happened kind of fast."

"Well, do you want to do it *again?*"

(No. Yes.)

Yes.

I grimace.

"Then there's your answer!"

"What the hell do I do with that, though? With all this, like . . ." I let it in for a minute, the swirling in me. "Looking at someone and just . . . remembering it all the time."

"Sounds to me," Ems says sympathetically, "like you've got a crush."

"Ew. No, I don't."

"Okay. You're blushing, but okay."

"I am not!"

"You are! Henry Hamlet with a crush. The world's not ready."

"I want to go home now, please."

"We definitely need coffee first."

"Home. Take me home—"

"And then I'm gonna try to guess who it is."

My stomach doubles over. "*No!*"

"Also," she says, suddenly serious again, mascara smudged under bright eyes. "You know what I mean, right? About us. Sometimes I look at you and think: you could literally murder someone in cold blood and you'd still be stuck with me, probably forever."

I exhale hard relief and let her have my hand again. "Back at you, kid."

I'm definitely not saying who. Probably forever.

———

When I get home, I go to *Gatsby*. (But only because we need to get our script done this weekend.)

I pull out my English notebook and lie in bed with the window thrown open, starting where Vince and I left off at the end of chapter two.

Nick gets stuck on a night out with Human Trash Tom Buchanan and his mistress, then goes off with the photographer guy, McKee. Even though it's cooling down outside, my face is white-hot when I write in my notes: *Nick in bed with McKee . . . looking at photos . . . then wakes up at train station.*

Next up is Nick meeting Gatsby. I write: *N describes G's smile like this is a Kmart romance novel.*

Gatsby's nervous reunion with his lost love Daisy and Nick organizing it even though he knows it's a bad idea: *N wants what's best for G; for G to be happy regardless of anything else.*

Daisy hitting Mistress Myrtle with her car and Gatsby taking the fall: *N thinks G secretly fragile? Protective. Doesn't tell him he was wrong to do that.*

102

We're basing our Nick script on chapter eight, the last time he sees Gatsby alive. *N tells G he's worth more than all the characters put together . . . Worships him?*

Lastly, I flip to chapter two again.

Nobody got it, in class, why the Mr. McKee scenes are the only bits of the book where the action's cut out by dot-dot-dots. I read through it again, chewing the cap on my pen and trying to think like a drunk novelist in the 1920s. The thing is, Nick's a decent judge of other people, but he's also pretty delusional about himself.

Afternoon cold blows through the window. When I close the book, I'm shivering.

I hesitate for a minute. Then I add to my notes: *Fitzgerald dot-dot-dots the stuff N doesn't want to feel.*

(Which is what, Hamlet?)

(. . . What?)

I throw the book over my face and inhale its paper smell until the room is washed by night.

After a while, I get up and go downstairs to sit with Ham. I pull him into my lap even though he's too big for it now, his sweaty lavender-smelling hair tickling my chin.

"Hen?" he says with his eyes on the Disney channel.

"What is it, buddy?"

He swivels to look at me. "Are the Jonas Brothers nice?"

"Um . . ." I try to pull my head into the moment. "Probably? Yep. Yes."

"Gran said they're man-fat heads."

I translate that. "Manufactured?"

"Yeah," he says seriously. "But I like them."

"Well, then you can."

"Oh."

"You can like whatever you want."

"Can I?"

"Course, Hambam."

"Then I do!" he declares, turning back to look at the screen.

Ham squishes into my chest like a log for a full hour. I almost manage to focus on him. (But of course, the best one out of these dudes would be called Nick.)

I flip open my phone and stare at Len's number. I start to type r the JoBros even real until I remember nothing is right now and throw my phone on the opposite couch.

———

Before bed I pick the notebook up again. I find a new page without switching on my lamp and try to write my way out of my thoughts, but all that comes is a mess of scribbled sentences all bleeding together:

I'M LOSING IT BECAUSE I KISSED YOU / BECAUSE I KISSED YOU I MIGHT LOSE YOU.

10

Our monologues are due the following week. We spend most of our lunchtimes practicing in the drama room and opt to perform ours first up on the day.

Vince unravels even more than me.

"Can't believe I let you talk me into this," he spits when we're standing side-stage.

"You're *Gatsby*," I remind him. "Literally all you have to do is die."

"I'm not like you, mate!" he cries. "I can't act. I dreamed last night that I sat up halfway through the performance and started talking."

"What'd you say?" I ask.

"I said, 'Fuck the police!' but I think that's just because—oi! Stop laughing."

"I'm not," I lie.

"*It's not funny*," he hisses. "I'm going to make a complete arse of myself, I know it."

I put my hands on his shoulders. "You're not, because I won't let you. I'm not losing my A."

"You ready, boys?" Ms. H. calls.

"Oh, Jesus," Vince whimpers. "Sorry, Jesus."

"Focus." I steer him toward the stage entrance.

We've brought Ham's wading pool in, filled and tugged to center stage with Ged's help at recess. Vince delivers his death soliloquy woodenly but word-perfect, then bursts the little packet of fake blood in his chest pocket and falls theatrically into the water while I wait in the wings.

I'm wearing gray slack-type pants and a white shirt with faded suspenders I got from Gran, and vintage glasses with lenses so strong I can't see (even more than usual).

I/Nick rush into the scene, making sure my face hangs with the appropriate amount of devastation.

I start my speech off slow, building momentum. After a bit of effort, I even manage to make myself tear up. I'm relieved that it's dead quiet when it's time for the final lines.

I understand where Nick's coming from. He's proud and naive at the same time. He resists how deep the connection with Gatsby goes—says he wants to stop lying to himself but runs scared, most of the time.

"You were more myself than I was." I sob over Vince's suitably lifeless body, then turn toward the audience. "We toil our days in vain dark, searching for a light whose very nature is to elude us: hope. You had it in spades, friend—and mine goes, here. With you."

I lean into Vince's wet chest. He doesn't start trying to sit up/rise from the dead until the lights dim and the class is clapping half-heartedly.

"Bravo, Henry!" Ms. Hartnett cheers.

We take our bows, linking arms under the shaky spotlight operated by a year-seven kid somewhere up the back.

"*Gayest* fucking thing I've ever seen," Jake Clarkson mutters.

106

"Jacob!" Ms. H. calls severely. "I have ears. And you now have a lunchtime detention."

"That was the *point*, dumb arse!" Ged hisses hotly.

"It's called *acting*," Vince spits.

Clarkson drops his voice and fixes his gaze on me. "Looked pretty real to me."

I flush fury red to my eyeballs. "Yeah, it looked like an *A*. Same way yours is gonna look like a *D*."

"Ooh! A *D*," Clarkson repeats in falsetto. He and Travis crack up.

Ms. H. calls out the next group, and Vince yanks me toward the change rooms.

———

"So, nice job," Len says when we're filing out for lunch.

I look up. (What?) "Yeah?"

The Boiyss run ahead, jumping on Vince and miming being dead.

Len stops walking. "Yeah. The bit about the two boats anchored together was cool."

"Oh. Thanks."

It stormed this morning but it's clear now, puddles on the footpath drying.

He reaches to pull off his school jumper. "Ah. Help," he says in a muffled voice when the jumper and his shirt are both half over his head, his face and arms swallowed by red wool.

Without thinking, I grasp the bottom of his shirt where it's come untucked and pull down. My fingers brush against his bare back on the dimpled bit, right at the base of his spine.

And then I am thinking. A lot.

I'm thinking about muscles under my palm and acting, and how the skin of his face feels softer or at least it did under my thumb. I'm thinking about Jay Gatsby, and are we really all just walking around in jumpers made out of nerves because right now *every single one of mine* is switched on.

There's no rule book for this. I mean, who gets it this bad for their best friend, after one stupid kiss? It's positively Shakespearean; the real Hamlet's got nothing on me.

Len's head finally pops back into view, hair mussed and his collar askew.

The sun makes his eyes glow almost green, color threading through carefully, the way light does in water.

———

Martin's emergency year-level meeting about the formal takes place the next morning, all of us stuffed between two of the science classrooms with the adjoining wall collapsed.

"As you know," he begins, "the formal is fast approaching. And due to some unforeseen admin complications, we now don't have a venue." He stares at me for backup.

I look up guiltily from scanning the pairs of eyes for Len's. "Er, yeah. That's right."

Martin looks livid. "So," he continues through his teeth, "we're taking a vote. Now."

I find him then—back row, legs dangling, sitting on top of a lab table with Harrison.

"Uh." I clear my throat. "Who wants to do the hotel function room and just pay the late booking fee?"

A few hands raise.

"Okay. And, uh, the community hall?"

A few more hands.

"Right, so . . . all those in favor of just using the gym, like they did last year?"

"Weren't we gonna do that anyway because then tickets are like ten bucks each?" Ged pipes up. Len leans forward, laughing, to whack him on the shoulder.

"Yeah."

Fifty hands shoot up. Martin's eyes start to water, his elaborate ballroom fantasy catching fire.

"Right," I call it. "It's decided, then! We're having it in the gym. Thanks, everyone."

This outcome is both good and bad. Good because it gets Martin off my back. Bad because it means all we have to do organization-wise is consult the list of vendors the Sniffer gave us, and I have to go back to regular school programming.

Except not, at all.

The space between Len and me dissipates post-*Gatsby*. He pulls in close again, as close as we've ever been. We sit together in every class we share. We pair off in conversations at lunch; we argue in modern history. The other guys don't question anything—it's just balance restored, things as they should be. As they've always been.

They are for *him*, at any rate. For me, it gets a bit . . . weird.

It's physically painful, all of a sudden, to be near him. I try to write it off as just another aspect of our friendship, but I look for him. Constantly. I'm tense until I know he's in the room. I clench my hands to keep from loitering by the lockers when I know he'll walk past.

There's something simmering under my skin too. It squirms in my chest every time I'm around him. And when I'm not. When I'm studying. When I'm sleeping.

I can't even begin to unravel what that means, so I push it away. Blessedly, schoolwork consumes us in the coming weeks, and I barely stop to shower, let alone think.

I put my uni preferences in—creative writing and journalism, though I'm not sure of either—at both the big unis. I squeeze formal and debating preparation into the limited free time I have, grateful for the excuse to keep my head as busy as possible.

Martin and I get special dispensation from the Sniffer to leave classes to confirm the caterer, decorators, DJ, etc. I milk it like an engorged cow, dodging the classes I share with Len as often as possible. The teachers are obliging, and nobody notices I'm barely ever where I'm supposed to be, except Finch, who can't snitch because he's doing the same.

Any leftover spare moments are dedicated to distracting myself.

I help Dad in the studio, spending hours chipping away at clay under his careful supervision. He's doing a series of people—a family he plucked straight out of his head.

I do housework with Mum.

I garden with Gran and Marigold.

At night, I rearrange my bookshelves alphabetically, then again by genre, until they're so neat they could belong to anyone.

My avoidance strategy works for a while, but then debating

finals hit, which means a dangerous number of hours needing to be spent with my gold-headed second speaker.

We've already got draft speeches, an airtight structure, a bunch of cases of crime-committing friend duos, and a long list of the opposition's possible affirmative points prepped for.

Still, we meet in the library every lunchtime to fine-tune our argument. Harrison smuggles chips in his bag, and Martin writes yet more pre-rebuttals on note cards.

On Thursday Len declares his argument is finished and picks up mine to proof, his eyes moving over my messy handwriting. "Yep. Good."

I light up like an oil lamp.

(Sitting next to him is fire now, every time.)

Martin leans over, shoving me out of the way. "Hamlet, you've grossly misused the word 'libel.'"

Nothing kills unwanted stomach-feelings like the Fincharoo. We have one last meetup at my place the night of the finals, to run through everything properly.

Len shows up an hour early, with a leather jacket over his NGS garb and rain in his hair. He reaches up and uses the excess condensation to slick it back from his face, and I realize this is going to be a disaster.

I don't know if it's nerves about the debate or the fact that we haven't been properly alone for what feels like ages, but it's a hailstorm in my stomach.

"What are you staring at?" He pulls off his jacket and sets it on the hook.

"You're wet."

(*Good god.*)

He lifts an eyebrow slowly. "So?"

"Er. They mark presentation."

(Nice save—not.)

"The debate's not till seven. I'll be dry by then."

Martin and Harrison arrive not long after. We cram onto the couch, our note cards spread out on the coffee table.

"I still think this needs work," Martin complains, pointing to a key pillar of my argument.

"It's too late," Len cuts him off. "Plus, there's not really another way to say that without—"

"Opening ourselves up to counterattack," I finish.

"Yeah." He smiles. "Exactly."

I smile back.

Martin eyes us disdainfully. "Do you two have original thoughts, or is that off the table when you share the one brain?"

"I'm really going to miss you, Martin," Len says. "Your cheery spirit—it's unparalleled."

He's sitting next to me. I let him, to test myself.

It's been going well, until he reaches into his pocket for a stray note card and presses the whole side of his body against mine. (*AAAH*.)

My arm twitches like a marionette's. I jump up. "I'll, er, go get drinks," I sing-song, my heart roiling hotly somewhere up near my throat.

I get out of as much as I can after that, ironing my uniform (again) while Dad entertains the three of them in the living room. I spend so long perfecting my shirt I almost singe off the pocket.

"Hey, Martha Stewart," Len calls. "Hurry up, we need to rehearse your bit."

"Coming."

He leans back on the couch, eyes finding me . . . with my shirt off.

"What are you even doing?" His mouth kicks up at the corner. "Get dressed."

I feel myself flush from chest to forehead and kick the door closed to get dressed.

We run through everything twice, then thrice at Martin's insistence, before leaving.

The finals are held in an old hall just outside the city center. Dad parks ludicrously far away, so by the time we've trekked up the hill, the other team is sitting down and ready.

Emilia waves at us, and we wave back. Then she mimes slitting her throat, narrowing her eyes exaggeratedly.

Beside her is Jamila Perdid, whom I know for a fact Ems can't stand, because she always goes for the kill shot in rebuttal, a blond flint-faced girl I don't know, and Lily.

Spew Grant memories of the last time I saw her shoot through me, but . . . that's all. There's nothing else when my eyes meet her black-lined ones. I look away.

Jamila "the Verbal Javelin" Perdid (not a real nickname, but it should be) is first speaker for the affirmative. She defines the topic, then opens her argument with "It can be elucidated that proposing anything but a resounding affirmative to this question would be morally bankrupt, for several reasons. Firstly . . ."

I clench my fist on the table. Len motions with his hand for me to stop, already scribbling a rebuttal.

When Jamila's done, he's filled three notecards in heavy-handed script. He pushes them toward me. I scan them rapidly, fitting everything together in my head and scribbling bits of my own. Then I pick up the cards and move to the lectern.

Harrison's playing timekeeper, and I'm more nervous than usual when he dings for me to start.

I keep my voice smooth and even, using Len's words to dismantle Jamila's case with razor-sharp precision. Then I go through my argument with minimal "ums" and "ahs," trying to look at my cards as little as possible.

Emilia's argument is technically perfect, but she's rigid, like me.

When it's Len's turn, he takes a moment to look at the audience before he starts, planting his hands on the edges of the lectern and crossing one leg behind the other so he's leaning jauntily to the side.

"It's such a loaded term, isn't it? 'Partners in crime,' which can be defined as two people so close, or bonded, that they do everything together. At its root, though, a partner in crime is more literal: a close associate, and/or . . . accomplice."

There's something about the way he speaks I've always been jealous of. He's cocky. Compelling.

People listen.

I see it, like a ripple effect—he's *charming* them.

By the time he's finished even the adjudicator, a harassed McGonagall type in her seventies, looks thoroughly captivated.

" . . . forcing married couples to testify against each other in court assumes close bonds are specific to them. They're not. In fact, most partners in crime aren't spouses at all—spouses are often kept *out* of such proceedings. When selecting a criminal accomplice, people are more likely to gravitate to those they have allowed *in*, from the outset of said bond." He pauses and looks up. "Friends."

I fight it, hard.

But I'm charmed too.

He runs through his examples and statistics off by heart, then gives the audience one last lopsided smile, before sitting back down beside me nonchalantly, holding his notes.

Across from us, Emilia's nostrils are flared. *Cheater*, she mouths at Len. He winks.

There's no real hope for St. Ad's after that. Lily puts up a good final fight, but she's against Martin. If Jamila's a javelin, Martin's a viper—he snaps and snipes his way to abounding applause, and our victory is sealed.

Aussie McGonagall awards us the cup (she hands it to Len, even though I'm team captain) and the audience, mostly tired-looking parents who'd probably rather be anywhere else, disperses while the teams shake hands.

"You play dirty, Cane," Emilia says.

"Never said I didn't."

"What about you guys," I say, pointing at Lily. "Nice casual use of 'amoral.'"

She laughs. "What *else* do you call letting spouses off the hook, hmm?"

"A winning argument." Martin tips his chin.

Jamila's face sours. "Oh, please. As if you won on merit."

"Jam," Lily says warningly.

"What else would you call it?" Harrison asks.

"You're manipulators! You did the exact same thing last year—you whore this one out," she stabs her thumb in Len's direction. "And the judges are putty in your hands."

"I was timekeeper last year," Len points out, mouth perched on a laugh. "How d'you figure that manipulated anyone?"

She looks so livid it's kind of funny. "Whatever you want

to tell yourselves. You're just lucky my dad isn't here—he's a lawyer. He'd sue all of you."

"So's mine," Ems says. "Pretty sure there's no legal recourse for a suit."

"Come on, J," the blond girl mutters. "It's our last debate. Just shake their hands, and then we can go."

With a jagged look, she reluctantly does so. Len holds onto her hand for too long, his eyes dancing, until she snarls and snatches it away. Emilia gives us yes-we-will-laugh-about-this-later eyes and follows Jamila to the back of the hall.

Lily shakes hands with me last.

"Good game," I say.

Her cheeks are flushed. "Yeah. Pleasure doing battle with you."

I stare into her eyes. They're celery green— pretty, but all I feel is . . . that her hands are clammy.

(*What is wrong with me?*)

"All right, well," she says, withdrawing her hand. "Message me, over the holidays. If you want."

"Absolutely. Will do."

She disappears after the others.

"Hook in," Len says from behind me.

"What?" I spin around.

"Lily. She's into you."

"Oh! Uh. Cool."

"Wow. Don't look so enthusiastic."

"No, I am, I'm just . . . tired."

He looks at me oddly. "Whatever you say."

"Gentlemen!" Dad calls, lifting up his camera to snap a flashy picture of us. "That was brilliant! Truly madly deeply. A win for NGS and the justice system alike!"

"You realize they won't actually *change* any laws," I tell him. "It's a simulation, for argument's sake."

"Still!" Dad enthuses. "You all spoke so well, it makes me excited for what's to come. A world ruled by young people—it'll be here before you know it, Hen!"

Harrison and Martin go home with their parents, and Dad seatbelt-straps the trophy in the front like it's a person, so it's just Len and me in the darkened back seat.

"Sorry we whored you out," I fake-apologize as Dad's pulling out of the car park.

Len rolls his head toward me, laughing.

The twenty-minute drive feels a hell of a lot longer than it has a right to.

It's so dark. He's so close; I feel it like static. How can a person who's always been there suddenly do that?

He leans back against the headrest, watching the road ahead. I look down at his hand, resting open on the middle seat.

Some of the simmering of the last few weeks abruptly boils over, and I make a snap decision. Or it makes me. Either way, I let my fingers walk, inch by inch.

Dad's quiet in the front. Somewhere in the back of my head, Rational Henry is absolutely screaming, but instinct drowns him out.

I inch further, until there's millimeters between us. Then (I can't help it), I touch his hand, brushing the edge of his palm with mine.

I wait a few breathless seconds, until seconds turn into a minute. Then two.

Softly, the movement barely perceptible, his fingers flex across and he *takes my hand*. (I think.)

His eyes never leave the road. Either he doesn't feel anything, or he doesn't care.

(I feel things. Things that could ruin everything.)

11

Formal finally arrives on its designated blustery Wednesday. I spend the entire day setting up with Martin. We strip all the athletic equipment out of the gym, pulling moldy mats outside with our sports jackets tied around our mouths, and spray everything liberally with disinfectant.

The Boiyss come see us at lunch.

"This takes the piss even more than your car," Ged says helpfully, casting his eye around.

"It's not finished yet!" I snap, and Harrison drags him away.

I can feel Len's eyes on me.

"Do you need help?" he asks.

I shake my head no without looking up. "It's okay. Don't want to take up your lunch."

(I do, though. I want to be near him. So much that I can't.)

"What the hell did you say that for, Hamlet?" Martin hisses once they're gone. "We *do* need help."

"Uh."

"God's sake. Hurry up then, if it's just gonna be us, or we'll never get all this done!"

When the final bell rings, after Martin's been close to dropping the F-bomb at least twice, things look decent enough for the vendors to come in.

A couple of hours later I'm showered and hair-gelled and almost ready to go. I've spent months choosing my suit. The result is an overthought black tux with tails and a bow tie Mum has to do up.

Ham's mouth is an egg when I come downstairs. "Oh my gosh," he says. "You look like James Bonds."

The parentals take thousands of pictures. Dad cries.

"Where's Len tonight?" Mum asks suddenly. "Does he have a date?"

"Of course he does, Bill." Dad chuckles. "It's Len. Right, kiddo? Who's the lucky girl?"

My hands ball into fists. "I don't know what his plans are, okay! We don't have to do everything together."

Mum's lips purse. "Oh, you could've gotten a date, darling—"

"Of course you could!" Dad says, too robustly for it to be convincing.

"I can go with you, Hen," Ham offers brightly.

Mum moves toward me. "Are you sure you don't want us to—"

"Yep, okay!" I back out the door. "Gotta go. Bye!"

Ged's other cousin owns a classic car company, and we arranged to go together in a 1966 something-or-other ages ago. He, Vince, and Harrison are already aboard when it pulls up outside my house, with a surly shaved-headed gentleman in the driver's seat.

I glance at Vince up front (he's restyling his straightened hair in the passenger-side mirror) and pull open the door to the narrow back seat.

"Hello!" I greet the driver. "I'm Henry."

"It's a hundred and fifty bucks an hour," he says without inflection.

"Fuck off, Kyle!" Ged responds, outraged. "Auntie Carol said you had to give us mate's rates."

"That is mate's rates," Kyle deadpans.

Ged folds his arms across his chest and huffs loudly. "Just get in, Hamlet!" he snaps.

I squeeze into the space between Harrison and the driver's-side back door.

"It's a left here," Ged instructs as we turn off my street. Kyle doesn't respond.

Vince produces a giant can of hairspray seemingly out of thin air and begins liberally dowsing his emo-mulleted head. He clips red extensions into the bottom too.

"What do you call this look?" I ask.

"Sick as fuck," he answers primly.

Then he says something else but I don't hear, because we're turning down Len's street.

He's waiting on the curb by the front gate—hair slicked to infinity, jiggling in the cold with his hands tucked under his armpits.

"Why aren't you wearing a suit?" I demand when he opens the door.

He looks down at his outfit. "This is a suit."

It's not, really—it's a houndstooth jacket over black jeans with a white shirt, sans tie. He's finished the ensemble with black loafers, no socks.

I look like a Regency-era footman in comparison.

"Cool jacket," Kyle says.

To make matters worse (better?), once we pick up Jess

(Harrison's date is meeting him there, for obvious reasons), the only way we can all fit is if we squash together. Len ends up half sitting in my lap.

In. My. Lap.

My thigh is aflame under his. Aflame. I grit my teeth, mentally instructing myself to be cool, at least for the duration of formal.

"Nice to meet you guys!" Jess says.

All I can manage in return is a wild-eyed smile-grimace. My leg continues smoldering unbearably for the entire torturous drive to school.

When we pull up near the gym, Len slides out the door with his back pressing into my chest. I jump out as soon as I'm free.

"I'm not paying you a cent," Ged hisses at Kyle, slamming the car door closed. "This isn't even the one from the photo you showed me!"

"What about my hundred and fifty bucks?"

"Tell your mum to ring my mum!" Ged yells.

The vendors have made some of Martin's ballroom dreams come true—there's a red carpet of sorts, made of shriveled streamers and plastic cups strewn along the ground toward the cavernous double doors. Lights hang on the manicured hedge that's shaped to spell out NORTHOLM.

Harrison tapers off. Ged lets Jess lead him away too, his giant hand resting low on her back.

Vince pulls a flask out of his pocket and takes a swig. "Shall we?"

He links his arms through mine and Len's and pulls us toward the sound of The Getaway Plan coming through the speakers.

Inside, red and gray streamers hang from the basketball hoops, and a collection of vintage disco balls pulse rainbows across the floor. I soak it in, deriving a faint satisfaction, despite the glaring tackiness and my lack of a date.

Willa Stacy's by the dance floor in a black sheer-bottomed dress, standing with her brother. She waves at Len, and he walks over without looking back.

I'm so jealous I can barely see.

Vince jabs me in the ribs supportively, misreading my expression. "Cheer up, mate. Someday you'll meet someone just as batshit as you are."

"Thanks," I mutter darkly.

"No prob."

"I'm being—"

"Listen. I'm just going to go meet that hot kayak girl from mixed sport outside. You be right on your own for a bit?"

"Yeah. Whatever."

There are rows of long plastic tables set against the back wall so uniformly I suspect Martin spaced them apart with a tape measure after I left. I grab a lukewarm Coke and some Doritos and make a beeline for one of them, settling in for a long night as the village outcast.

I pull out my phone and play Snake for a good twenty minutes, hoping it looks like I'm texting my significant other who couldn't be here because they're busy modeling. In Paris.

I get a text from Mum: **How is it? R U OK?**

I don't answer.

Mr. Schiffer is here in fine form, standing by the entrance and policing new arrivals for any signs of fun. He has a sack of mobile phones slung across his back, so I stash mine back in my jacket pocket.

Len reappears some time later, plopping down beside me

heavily. His face is flushed, hair coming loose from its style. "Tell me you're not playing Snake," he says, breathless but still sardonic.

(Be normal.)

"Guilty." I hold up my phone. "I'm almost at the final level."

"It's your last ever high school dance. Get amongst it."

I look over at him. "You mean like you? Willa looks especially . . . spidery this evening."

"She's actually a cool person, if you'd bother to give her a chance."

The green monster in me roars. I manage to keep my face smooth. "Right. I'll be sure to do that, seeing as she'd totally let me after Vomka-gate."

He smirks. "You've got a point."

"I know I do."

"Because you're always right, and everyone else's opinion is just secondary evidence?"

"Yep. Exactly."

Len picks up my Coke and takes a long sip. He sets it back down slowly, staring at me.

"What?" I ask.

"Sometimes you're wrong."

His voice is soft but his eyes on mine aren't flinching. It's so unexpected I stare back. There's a moment slipping through my hands like water.

"Nah," I say awkwardly after a pause, my voice vaulting through several octaves. "Don't think so."

He looks away, then stands up with sudden finality. "You okay here?"

I shake the fuzz out of my head. "Why does everyone keep

asking me that? I'm sitting here by choice," I say, a little too forcefully.

"I'll leave you to it, then."

I slump back in my chair, watching as he rejoins Willa. Vince and his date are on the dance floor too, vigorously shaking it to Metro Station.

Willa brushes Len's sleeve with her black-painted fingers, tilting her head to laugh at something he's said. His left hand cups one of her bare shimmering shoulder blades.

I feel sick.

I flip my phone open and closed to distract myself, and it buzzes with another text.

Mum: Henry?? Hellooooooo

Dad: Narrowly managed to dissuade Mum from calling. Welcome.

I'm just punching out a reply begging them to pick me up early, when a familiar voice calls, "Henry!"

Emilia, ever my guardian angel, is crossing the dance floor, narrowly avoiding Ged and Jess, who are gyrating by the drinks table.

"I thought you were busy tonight," I accuse half-heartedly. I never officially asked her to be my date. It seemed too blurry a move to make in light of everything else.

She blushes slightly. "I'm sorry I didn't tell you. It's just that I'd already said yes to Martin."

"Wait, Martin as in the *Fincharoo*?"

"Oh, don't! He made me promise months ago. You know our mums are friends, and—"

A tweed-clad arm appears out of nowhere and winds its way around her shoulder.

"Evening, Hamlet," Martin snivels. "You know my date, I presume."

Emilia widens her eyes at me warningly. Tonight has been just shitty enough that I focus on Martin.

"Fincho," I return. "I didn't know they did entire suits made out of tweed."

"Yes, well—Buckingham Palace called, looking for you."

"*Martin*," Emilia interrupts with put-on sweetness. "You said you'd go get me a Sprite, remember?"

He looks at her like he just remembered where we were. "Yes."

"Do you want to maybe go do that?"

"Fine. But no dancing with my date, Hamlet."

"Wouldn't dream of it."

He stalks off, and we only just make it until he's out of earshot before we both collapse into laughter.

"Shut up!" Emilia whacks me on the arm with her tiny jeweled purse, which sets me off all over again.

"I'm sorry." I wipe my eyes. "I'm done, I promise."

She purses her lips. "And who are *you* here with, hmm? Don't tell me I was your best option."

I put my hand over my heart. "Ouch. I don't know which of us should be more offended by that."

She makes a soft tsk-ing noise.

"You look nice, by the way," I say, because she does. Her hair's piled on top of her head in glossy waves, and she's wearing a silvery Cinderella dress that flares out at the knee.

"No flattering Martin's date," she orders, but she's smiling.

We sit companionably, until Martin laser beams in on us from over at the drinks table, motioning for us to separate.

I move over, scrunching my face as a disco light stabs my eyes.

"You look sad," Ems says after a beat. "Let's dance. Stuff him."

They're playing "Don't Dream It's Over." Everyone's singing along disjointedly.

"*Very* much not in the mood," I bite out.

Ems smooths her dress over her knees and drops her voice. "Is this about the stuff you told me at the open day?"

I jiggle my foot in its pointy shoe. "No."

"Come on. Talk to me."

I don't know if it's the music or the way it felt to be so close in the car. Or maybe because it's Emilia, but I want to tell her everything. Right now. Let it out into the world, to see if it's real.

"Henry?" she asks again when the song ends.

The stereo clicks and switches to "Bleeding Love" by Leona Lewis. I cringe inwardly. Not the best backing track.

I take a deep breath and look up.

(Now or never.)

(*Now.*)

(. . . Or never.)

"I think I properly like him."

Emilia stares at me hard. "*Martin?*" she says. "But I thought—"

"What? No! Of course not Martin."

"Then wh—" She follows my gaze, across the dancers, to the place it hasn't left all night. "*Oh.*"

I clear my throat. "You . . ."

I wait.

"*Len?*"

"Yes."

Emilia puts her hand over her mouth, then down again. "You think, or you know?"

"Know."

"Oh!"

"Can you say something besides 'oh'?" I ask.

"Sorry." Her styled hair is jiggling. "I'm just . . . I'm processing."

"Okay."

"How long?"

"I don't know. Recently?"

"After you . . . *kissed*? Len is who you kissed?"

"Kind of? Yeah."

She pauses, eyes wide. "And now you . . . Have you told *him* any of this?"

"Ems. I can't."

"Why not!?"

"It'd wreck everything," I say, because it would.

"You don't know—"

"Yes, I do, okay? I just do."

Ems sighs, frowning. "Okay."

"Sorry, I didn't mean to—"

"No. I get it."

I look at the streamers over her shoulder and sniff loudly. "It's fine, though. I'm sure I'll get over it, or . . . something."

"Right. I'm going to go try to ditch Martin, and then we're gonna leave together," Emilia says decisively. "Okay?" She squeezes my shoulder before disappearing.

(It feels realer than ever. A solid, in-the-world thing.)

I can't sit still.

I get up and find Vince on the dance floor to say goodbye. Kayak girl had to leave early, so I hang out with him for a bit, "dropping it low" as he insists on putting it.

"I just—" he says over the music, pushing an inky strand of

hair out of his sweaty face. "I mean, it's whatever. It's not like we're *exclusive* or anything."

"Mmm."

"But you'd think she could at least tell me we weren't. I did physical exercise for that woman." He takes a swig from his flask.

"How much of that have you had?"

He gives me the finger and chugs more. "Dude, if the Sniffer sees you—"

"He's not gonna see me. I'm *stench*."

"D'you mean stealth?"

"Whatever."

I snatch it off him. Then, without thinking about it, I drink what's left.

Ugh. Whiskey.

Vince whistles once. "You really are batshit."

"Yeah, well. Come on—it's awards in a sec."

We head over to where there's a crowd gathering in front of the stage.

Ged and Jess take hottest couple, and Vince wins best dressed for his pantaloons-and-cape ensemble. There's no certificate for most successful awkward loner, so I settle for photographing my friends.

Couples flock for the DJ's final set—all slow songs, mostly sappy and only a few from this century. I go back to watching. Len and Willa are talking and dancing nearby; I try to look like I'm having at least a shred of fun.

"Gatsby!" Jake Clarkson calls from the opposite end of the dance floor. He's flanked by Travis Burrell and three other guys.

"Oi!" he calls sloppily, coming closer when I don't respond.

"Sick burn, but I was Nick." I try to turn away. I'm hot.

"Nah," Clarkson insists. "You're Gatsby."

"Right. Cool."

He raises his voice to a holler and points. "Mr. GAY Gatsby!"

My blood boils like it's going to shoot out of my ears.

It happens fast. One minute Len's in my periphery, then there's a flash of white shirt and he's here, his jacketless shoulder pushed up against mine.

"Hey, Clarkson?" he says. "Shut the fuck up."

Clarkson's face twists. "Or what?"

Len moves forward so he's in front of me. "Or I'll make you."

Clarkson's eyes dart between us. I don't know what he sees in Len's—what I'd see, if I *could* see them—but he falters.

"It was just a joke, Cane. Get a sense of humor."

The back of Len's shirt makes little movements—he's breathing fast. "Get out of my face."

"Are you serious?"

"Do you wanna find out?"

Clarkson waits a beat, then holds up his hands before backing away exaggeratedly with a sickly smile.

I'm shivery-scalding. I sidestep away before Len turns around, and bolt across the sticky gym floor.

The outside air hits my face like a wall.

I undo my top three buttons with numb hands and head out to the car park to wait for Emilia.

Willa Stacy is waiting by her brother's car wearing a leather jacket and a pissed-off look.

(*No!*)

I try to walk past without her noticing, but she calls, "Hamlet!"

(Dear god, no.)

"Oh! Hello. Didn't see you there!" I shout.

"Wow. You really *are* touchy." One side of her scarlet mouth lifts.

"Who said I was . . ."

Willa wraps her fingers around a stub of cigarette. "You know he and I broke up, right?"

Revelry white-noise crashes in my ears. "Tonight?"

"A while ago." Willa watches my face, tilting her head so her hair slips over one shoulder. "He didn't tell you? Interesting."

"How come?" I sputter.

She exhales smoke, wrapping us both in gray. "He's the best, but all walls." Her eyes flick away. "And I'm not into chasing people who don't want me to catch them."

I open and close my mouth. "Why're you telling me this?"

Willa gives me a long look. "Don't be obtuse, Hamlet."

"Henry!" Emilia appears in the doorway behind us. "Are you out here?"

"Seriously," says Willa, and she melts away, stubbing out ash under her heel.

Ems links her arm through mine—it's warm and familiar. "Excuse me, but what did I just witness?"

"I genuinely have no idea."

"I think," she says, pulling me away, "the only thing for us to do is get McDonald's and watch half of *The Exorcist* until we fall asleep on the floor."

We end up making it through closer to three quarters, Emilia peppering me with her lawyerly questions until my eyes slip closed. *When? What? How?*

She starts snoring first but keeps one hand out of the blankets, holding my shoulder, the whole night.

12

After leaving Emilia's, I go through the next day's classes half asleep, unable to keep my eyes open by the time I hit fourth period.

At lunch I find my usual seat with the guys by the quad. Ged and Vince are already there nursing their heads and looking dejectedly at their food.

"Oh god," Vince whispers. "I'm never drinking again."

"You say that every time," I remind him.

He throws a chip at me.

"How did you do last night?" I ask Ged.

His entire face and neck turn pink.

"I take it Jess and the Hilton were a success?"

"The woman's magic," Ged says dreamily. "Perfection in every way."

"Cut the sappy stuff, please," Harrison says, sitting down carefully. "I feel sick enough already."

"Can't help it, mate," Ged says. "I'm in love."

"That's nice," I say, concealing the confusing spurt of jealousy I feel.

"Where's Cane?" Ged asks.

My stomach tightens. "Don't know. I left early."

"I think he was talking to someone," Vince says. "Jamila, or something? Jam doughnut? Might've been a *late one*."

I exhale so sharply into my meat pie that I carve a hole in the tomato sauce on top.

Harrison points across the quad. "There he is."

Vince says, "I'm just gonna go to the loos for a mo." He rushes off, hand over his mouth.

"Poor bloke," Ged says. "He doesn't know what love is."

"It's from whiskey. Not lovelessness," Harrison says, a little green around the edges himself. "Why do *you* look so chipper?" he asks Len as he sits down next to me.

(My whole body's tense now.)

"I've decided," Len announces.

"Decided what?" Ged asks, his mouth stuffed with lasagna.

"My major artwork," Len says. "I'm going to do portraits. Black and white, on film."

"Of who?" Harrison asks.

"Myself. Life. You guys."

"Sod off," Vince says weakly, plopping back down and paper-toweling the edge of his mouth. "I'm not posing with my meat and two veg on display just so you can get an A."

"You wouldn't be *nude*, Vincent van Hoe. I was thinking more like a series of profiles, close up."

He used to do portraits like that when we were younger, obsessing over lighting, getting every freckle and fine line.

"Of our faces?" I ask, and then regret it when our eyes meet. I pull mine away.

"Exactly. I think that's probably my best bet at getting into the gallery show at the end of the year."

"As long as you only shoot me from the left," Vince grumbles. "I don't want the whole school seeing my bad side."

"Sounds awesome," Ged says. "Doesn't it, lads?"

"Yep!" I say, standing up quickly and grabbing my untouched lunch. "Awesome. I've just gotta go . . . do some stuff. I'll see you guys later."

———

I manage to dodge him for the rest of the day, both miraculously and out of sheer necessity.

I only need to make it through an awkward modern history lesson clutching the corner of my desk before I can retreat to the library.

It's study period last up and the supervisor's away, so we scatter off to do our own thing and my brain goes into overdrive.

He didn't bring it up, but last night's still in my skin. Emilia's questions.

Clarkson's face.

Len's shoulders covering me.

(Why did he do that?)

(When did we stop treating each other like we were radioactive?)

When the bell rings, I don't go home.

I drive the streets around school where the houses are older and huge until sunset. It's after five-thirty by the time I pull up at home.

I take my time getting out of the car, gathering my school stuff and whatever's left of my wits.

Someone clears their throat when I lock the door.

I look up to find Len waiting, leaning with one foot against the siding.

"God!"

"Hey."

"Hi! Uh. You scared me. What are you doing?"

He smiles in the falling dark. "Robbing you."

"I've got five bucks and a hairy stick of chewing gum," I say with affected drama when I catch my breath. "Leave my family alive, and you can have it all."

He tilts his head. "Tempting. I think I'll go for the murderous rampage, though."

I click my fingers. "Damn."

We're both quiet for a minute. A colony of bats screeches past overhead. We tilt our faces up, watching their shapes cut across whitening sky.

"What's up?" I ask.

Len swallows, his Adam's apple bobbing for a beat. "I didn't mean to go off yesterday. I know you can handle yourself, or whatever."

"Are you . . . *apologizing*? I don't think you've ever apologized to me about anything."

He looks uncomfortable, digging his hands into the pockets of his skinny jeans. "Yeah, well—don't be annoying about it."

I fold my arms. "I'm annoying, now? I think I need another apology. I can't work under these conditions."

He rolls his eyes. "You know what? I take it back."

"No, I forgive you. I'll live to fight through the maltreatment another day."

He looks up at me with such a sardonic expression on his face that I laugh.

"I mean it," I say. There's light in my limbs, now that he's here. "It's fine."

"Yeah?"

"Yeah. You should come inside." I want, suddenly desperately, to just hang out. "Have dinner."

I pull him to the back patio, where the outside light bathes us in warm. Ham catches sight of us and rushes over to blow bubbles against the glass sliding door.

We slip inside and Dad whips around from where he's standing at the stove; the movement causes brown liquid to slosh onto the floor.

"My main men! I haven't seen you in a while, Vladimir Lennon," he says.

"Hey, Reuben."

"Where's Mum?" I ask.

"Working. No matter—you're just in time to taste this culinary masterpiece."

"What is it?" Len asks, eyeing the solidifying stain at our feet.

"Noganoff," Ham says helpfully. "With human meat."

"*Mystery* meat, Hambam," Dad corrects. "First one to guess what it is gets a prize!"

"Is the prize not having to actually eat it?" I say, dumping my schoolbag in the hallway.

"Don't be silly," Dad says. "That would be a punishment, a travesty. Not a prize."

"Len!" Ham shouts. "Come look at my drawings."

"Sure thing, little man," Len says.

"Do you need any help, Dad?" I call.

"No, no. I'm almost done dishing up."

He appears a moment later, arms laden with several plates

of what looks, at first glance, like deep-fried balls of drain hair.

After fifteen minutes of pushing our "food" around with our forks, Dad gives up.

"I've stuffed it up again, haven't I?"

"Yes!" Ham says.

"What am I doing wrong?" Dad whines. "I followed the recipe exactly."

We murmur sympathetically. Over the years, Dad has developed several truly odd, verging on poisonous, dishes that he pulls out when Mum's busy at work, and he's feeling guilty about ordering takeaway. Always, it ends with the food going in the bin.

"I mean, let's start with the concept of mystery meat," I say. "Why does it have to be a mystery? Is the mystery whether it's meat at all?"

"We should have had chips," Ham adds. "I *love* chips. Mummy makes good chips."

Dad glares at me. "Betrayed by my own sons. What did you think, Len?"

"Leave me out of it," Len says. "I'm just here for the . . ." He looks down at his bowl uncertainly. "Hair."

"It's shaved zucchini!" Dad says. "I think, anyway. I'm not sure actually, but the guy at the deli gave me a really good deal on it."

"I'll bet he did," I say, prodding the congealed mess one more time.

"You know what? You two can clean up the kitchen. Come on Hambalam, bath time."

I don't protest. Honestly, I'm relieved. In the past, he's insisted on watching us eat every bite. This is far more preferable to dying of salmonella.

Dad carries Ham upstairs, and Len and I survey the damage, scraping plates into the bin and tipping the contents of the crockpot out. I fill the sink with hot sudsy water and we set about doing the dishes.

I wash and he dries. We're a well-oiled machine born of years of similar forced labor.

"You sure you're fine?"

"Why'd you get so mad at Clarkson?" I ask before I can stop myself.

His face gets very complicated. "I didn't want you to get in the shit. It was my dare. The . . . you know."

"Since when have you not enjoyed me getting in the shit?" I joke, even though I'm being set on fire by the words he didn't say.

Then he reaches for the plate at the same moment I move to hand it to him. Our hands smash into each other.

I pull back as if he's shocked me. It feels like maybe he did.

"Jumpy much?" he murmurs.

I spin away from the sink. "Dad can deal with that," I say, referring to the mess that used to be Mum's good crockpot.

"Dad can deal with what?" Dad asks, bounding downstairs.

"The monster from the black lagoon that's on the stove," I answer, my voice only slightly too high. "It's probably full of E. coli."

Dad pokes his tongue out at me. "Len'll help me, won't you mate?"

Len looks back at me for a moment, another unfathomable expression on his face. "Sure."

"I'm gonna go have a shower," I say, jumping the stairs two at a time without waiting for a response.

I shower meticulously, washing my hair twice with Mum's

expensive shampoo even though it makes it go all wiggy. It smells like her, a temporary distraction from the riot in my head.

My heart is beating double time, the blood being ferried around my veins with palpable heat. I lower the water temperature until it's close to freezing, but even that doesn't stop the burn.

I close my eyes tightly, concentrating on the feeling of the water streaming over my skin.

This is fine. Everything is fine.

As long as I stay in the shower forever.

"Henry!" Ham bangs on the door a little later. "I need to brush my teeth."

I turn the water off and scrub my face dry, wrapping a second towel around my waist.

"Henry!" Ham bangs again.

"I'm coming!" I shout back, throwing open the door. "God."

Ham's lip quivers like he's about to cry; I almost never shout at him. He pushes past me into the bathroom.

(How do people function like this?!)

"I'm gonna go," Len says suddenly. He's leaning against the banister at the top of the stairs, all the warmth and normality from dinner evaporated.

"Wait!" I say frantically. "I'll, uh, walk you."

His forehead scrunches. "Why?"

"Just—give me a sec."

I slip into my room and pull on clothes in a frenzy—jeans and a green hoodie and sneakers that are too small—then draw a deep breath, trying to center myself the way Mum does with Ham during his tantrums.

Len's eyebrows are in his hairline when I emerge.

"Okay," I trill. "Let's go!" I grab my keys and swing the door shut behind us.

It's one of those nights you can drink, late enough for stars to stretch out from the top of the hill. We wander in unwieldy silence for a bit, him on the road and me balancing on the edge of the footpath.

"Do you think," I ask, needing to fill the silence with something besides my rapid heartbeat, "that alien life forms would be impressed by us, or horrified?"

Len shoots me a look reminiscent of Vince in English.

"What?" I stumble a bit and hold my arms out for balance. "I had a dream about it. Or wrote something about it—I can't remember. But I realized we don't know, do we? What we look like from the outside. No one does."

He hesitates, pushing up the sleeves of his jumper. "What, like, the human race 'us,' or us specifically?"

"Both, I guess."

Len stares at the clouds, thinking. "I don't know. Purely from a scale perspective, modern life is pretty unbelievable. But if you go beyond that, there's too much suffering for it to be impressive in any real way."

"Our lives, or the human race?"

He stops under a street lamp, momentarily washed gold. "Both."

"Hmm. I still think blob-people would be at least a bit intimidated by the three and a half badges on my blazer."

Len shakes his head. "*Especially* the half."

We turn down the top of his street. It's cold in a lazy kind of way, still but with a breeze tweaking our hair and making

140

white spirals of our breath. A train horn sounds in the distance, fanning out across the quiet.

"So," he says. "Are you gonna tell me what that was about, back there?"

My insides contract. "What was what about?"

"Your little meltdown."

"I didn't have a meltdown. I had a shower."

Len raises one eyebrow, as if to say *seriously?*

I turn away from him, examining the deserted street, half of it lamp-lit and the other blanketed by trees. My body temperature skyrockets under my hoodie.

"Henry," he says. "Stop."

I'm so surprised by my real name that I forget not to look at him. "Stop what?"

He chews his lip, eyeing me like I'm a startled animal. "Just . . . stand still, for a second."

Len steers me sideways, under the cool canopy of a fig tree. He props one leg up against the trunk. "You're freaked."

"I'm not. Is that why you came over?"

Len looks down the street. He takes two breaths, both of them winding up into the air. Shrugs. "I wanted to make sure you were okay."

He's looking at me and is so close I can smell him. His eyes are wide in the half-light. His hair's as perfectly styled as ever, but with one strand coming loose at the front. I wonder what it would feel like in my fingers if I pushed it back.

"I'm not," I say, sharp and sudden.

Len frowns. "What do you mean?"

I pull at my own still-wet hair, enraged suddenly. By my life, myself, the world.

He waits.

"I just," I start. "I mean, do you ever feel like you're not who you're supposed to be? Like, people have this idea of you, but it's so different from the truth you can't correct them?"

"All the time," he says.

"Ha. Right. I'm serious."

"So am I."

I tug at my hair some more, raking my eyes out over the night. "Everyone thinks I'm this model student with this perfect bright future. Study something pretentious. Marry good woman. Have two-point-five perfect children with similarly ridiculous names to mine. Make terrific mark on the world."

He doesn't ask, *What's wrong with that?*

I answer it anyway. "It's not *me*. At least I don't think so. I don't even know who that is anymore. Or . . . yet. It's like I'm on this constant spin cycle with no off switch, every single day."

I'm rambling, which should be embarrassing but oddly isn't. It's just us and the dark.

"I get that," he says eventually.

"You *do?*"

He nods like it should be obvious. "Perfect Lennon Cane with his perfect life and his perfect girlfriends? It's not real, not even half of it. People think what they want."

I digest that for a minute, narrowly stopping myself from asking, *Which girlfriends?* "And we thought this year would be boring."

"With you present? Unlikely."

"True." I tip an imaginary jaunty hat. "I am the original triple threat entertainer: writer, debater, neurotic mess."

He pats me on the shoulder. "Whatever you say."

It happens again, the shivery feeling when he touches me. I shrink back out of reflex, surprising him, and his hand slips down my arm. It's warm even through my hoodie.

My breath catches. Audibly. His eyes shoot down to my mouth.

I think, *this is going to be so embarrassing when he pulls away.*

Except he doesn't. We both stand there, inches apart.

I lean in, gravitating toward his warmth despite myself.

Len does too.

My hands hang uncertainly between us. His are moving, reaching across to hover over my wrists. Holding them there.

Our foreheads touch. Then our noses.

I bump my chin into his, too hard. He cups it with one hand and bumps back, unyielding, the rest of us winding together like the roots under our feet.

It's slow and soft but so *hot*, even though my fingers are cold. For a minute, my jangling brain goes radio silent. I just grip him by the collar, both of us breathing the same air, until his mouth glances down on mine.

He pulls back to look at me after a second, red-lipped with his pupils blown wide, and asks, *What are we doing?* with his eyes.

I want to tell him not to stop, but I can't make my voice work. My limbs are concrete. It's like I want it so badly it freezes me solid.

Len steps away.

It's a blink and five years before he says haltingly, "I should go."

My head's doing that thing where it's so full it's almost blank. Mostly there's just this *feeling*, right in the pit of my stomach. Of having been running, away from and toward this, for the longest time. Pelting-downhill running. The kind where you don't realize you're even doing it until you try to stop.

"I . . . um. Yeah—okay."

We cross the road without looking at each other.

"I'll . . . see you tomorrow." He disappears into the wet-denim black.

And then I'm standing on the street and it looks the same as ever, sleeping-tablet still. Traffic light spots flash across house fronts.

Green. Red. Green.

Nothing's changed except all of it.

13

I don't know why North chooses to hold forced team-building camp in the year twelve penultimate school term, when we truly have enough problems to contend with. It's sadistic. Most of us have been together for seven years by now, anyway.

It's the same people in the same classes. But still the year-twelve homeroom teachers gather each year and plot our last peppy hurrah, chucking it in whichever week is sufficiently close to the End and doesn't clash with any assessments.

I usually look forward to these types of things, but this year the timing is uncanny.

I can't stop thinking about last night.

It's making my jeans very uncomfortable.

I need time to digest. To figure out what the hell's going on with me. Us. Instead I get three days in the wilderness, under the watchful gaze of our entire year. (Bar the guys who've had too many detentions, including, thank god, Clarkson and Burrell.)

"At least it's in a good spot," Harrison says when we're clustered outside the bus at six-thirty, jumping up and down to keep warm.

This year's camp is on Fraser Island, a decision I'm sure came straight from Mr. Lewis, who arrived from the UK at the start of the year and has been talking about "sunbathing" for the last month.

I wait for the guys to notice some fundamental difference in my face, but they're as crabby and sarcastic as always.

The rickety NGS bus is the same. School is the same—red brick and vine covered exactly as it was yesterday.

Nothing's changed except all of it.

Vince arrives late, dressed in mourning black. Len pulls up a few minutes after him in charcoal tracksuit pants and *my* My Chemical Romance shirt from the concert we went to last year.

My eyes pop a little and heat rushes over my skin. I've been asking him to give that back forever.

"Bollocks to this," Vince grumbles, dropping his heavy bag down in the dirt. "What is the point?"

"Come on, you lot," Ged says. "An entire weekend with no homework, no Sniffer, and no worries. Get excited!"

Len and I throw unimpressed eyes at him in unison. Other than the shirt, he's giving no indication that this is anything other than a normal day. I don't know what that was, last night (*last night*) or what it means from here.

I don't know anything, except that this is going to be a long-arse three days.

Mr. Lewis saunters over to us. He's wearing a bright-red NGS tracksuit and an Akubra hat with actual corks dangling from it.

"Morning, boys!" he chirps in his Yorkshire accent, slathering pink zinc all over his nose and cheeks. "Glorious day to be heading off to see some of Awe-stralia's majesty, isn't it?"

"Sure is, sir," Harrison says.

"Glorious day to see some of the Adele's girls' lovely bunch of coconuts," Ged mumbles under his breath.

146

It's a long-standing tradition that NGS and our esteemed sister school hold their senior camp in the same week. Of course, this invariably results in anarchy and depravity; Lacey swears a girl in her year conceived her baby in the dingo sanctuary.

"What was that, Gerrard?"

"Glorious day to see some coconuts, sir."

Mr. Lewis frowns. "I don't know whether they'll have any, I'm afraid. Not quite tropical enough. Should be lovely weather for some *sunbathing*, though."

We all agree with false enthusiasm until he moves farther along the line to chat to another group.

"You're not really gonna try to get into the girls' camp, are you?" I ask Ged once sir's out of earshot.

"Jess a stone's throw away and no parents walking in on us? Of course I bloody am."

"You're sick."

"*You're* a monk. You don't get it because you're voluntarily celibate."

"I am not." I can feel my cheeks starting to flame.

"Please. The closest you've ever got to a chick is spewing on her."

"Yes, well— there's more to life than girls, Gerrard."

"Monk."

"Don't you have to be religious to be a monk?" Len interjects.

"Oh, yeah," Ged says. "Guess you're just a loser, then."

Vince and Harrison snigger. I punch Ged in the arm but avoid looking at Len. I want to avoid him for most of this trip.

(And also, I *don't*.)

We shuffle forward in line, and Mr. Lewis calls everyone to

attention. Accompanying him are Ms. Hartnett and Coach Jamieson.

"All right, listen up!" Mr. Lewis shouts. "The buses will be departing in five minutes, but before you hop on, I just want to alert you to the way the seating plan is going to work this year. In the past it's been alphabetical, but this year we've tried to keep you with your mates. Your name will be on your allocated seat."

I groan internally. Please let me be with Vince. Or Harrison.

Or even bloody Ged, if it'll get me out of spending six hours at excruciation station.

Mr. Lewis seems to be anticipating applause for being such a "cool" teacher. He waits for a few more seconds before giving up and waving us onto the buses. I hitch my bag over my shoulder and follow the rest of our homeroom onto bus three.

I search the seats, wishin' hopin' prayin' . . .

"Looks like we're bus buddies," Len says from behind me. I turn around unwillingly; he points to a seat near the back of the bus with *LENNON AND HAMLET* scrawled onto a Post-it on the headrest.

"Sit down, Hamlet!" Coach J. says. "For the love of god."

This trip will kill me.

"Great," I say, weakly. I shove my bag into the overhead compartment and slide into the window seat. Len does the same and sits beside me, his arm brushing mine. I grip the armrest hard enough to snap it off.

Any initial confusion has congealed into a blob of intense, searing embarrassment. I know it's not the same for him; he does this sort of stuff all the time, with all sorts of people. But I become a mess of weird wanting, and then I freeze. (Why am I *actually* beyond help?)

I scoot as far from him as I can. My face is practically pressed against the glass.

"Hamlet."

I can feel him rolling his eyes at me, but I don't look up. I resolve to sleep the entire journey.

I make it as far as the bus pulling out of the school parking lot and onto the road before he coughs conspicuously and leans in, lips so close to my ear my spirit actually leaves my body, and whispers, "Are you really gonna ignore me the whole way?"

I don't answer him.

"You realize you are the chattiest person ever on road trips."

I prop my head up to face him. "Maybe I don't have anything to say."

His eyebrows lower. "Why are you pissed at me?"

(Because we're pretending like nothing happened.)

(Because maybe nothing did.)

(Because you're wearing my shirt and it makes me want to blow my cover in front of everyone.)

"I'm not."

"Right. Except, you are."

"Why is nothing a big deal to you, ever?"

His eyes darken with something. "What do you mean?"

I lean back against the window and close my eyes. "Forget it. I'm tired."

"Fine. It's not like you're not gonna crack in twenty minutes and be at me wanting to play Cruise, Marry, Shag."

His prediction doesn't come to pass. I manage to fall asleep, waking only to groggily get on the ferry to the island.

———

Vince, Ged, Len, and I end up sharing a cabin—Harrison goes with his soccer friends. I take the bunk underneath Ged's, at which Len makes a face but says nothing.

The cabin is pine-y and decent, and there's a wide bay window framing the bright turquoise sea. Ged pushes it open, salt air filling the room.

Coach J. pokes his head in the door to bark, "Dinner's at five-thirty, lads. Free time till then."

"*Excellent.*" Ged claps his hands together.

Coach J. turns a watery eagle eye on him. "Go anywhere near those girls, McConnell, and it's immediate suspension."

Ged puts his hand on his chest innocently. "We wouldn't dream of it, sir."

Coach grumbles away, unconvinced.

"You are so full of it, mate," Vince says. He's reapplying his eyeliner in the smudged mirror by the door.

"And who's that for, Vincent?" Ged asks. "Me?"

Vince puts the cap back on the thick black pencil. "That Maia from lacrosse might be there."

Maia is basically Vince's emo kryptonite and has officially replaced kayak girl in his affections.

Ged pulls off his tracksuit bottoms and steps into a pair of black skinny jeans so tight they barely zip up.

"You guys coming with?" he asks.

I look at Len lying with his iPod earbuds in on the other bottom bunk.

"Nah."

"Your loss." Ged winks. "Come, young Vincent—let us go in search of nirvana."

"Tosser," Vince says, fluffing his choppy hair a final time.

I look at Len again. If he realizes this is the first time we've been alone since last night, he doesn't let on. I, on the other hand, am so aware of him it hurts.

The cabins are completely *in*decent, upon second inspection. His bed and mine are only about half a Ged-leg apart. I need to get out of here. I stand up restlessly.

He pulls one earbud out. "Off to find nirvana too, are you?"

"Going for a walk. I'll be back at dinner."

He smiles. (I think.)

I step outside and breathe in salt smell. The rest of the guys are milling around, engaging in various sporting activities or stripping down to go swimming, despite the chill setting in. Ms. Hartnett waves at me—she already has the stressed look of someone who's just realized they've bitten off more than they can chew.

The cabins are surrounded by bush on all sides. I set off to the left of ours on a kicked-dirt pathway leading into the trees. My boots crunch satisfyingly, and as I wind farther and farther away, I can finally feel the tension in my stomach start to unfurl a bit. I'm careful not to veer off the path too much, stopping after fifteen minutes or so. There's a big boulder perched next to a wiry gum tree, so I use the low-hanging branches for purchase and climb to sit at the top of the rock, glad Mum insisted on me bringing Dad's heavy-duty hiking shoes.

From here, I can see over the treetops to a strip of blue. It's beautiful—untouched in a way that slips into your bones.

I sit crossed-legged, listening to the cackle of kookaburras overhead. I stay like that for a long time, until the light through the trees burns out, and I start to wish that I thought to bring my jumper.

Darkness is leaking milkily across the horizon when I go back for dinner. The trek through the trees turns out to be significantly more challenging sans light, and I fall over and scrape my shin. Twice. I wince at the pain when I sit down on the log with the Boiyss by the fire.

"Jesus, what happened to you?" Ged asks, looking at the blood dripping down my leg and into my sock.

"Dingo eat your baby?" Vince enquires around a mouthful of sausage in bread.

"I went for a walk," I say defensively.

"To where, Jurassic Park?" Len joins in.

"I fell!" I throw up my arms, red-cheeked. "I'm a child of the city. I'm not built for the great outdoors."

"You should probably get that looked at," Harrison says. "It might get infected."

"It's a scratch. I'm fine."

I get up and stride over to the food and drinks table. I pile my plate high without looking at any of it and end up with a mountain of pasta salad and three tofu sausages. I sit back down, shoveling mayonnaise-y goo into my mouth dejectedly. The tofu sausages taste predictably like nibbling Ged's big toe.

Len pushes his plate toward me. "Here. The actual meat went early; I saved you a steak."

I lift my eyes in surprise. "Thanks."

The steak oozes its juices at me invitingly. I snatch the plate from him and dig in, pushing the texture of the tofu from the back of my throat.

"How was nirvana?" I ask with my mouth full.

Ged looks smug. "Let us simply say that the girls' camp is quite close by and, mercifully, secluded."

I wrinkle my nose.

"Emilia said to tell you hello," Vince says. "After she was done beating us about the head with a stick for being perverts."

I choke on a laugh. "Did you talk to Maia?"

"Off swimming, wasn't she?" he responds dejectedly. "But we're going back next time we get the chance."

"You're gonna get caught," Harrison says.

Ged cries, "Don't ill-wish us, cuz!"

"I'm going to be there to tell you I told you so when you do."

"Singalong time!" Mr. Lewis calls from where the teachers are clustered over the other side of the fire. "Who's for some Toto?"

He starts strumming the unmistakable first few strains of "Africa." Vince murmurs something that sounds like "merciful god."

My shin is starting to burn dully. I squint down at it. "Ugh," I groan, mopping the grazed part ineffectually with a napkin. "Gross."

"There's a first-aid kit in all the cabins," Harrison says helpfully.

Ged's eyes light up with an idea. "Miss H.!" he calls across the fire. "Hamlet's screwed up his leg—can we go back to our cabin and fix it?"

Ms. Hartnett stops shouting at Derrick Somers, who's trying to set his beach towel on fire. She shields her eyes from the flames and appraises my leg for a moment. It must look sufficiently grim. "All right, but be back in half an hour."

"Of course, Miss."

We leave Harrison by the fire and the guys help me hobble down the path to our cabin.

Ged turns around at the door, and whispers, "Can you chill here for twenty minutes or so?"

I look from him to Vince and back again. "Where are *you* going?"

Vince lights a cigarette guiltily.

Ged grasps Len's shoulder and mine. "If anyone asks, the leg was so messed up we went to look for natural bush remedies," he says meaningfully.

"Oh, brilliant. I'm going to be an accessory to the second dingo-sanctuary offspring."

"Come off it," Ged snorts. "A gentleman never travels anywhere unprepared."

Vince sings, "Don't be silly, wrap your—"

I slam the screen door in their faces.

Then it's just the two of us again in this too-small room.

Wordlessly, Len pulls the steel first-aid box from the top shelf in the bathroom.

My pulse lights in my neck, my ears, my wrists—but mostly in my leg, which is really starting to bother me.

He sits down on one of the bunks and opens the kit on his lap. "Come here, then. Let's see." He gestures for me to stand in front of him, between his legs.

I swallow loudly but do as I'm told.

Len blots something that smells like bleach onto a piece of gauze. He starts dabbing at the gash gently, brow furrowed in concentration.

I hold my breath, partly to stop myself from inhaling him and partly because *freaking ow*. He gets a spot of blood on the back of his hand.

I am literally bleeding love.

"Sorry." He leans in closer and staunches the wound with more antiseptic. It's a mess, really, but unavoidably intimate.

I'm still holding my breath.

"It's not deep. Just a sec." He finishes cleaning me up and spreads something else onto the cut itself, his fingers quick and careful, then covers everything with one of those stick-on bandages. "There. We won't have to amputate after all."

I step back, admiring his handiwork. "How come you're always looking after me?" I ask, still feeling off-balance and chicken-shit, the blood loss making me bold.

"Cause you're hopeless." He smiles sideways.

"I'm serious. Why?"

Len shuts the metal lid and sets the box aside. He stands up, slowly, and leans forward so we're face to face, his gaze locked on mine. "Why do you think?"

"I don't know what to think!" I say honestly. I can't look directly at him.

"Because you're *overthinking* it." He moves closer still, nothing separating us but an inch of charged air.

"You're pretending everything's normal," I accuse in a whisper.

"We were on a *bus*," he counters softly. "Also, I'm not pretending."

I can smell his breath. I can't catch mine. "I . . . Still . . . You . . ."

He tilts his head. "You are so dramatic, Hamlet," he breathes. "Not everything has to be a big thing."

I gulp.

"What is it, then?"

He doesn't answer, just moves his palm to my shoulder. We're standing so close he barely puts any pressure on it and my head dips forward.

Len kisses me once, lingers for a minute, then leans away. It's just like last night. No, it's *better*—what's up with *that?*

This time I pull him back to me by the front of his shirt. His lips smile under mine. I forget to be embarrassed, or confused, or human. I'm a mouth and hands and a heart that's a beating drum.

We kiss fast slow fast, until all the bones in my body are mush (well, *almost* all of them).

His tongue searches for mine. It's still as much of a line as it was in truth or dare.

This time I cross it. Then I cross it again.

I grip the small of his back to keep from falling over, staggering back toward the window.

Len makes a humming noise and steps sideways, yanking the curtains closed. He pushes me up against them until we're connected, chest to hip.

Does he have to be as good at this as he is with everything else? I'm dizzy. I break away to breathe for a second, which just makes him move across to my jaw. He grazes it with his teeth, which is *holy*—

Merciful god, there's footsteps outside.

We spring apart like a bomb's fallen between us. Ged clatters the door open, the sound reverberating through the room.

"The girls've gone inside already!" Vince shouts from behind him.

"Wait. Why do you look weird?" Ged's eyes dart from my beetroot face to Len leaning against the wall with his arms folded, and back again. "Did you spew somewhere from the blood?"

"Yeah," I lie. My voice comes out raspy. I hope it works to sell the effect.

"Fucking hell, mate." Vince grimaces. "Even I can camp in this godforsaken country without completely losing my shit."

"Mmm." I don't look at Len. Or I *will* lose it, all of it, everything.

"Shall we go back, then?" Ged asks. "Maybe a couple of bars of the rains in Africa will earn us some marshmallows."

"You guys go," I say. "I'll be there in a sec."

Ged and Vince step into the cold, the screen slamming again.

Once I'm sure they're gone, I brace my hands on my knees. I hear Len step away from the wall, his soft footfalls coming to a stop in front of me.

"So dramatic," he murmurs again in mock-reproof, and walks out the door.

———

The rest of camp is a blur after that. We're surrounded all the time.

I pretend—through breakfast, lunch, and dinner. I pretend to care when Jess dumps Ged, and when she takes him back again after he finds her some questionable-looking flowers.

I pretend to be responsible while delegating tasks with Martin, and when Vince gets caught smoking in the shower block.

But at night the thoughts slip in, uninvited. X-rated flashbacks that wash through me like the moment when you turn on a tap but forget to adjust it, and the water's so hot on your skin it's ice. I don't think I sleep more than a few hours the entire trip.

I put on my best-mate face when Len comes first in the swim challenge on the last day. I holler the blokiest cheer I can muster.

(I watch him, though. His wet collarbones. His school bathers. Did he always have such good . . . thighs?)

It doesn't feel like a phase.

It feels like *alive*.

We're not alone again until we're on the bus back to school, countryside spinning past the window.

The chatter around us is light after the exhaustion of the last few days; half the guys are already asleep. His nearness makes me feel hot and twitchy and wide, wide awake.

I plug my iPod in without turning any music on.

"Cruise, Marry, Shag," Len says softly.

I pull one earbud out. "Hmm?"

"Come on, I made it up to you. Play with me—I'm bored."

My cheeks flush. Is that what he thinks the other night was? Just "making it up" to me? I want to ask. Also, I don't. If he's going to be weird and evasive, so will I.

"Fine." I wind my headphones into a ball and shove them in my pocket.

"All right . . . the chick from Paramore," he starts.

I wrinkle my nose.

"Dame Edna, or . . . Grace Kelly."

I tap my chin, considering. We've played this game a lot; I know from bitter experience that one false move and he'll tease me about it for the foreseeable future.

"Cruise with Dame Edna," I decide. "Marry Hayley Williams so she can sing me to sleep every night. And . . . I guess I'd sleep with Grace Kelly, wouldn't I?"

"Predictable."

"Who would you choose, then?"

"Nope. Not my turn. Give me a new list."

We play for half an hour, until my mouth is dry and my nerves are frayed, and I'm running out of random women to imaginarily set him up with. We decide it's a tie, to be broken by one last round.

I pinch my chin. "Um . . . Brendon Urie . . . Pete Wentz or Barack Obama."

As soon as the words are out I want to claw them back in.

"Cruise with Pete, marry Obama, shag Brendon," he says, without hesitation. "Obviously." A smile plays at his lips.

"Er, right. Good choice. Your turn, then," I manage to choke out.

"I think I'll save mine—sit on the almost-win for a little longer."

"That's not a thing! You can't just not break a tie so you look like the winner."

"It's too juicy to waste on a bus trip. You'll just have to wait."

I roll my eyes, unraveling my headphones again. "Whatever."

He picks up an earbud and slips it into his ear, then reaches into the pocket of my hoodie with his other hand like it's nothing and retrieves my iPod. I'm too stunned to respond as he scrolls through the songs.

"Okay. These are all bootlegs from musicals."

I inhale. This, at least, is familiar territory.

"Not *all.*" I grab it off him. "You're in the musical theatre playlist."

He rolls his eyes.

I scroll around until I find something alternative enough for his snobbery: "Between the Bars" by Elliott Smith. There. That ought to shut him up for a bit.

I've never thought of this song as remotely sexy—it's sad, if anything. Actually, it's one of my cry songs (not that I'd ever tell anyone that). But there's something about sitting together.

The slow melody. His shoulder against mine. I look at him, then have to look away because he's staring at me.

I wish I knew what he was thinking. Or that everyone else would disappear, so I could touch him.

We stay like that, our faces dipped toward each other. The song ends, and Katy Perry bulldozes in after it.

Night falls in a sudden wave outside; the lights on the bus flick on. I can see my reflection in the window, but I don't recognize the hectic eyes flipped back in the glass.

———

Mum picks me up from the school parking lot wearing her dressing gown over scrubs. Several other mothers in expensive-looking coats stare at her haughtily. She doesn't notice.

She pulls me into a hug and sniffs my hair.

"Mum, let me go."

"Sorry! Think I fell asleep for a second. Double shift."

Len's eyes are fixed on us when I look up.

Then he turns away.

I try not to look disappointed as I follow Mum to the car, past where Vince's dad is rapping him on the back of the head and lecturing him. "*Cigarettes*, Vincent? If you're going to be a ruddy delinquent, at least do it well."

I'm so wiped from not sleeping that I fall into bed as soon as we get home. I pull my boots off in the dark and worm under the covers fully dressed.

I'm half asleep when my phone vibrates.

Hamlet—are you awake?

Len never uses text speak. Always full words and sentences.

Am now >:| I type back, squinting in the dim light.

Sorry. Go back to sleep.

Awake. Wat is it?

Nothing.

Giving u the finger.

No, you're not—you were just asleep.

Figuratively giving u the finger.

You can't figuratively do that.

Wat. Do. U. Want?

Just to ask you something.

Thud thud thud.

Ask then.

He takes so long that I drift off again for a bit. The buzz of his reply only just wakes me, but I stare at it for ages.

Grace Kelly or me?

Part II

It is also good to love: because love is difficult. For one human being to love another human being: that is perhaps the most difficult task that has been entrusted to us, the ultimate task, the final test and proof, the work for which all other work is merely preparation.

—Rainer Maria Rilke

14

The start of the last week of term is entirely ordinary. At least on the surface.

Gran mails save-the-date cards for her wedding after always insisting those were arbitrary, and Mum pretends not to be furious. Dad finishes the biggest of his sculptures and starts eating dinner with us again. Ham is Ham.

Exams start on Tuesday. We're studying so much I don't really get an opportunity to assess *other things*.

There's a collectively frantic air hanging around the senior classrooms. These are the big exams, really. Next term's just a four-week-long closing ceremony. This is it.

The lockers become a hub of shell-shocked guys rubbing their bloodshot eyes, demanding to know just how the hell the rest of the class got *Hiroshima* as the answer to question twelve when they put *1750*.

I go into full Reuben Hamlet blackout mode, bunkered down in my bedroom with notes spread everywhere, my phone locked in a cupboard so I can't text him.

Len and I don't say it, exactly, but the game's switched . . . so far up. Whenever we see each other there's this burning anticipation that's almost unbearable.

I was half-hopeful and half-afraid the feelings would mellow now I've given into them, but, if anything, they get worse. I nearly have a stroke every time his knee brushes mine. Which is often, because he sits next to me at lunch whenever he gets the chance.

(Is *that* a sign?)

(Do we need signs, at this point?)

Thankfully, tests and study periods are all seated alphabetically, so it's just me and H through J for most of the week.

———

My exams go okay, in the end. English is the best because I get to go on a long anti-capitalism rant about the American Dream. I manage to nail the short essay section in modern history. Math is a complete shit show that I *think* comes together in the written questions.

On Wednesday afternoon, Ged decides we're in dire need of a McDonald's run. The one Harrison works at is only about a kilometer from school, so we set off on foot in search of chicken nuggets to help us retain knowledge ones.

Len walks next to me, mirroring my steps and trying to trip me over. He used to do it all the time when we were younger; all the guys did—I'm an easy target. I wonder if any of them notice, now, that he's twisting our thighs hard together. Or that I have to bolt ahead and strike up a conversation with Vince about the Red Jumpsuit Apparatus so I don't pass out.

When we get there, Harrison shoots Ged a look from behind the counter that's all daggers; last time we were here there was an incident with some hotcakes being flushed down the toilet that Ged maintains innocence on.

The place is empty, apart from a couple of other North guys milling nearby, hollow-eyed and inhaling life-saving trans fats.

"Good morrow, Harrison Ford!" I greet Harrison when it's our turn to order.

"What are you guys doing here?" he asks grumpily, still looking at Ged.

"Visiting you, our worker bro!" Ged says.

"Cause it's so funny that I work, right?" Harrison snaps.

"No," Ged looks confused.

"Some of us have to, you know, because there's no other option."

"Oi," Vince cuts in. "We didn't mean—"

"Forget it," Harrison says, tapping the screen in front of him. "What do you want?"

We order frozen drinks, nuggets, and chips, watching as Harrison's hairnet-framed face turns gradually redder.

"All right," Ged says once he's handed over his money. "What's up yours?"

"I mean, I tanked chemistry today," Harrison says in a rush. "So, there's that."

"I doubt you *tanked* it . . ." I start.

Harrison leans against the sticky counter. "I blanked. Completely. My average is gonna be screwed, and I've already put down engineering for preferences."

"Shit a brick," Ged muses softly.

"It was a bad exam," Len says. "You can make it up next term."

Harrison eyes are wide. "I'll have to. I have to do well."

We all frown at him for a second, eating our nuggets in respectful silence.

"Would you . . . perhaps like some of my gum?" Ged eventually asks delicately.

I don't know why it's funny, but suddenly we're cracking up.

"Yes," says Harrison, pulling at the name tag on his chest. "Gum's really gonna fix all my problems."

"Oh, you'll be right, mate," Vince says, rallying. "If anyone can pull it out of their arse at the eleventh hour . . ."

We make noises of agreement. Harrison chews the gum savagely.

"Oh, shit," says Len. "That reminds me. I've still gotta do those portraits of you guys."

"When by?" asks Ged, blowing a bubble that snaps and gets stuck to his nose.

"Friday, probably. Then I can edit over break."

"God's actual sake," grumbles Vince.

"We can just do them in study period tomorrow," Len says.

"You can call mine 'Essence of Failure,'" Harrison says glumly.

"Or," I respond cheerily, "The Comeback Kid. *Eau de Resilience.*"

"'Real Aussie Battler,'" Ged joins in.

"Nah." Vince shakes his head. "You killed it."

Harrison pushes himself off the counter. "I'd better get back."

We do some more sympathetic grunting, then go and sit to eat. Ged and Vince still look shaken. I am too. If Harrison Ford—follower of any and all instructions to the letter—can fail at anything, none of us are safe. This (really) is it.

"Sheet," Ged hisses suddenly.

"What?" asks Vince.

"Fantalanche!"

Frozen orange liquid is seeping out of his knocked-over cup, across the white tabletop and all over the floor.

"Abort mission!" says Ged. "Quick, let's go!"

After Len mops up the worst of it with some napkins, we hastily wave to Harrison and leg it back to school still carrying our food.

In the student car park, Vince skids off in a spectacular donut, and Ged chases his car for a bit. I don't look up at Len, but I sense him behind me in the fading day. Shiver with it.

Our cars are parked two empty spots from each other.

He touches my arm. It's barely anything; it lights up everything.

"Your portrait," he murmurs. "Friday night. Dad's away."

"Okay."

"What'd you say?" Ged bellows from up the road.

"I said you're a disgrace," Len says, without missing a beat.

———

On Friday afternoon I spend longer than necessary packing up my stuff, feeling nervous suddenly. I've stayed at Len's hundreds of times before, especially when John's away. But this is different.

I find him in the school darkroom.

It's not a proper darkroom as much as a soundproofed cupboard behind the art room with works-in-progress hanging over spare desks. But it is dark.

Len turns around to look at me as soon as the door shuts. He's doing his smoldering face, and it shouldn't work on me— but it does.

I lean on a desk for support and do a sort of cough.

"Don't know if you should come over." He pretends to dither. "I mean, if you're sick."

"I am." I swallow. "Sick."

Len raises his eyebrows. "Are you, like, trying to be sexy?"

I turn away, cheeks flaming. "No!"

He pulls me back by the crook of my elbow. "Stop."

"What?"

He lets go. "Don't be weird."

I look down at my hands, irritated by how transparent I am.

I have no idea, as in none at all, how to do this.

We sit down on opposite desks, facing each other with our legs dangling. Len stretches his foot out to touch mine with the tip of one pointed black shoe.

"What do you want me to do, then?"

"Nothing."

I try not to look disappointed. Then he says, "I want you to be you."

The words *I* and *want* and *you* make my stomach drop to the floor.

"Annoying," he continues, kicking his foot against mine. "Know-it-all, irritatingly handsome, you."

"Did you just refer to me as *handsome?*" I try to sound nonchalant, but it doesn't come off that way. At all.

His mouth quirks up as he shrugs. "Are you planning on staying here all night, or can we go get some dinner?"

————

We end up at a pub on the river that has flickering torches on the walls and big leather booths. We sit in the back, tucked between the wall and a window, watching as workers hop on the end-of-day ferry. My eyes are starting to burn dully, so I pop my contacts out and pull my glasses from my blazer pocket.

Immediately, this strikes me as the least attractive thing I've ever done in my life.

(Should I have done that? Do I look better or worse? Does he care what I look like?)

He orders the same thing as always (parmigiana without the parmigiana).

My stomach is in knots, so I settle for something bland: cheese pizza with salad. The waiter stares at our uniforms.

It feels different now, the two of us sitting here, alone. Like a date.

(I hope it's not. I'd have worn better shoes.)

Len folds his arms on the tabletop and leans forward slowly, tilting his head to the side. "What are you thinking?"

Whoever said being friends first is key to successful romantic relationships was sorely mistaken. There's nowhere to hide.

"I was thinking . . . I definitely misquoted Winston Churchill in the year-level assembly this morning."

He snorts. "As if."

I push my hair out of my eyes. It needs a wash; it's clumping together in untidy waves across my forehead. "I'm really not leadership material, am I?"

"You're the smartest person in that room, and you know it."

I blink at the second unexpected compliment, embarrassed and (pathetically) elated. "Er, thanks."

He pauses, eyes intense. "What were you really thinking?"

"Just . . . I don't know. This is weird."

"It's not like we haven't had dinner before," he points out. "A lot."

"*Yeah*, but—"

"But what?"

"It's different now, isn't it?"

"Different?"

"More."

"More."

"Can you stop repeating what I'm saying?"

He smiles again. "Sorry."

Our bread arrives, and we're quiet for a while, chewing and scraping.

"It doesn't have to mean anything," he says, looking at me. "If you don't want it to."

"Don't you say I'm always obvious?"

"Not always," he demurs, but then the waiter comes back and the moment slips.

———

When we get back to Scott's Corner, it's still light outside. The air smacks of freedom—two weeks of holidays stretched like a little infinity ahead of us after so much study.

"The portrait?" I ask after a long pause, hoping/wondering if it was a ruse.

"Oh, yeah." Len nods. "This is perfect, actually." He points to the arched window in the kitchen leaking orange. "Golden hour."

We settle on the balcony, cars drifting past on the road below us. As soon as he looks at me it's a flame licked between us. Him mapping the contours of my face with his mind, now, is like making out on high.

Len swallows like he feels it too and lifts up his camera. "Relax," he orders. I don't know which one of us he's speaking to.

172

I try to keep my mind on permitted topics—groceries we're low on, Gran's bunions, global warming. Definitely not the way the waning sun makes his hair glow silver, or the movement in his forearm.

He stares intently, his teeth worrying at his lower lip while he snaps this way and that.

The flash rebounds off my glasses. I reach up to take them off.

Len tilts his head and smiles sideways. "Yeah."

I grip the chair underneath me. Global warming. Financial recession. Ham's dirty soccer socks.

A few shots later he gets up and unscrews the big lens, and I think we're done, but then he reaches across toward my face.

With the lens, he guides my chin upwards and to the side. *With the lens.* The metal and glass are cold on my face, but his fingertips are feather light. His breath fans across my face, and I can smell it—a *himness* that absolutely kills me.

I hold my breath and try to look like this isn't the hottest thing that's ever happened on a semi-wraparound suburban verandah.

"Sorry. The light," he says softly, sitting back down and gesturing to the sun, which has sunk westwards and left me here to spontaneously combust.

I gulp. "It's okay."

The day dies around us as he works, the sky turning bruised behind his head. I feel his eyes on me; every time they home in on a new section, their focus leaves a trail of warmth.

"Okay," he says finally. "I think I just got it."

"Cool."

We're quiet for a minute. Len looks almost . . . nervous, or something. But that can't be right. I must have entered a phase of turned-on where you hallucinate.

"What now?" he asks, rubbing his thighs.

I take a breath and stand up. "I kind of want to go to bed."

I have no idea where this is coming from. Some smooth-talking alter ego who's been lying dormant until this exact moment. I hope he sticks around.

Len swallows. "Okay."

We take the stairs slowly. Even though it's still early he flips off the lights, dimming the heavy chandelier until we're being guided only by the foggy glow of the street lamps outside.

"You can sleep in Lacey's room, if you want," Len offers quietly once we're on the landing. His eyes are glow-in-the-dark bright.

I shake my head; it's still buzzing. The dead-silent house eggs us on, a beacon.

"We probably should. Sleep, I mean," Len continues. There's no conviction in it.

How much build-up is too much? Bridging the electric gap between us feels actually impossible, for a minute, but so does not doing it. My hands sweat with the strain.

"I'm not really tired," I whisper.

Len takes an unsteady breath. "Henry . . ."

I kiss him because I can't *not* for another second. He kisses me back like I'm air.

He shudders under my hands. Gasps into my mouth. Push-pulls at me until I loop one arm around the back of his neck.

A memory flashes through my head: Rodin's statue at a museum I went to with Dad. The figures' arms wrapped around each other with such easy possessive grace that I was jealous, just for a second. Like they'd stood together that way a thousand times, one-person tight. Like they'd never stop.

Later on, he snores as soon as his head hits the pillow.

I'm rigid at first, stretched out on top of the covers in his room. It's been years since we've slept next to each other.

It feels strange. Nice. Strangely nice. His skin is hot and vital, and the rise and fall of his chest is the only sound in the room.

After a while I grip my fingers around his softly, watching that his face is still smooth in sleep. They're pianist elegant where mine are all nails bitten down to the quick. I want to thread them through at the knuckles to see if our hands fit, but my eyes shutter closed.

15

How to maybe-date your best friend: don't.

Kidding. Kind of. But usually (from what I've seen, anyway) this part is the requisite getting-to-know-you phase. Coffees and questions about where you both grew up, your neuroses with your parents, bosom dreams, etc.

We skip that altogether, given there's no mystery there. There is a lot of coffee, but beyond that we head straight for the next level. All of the levels.

There's hours at his house, pushed up against each other in front of the TV. Holding hands in my room. And the kissing— that's probably the strangest thing.

I keep waiting for the other shoe to drop, for it to transition into something more like what I expected kissing would be (sedate, the way elderly couples in films do it), but it's never *not good.*

The touching is taking some serious getting used to—I'm jittery, stiff. There's normal touching with other people, and then there's ... *feely* stuff. But once it's happening, it's also a bit like a part of me's been waiting to feel this way: ripped-apart good. To be made out with like that scene in *The Notebook* on performance enhancers.

We do ordinary stuff too—I mean, we're not animals. I sit at the café and watch him work. Text him dumb things. Stay up too late at his house playing PlayStation. But it's always there in the background: a living thing.

I'm definitely not thinking about *feelings touching kissing* when I drag him to family brunch, holiday edition, at Gran and Marigold's in New Farm on Tuesday afternoon. Definitely not hyper-aware of his arm next to mine the whole drive there.

"My beautiful boys!" Gran coos when we walk in, hugging us both so hard our heads smack together. Without warning, she thrusts a worn paperback at me.

"What's this?"

"Rilke!" she says.

"Who?"

Gran recites something in German, of which I only catch the word "blood." "He's prolific, Hen. Honestly. Sometimes I despair of you."

I read the cover. It's in German.

"You realize I sucked at German, right? And French."

"You were all right in French, weren't you?"

"No. I told the examiner *je suis douze les chats.*"

Len snorts softly.

"Well, there's an English translation in the back!" Gran snaps. "I want you to pick a quote for me. For your reading at the wedding." She grabs me by the book-hand and whispers in my ear, "Might help you sort your nonexistent love life."

"Let him go," Mum says. "He's been through enough this term."

Gran does as she's told, releasing me only to grasp Len by the hand. "And Lennon! I've been meaning to talk to you, actually."

177

I stare at her. "Why?"

She ignores me, and beckons Marigold over. "Speaking of the wedding, we have something important to ask you, but I wanted to do it in person."

Len sucks his teeth, looking between them. "Okay."

Gran clasps her hands together under her chin. "I've been looking through all these wedding picture people, and they're just crap, darling. We want it to be someone we know, someone good. We want you to do it. Will you? Please?"

Len looks thoroughly taken aback for a minute.

"If you'd like to, of course," Goldie qualifies.

"I . . . Yeah. I could do that."

"Wonderful! Then it's settled." Gran beams and kisses him on the cheek before disappearing into the kitchen where Mum's sorting out brunch.

"You don't have to—" I start when she's gone.

He smiles and holds up an "it's fine" hand. I want to say more, but then Ham drags him into the backyard.

"How are *you*, Henry?" Marigold asks me suddenly, handing me a glass of red wine.

Gran doesn't have anything remotely resembling a romantic pattern. My sketchy memories of Pa are that he was stoic and sturdy. Goldie is an ethereal, fairytale type, with her big honey-dyed hair and magnified glasses. Her conversation starters are always sudden, like she was in another realm before focusing on you.

"Uh, good," I say, shrinking back from her penetrating gaze.

"This is your last year?"

"It is, yeah. We just finished the big exams."

She peers at me over the top of her drink, in full retired-psychologist mode. I'm wearing my heaviest gold-rimmed glasses; hopefully they conceal the Len-thoughts behind them.

"You're handling everything else okay? Growing pains can be tough."

"Um. Handling it pretty well, I think," I blatantly lie.

She squeezes my shoulder; the brass rings on her fingers press into my skin. "It's all relative, you know," she says in her soft voice. "I dropped out of school when I was fourteen; my brother went straight to university, and then he dropped out of that. Now he breeds horses. Don't feel too pressured to have it all sorted right now."

"Er. Thanks, G," I say, awkwardly gripping the neck of my still-full red wine. "Will do."

Dad brought a sketchpad with him and is idly tracing the outline of Len, Gran, and Ham playing tag in the garden.

"Reuben!" Mum calls from the kitchen. "Come and try this. It's nearly ready."

"What?" Dad clatters through the sliding door, stamping his boots on the welcome mat.

"Honestly." Mum holds out a slice of Gran's vegetarian nut loaf. "Sometimes it's like being the wife of a ghost."

Dad wraps his arms around her waist. "A hot, cool, *flexible* ghost."

Ham's standing at the door covered in mud. "Ghosts? There are ghosts here?"

"Now you've done it," Dad murmurs into Mum's shoulder.

"No, Hambam," Mum soothes. "It's a saying."

"*A séance?*" Ham screams, running off.

Mum looks exhausted.

"I'll get him," says Dad.

Gran watches all this with a faint line in the middle of her forehead. "Right. Billie, sit down. Goldie, pour her some wine. Boys, come and help finish lunch. This gravy is cement."

Len and I exchange a glance. It sparks, despite the five intrusive Hamlets.

"Yes, chef."

───────

It sparks again on the drive home. All my skin goes sunburnt. (His face doesn't look like the one I've known basically my whole life. He looks how I feel: *hungry*.)

Mum and Dad make small talk I don't hear and carry a sleeping Ham inside.

"Let's go somewhere," Len says, clicking his keys.

The suburb's sleepy around us, toffee-apple twilight almost completely silent. There's *atmosphere*, so much that I think it might swallow me. I crack a window, just in case.

I don't say anything when he drives us out further bush than the Reserve, pulling to a stop at the edge of what looks like a cricket pitch. I'm grateful for dusk's cloaking purple, obscuring the fact that my face is the exact same color.

He's so . . . confident. The way he opens my door, leaning against the car, so I'm face to face with him when I step out. It makes me nervous. More nervous.

The field is iridescent green under the muted glow of old floodlights. He pulls me to the center, then flops down onto his back. The stars are waking up, a sequined blanket thrown over our heads.

He holds out his hand to me.

"Is it wet?"

"Relax. I come here all the time."

I hesitate, still squinting at the grass.

"Hamlet," he says. "It won't kill you to live a little." He closes his fingers around mine and pulls me down. I shift awkwardly for a bit until my head rests near his shoulder.

A car speeds by, lights washing the grass. It makes me jump, and I jerk my head away from his reflexively.

Len laughs, moving the earth underneath us. He finds my reactions to physical intimacy infinitely funny.

"You said you come here?" I ask to distract myself, settling back down.

He tips his head toward me. "Couple of times a week, since Mum."

I feel my face go slack. He's only ever talked like this a handful of times. The weight of it nearly makes me say, "it's okay to miss her," but then I stop, because who am I to tell him that, or anything.

He looks away from me and nods like I did say something.

A shape dances across the sky, a lightning-colored thing that's either astral or a metal tube carrying people to Europe.

Len pauses. "Looking up helps me think. Reminds me we're all just tiny specks of nothing, and soon our petty problems will be puffs of dust."

The words hang in the air for a moment, then sink down.

We look at each other and burst out laughing.

"Deep," I compliment. "How long did it take you to come up with that one?"

He smiles easily, and leans in closer, so that my head's pressed into the base of his neck.

I shiver. (From the cold. I'm *not* jumpy.)

"Really, though. It's like a pocket of calm in the sea of chaos." He moves his fingers until they're wrapped around my wrist.

The sensation is so stark that I shut my eyes for a few seconds.

"Is it always like this?" I blurt out eventually.

Because it's Len, he doesn't need more context to know what I'm asking. He looks at me for a long time (it's such a look), and says, "No. It's not."

I take a breath so big it hurts.

"Do you bring all your conquests here, then?" I ask, trying to lighten the mood.

"Please. It's my thinking place. Not my—"

"Secret make-out place?"

He laughs once through his nose, and it vibrates through both of us. I join in, even though nothing's particularly funny. Everything feels hilarious all of a sudden, the whole blurry world a carnival. It must go to my head, because the next words to fall out of my mouth are, "I'm curious, though. Have you ever . . . ?"

Heat immediately washes through me.

"What—brought someone here?" He wrinkles his nose. "Nah."

I sit up more, steadying myself with a hand on his chest. Before I can wuss out, I push on. "No. I mean like, *have* you *ever*. As in, with . . ."

I know the answer, of course—he's Len. NGS's resident Don Juan, with a jar of hearts from every school in the area. Still, a tiny screaming part of me hopes he'll deny it. Then maybe I could pretend we're at least marginally in the same league.

"Yeah," he says, unabashed. "I have."

(Right.)

He looks at me, leaning back on his elbows. "It's okay that you haven't."

I want to say something—a nonchalant remark, anything—but my tongue is stuck somewhere between my throat and the stars. I flop back down, more heat rushing to my face.

"Okay," I repeat.

He squeezes my wrist once.

"Yeah. It's cool."

I glower up into the backlit black. "It is far from cool."

Len rolls onto his side, our faces almost touching. "You know, right?"

"What?"

"I don't, like, expect anything."

"I . . . you . . . I wasn't—" I huff. (Why am I like this? This isn't at all the suave exchange I hoped for.) "I mean, yes. I know."

"Good."

I clear my throat. "Um. You can, though."

"What?"

"I mean," I mumble. Swallow. "Like, obviously I have zero experience. Sub-zero. Sub-Saharan Africa, that's how much of a dry spell my life has been. But—"

"I know," he puts me out of my misery. "I was there."

"Right. Yes." I nod rapidly. "But like—you can. Expect things. If you . . . want."

He smiles slow with mischief and runs a hand over my sternum. I wonder if he can feel the shattering beat in my chest. How, when he dips his head, I swear it's like the sky pours down on me.

"Noted."

I wake up jittery-early the next morning and lie in bed for a bit before I find myself jumping up and straddling the ledge outside my window while the sky wakes up.

It's a dewy-wet climb onto the roof, but I manage to swing myself onto the flat bit with only one and a half near-death slips. Once I'm at the top, Brisbane spreads out ahead of me.

For spring, the city blooms fuzzy purple hope.

It's corny, but jacaranda trees kind of fascinate me. How quickly they paint the tired face of the city. That they're beautiful, and we don't even notice, most of the time.

It happens gradually every year. A few pop up, then some more, until everywhere is ruptured color while winter shakes its fist in the background.

I'm a little too soon in the game this morning, but there's enough to stare out at while the sun rises. To trace the bright violet thread through houses and roads right up to the horizon.

I watch the light change colors, until it's on me.

16

My first major hurdle as friend-turned-more is his birthday. The September date looms ahead of me, a question within a question. "Fraught" is the word I would use.

Also: "fragile."

(I've held him while he slept, practically clung to him, but . . . do I do the birthday?)

I finally have a brainwave a few days before: Ged's parents' holiday house. We talked about maybe going away together before the end of the holidays. If we *all* go for the weekend, it's not me overstepping the mark.

I dial Ged's landline.

"Jess?" he answers hopefully, followed by, "Oh. It's you."

Our proceeding conversation unfolds approximately thus:

G: *What d'you want?*

H: Len's birthday.

G: Jess is gone.

H: I know, man. It sucks. Listen, though, remember when we were going to go to the mountains for end of term?

G: Everything is meaningless.

H: Maybe we should go now. Double celebration. It might cheer you up.

G: Life sucks.

H: Is that a yes?

G: Life sucks, and then you—

H: Aw, come on—

G: Die. Like I want to.

H: And I want to talk to you about it. At length. But first do you want to maybe ask your mum?

G: Mum! Can we go to the mountains for Len's birthday! It's this weekend definitely no alcohol and no (dry sob) *girls*!

. . .

G: She said yep.

H: Brilliant! So, Jess?

G: Whatever. I don't really wanna talk about it.

———

Hurdle number two is Lacey, who blows back into town like a hurricane on birthday eve-eve.

We meet her at Scott's Corner, smudge-eyed and carrying several garbage bags of luggage.

"God," Len says, hugging her hard and regarding her outfit: a pilled blue jumper held up over threadbare jeans with a thick belt. "Did you do *any* washing while you were away?"

She kisses him on the cheek. "I have you for that."

Len clicks the kettle on to boil.

"Tell me *everything*," Lacey commands, perching on one of the white leather stools at the counter. "How's the great and terrible year twelve coming along?"

"No school talk," I beg. "It's too awful for words. Tell us about you, out in the big smoke."

She wrinkles her nose. "Well, firstly, nobody calls it that unless they're ninety."

I poke my tongue out at her.

"Of course, the workload is kicking my arse. Lots of arguing about ethical dilemmas that end in tears."

"So you love it," I surmise.

"Yeah. I really do."

Len puts a peppermint tea in front of her.

"I need espresso pronto."

"Told you," Len says. "You're full Melbourne. You'll be wearing all black and buying a nine hundred thousand dollar terrace house in a drugs district next."

Lacey rolls her eyes. "I'm actually not loving that part of things, to be honest. Very cold, gloomy, et cetera. I'm thinking of moving back at the end of the year if my credits transfer. Home is where the heart is, and all that jazz."

"Believe it when I see it," Len says, turning back around to make our drinks.

Lacey sips her tea.

"Henry," Len asks after a minute, "can you pass me the milk?"

"Yeah." I jump up too fast, trying not to otherwise react to his casual use of my name.

We drink and talk for a while, before Len disappears upstairs to get some photos to show Lacey. I start cleaning up, clanking cups against the sink.

Lacey comes to stand behind me, smelling like musk and city rain.

When I turn to face her, she looks so like Len for a moment that I start.

"You're doing my brother," she accuses point-blank.

I'm so shocked that I slap the counter in my rush to deny it. "I—no—we're not! I mean, we haven't—"

"You *haven't*? Bloody hell. It's serious, then. I didn't think you had it in you."

(Why can't I ever lie convincingly when it counts?)

"No! There's no . . . it's—"

"Cut the shit, Hamlet. I'm getting mad vibes from the two of you. Who the hell calls you 'Henry?'"

"It's my name!"

"Plus, he told me. Last week."

My eyebrows contract. "He *did*? What did he . . . ?"

"Not important. The important thing is that you both realize how monumentally you could fuck this up."

"I—"

"I mean," she continues, "you've been a thing since forever. BFFs or whatever. Is it worth it, risking that?"

I replay his "Henry" and feel a squeeze of affection in my gut. "Yes."

"Break his heart, and I'll kill you," she says warningly.

My eyebrows squish even further together. "It's not likely to be me breaking hearts, is it?"

Lacey shakes her head indulgently. "He is quite the commitment-phobe, my brosephine. Learned it from me." She picks up a cup and dries the inside of it for a minute. "Worse after Mum, though. Like . . . I don't know. Maybe he thinks he'll feel all of it again, if he feels anything, ever."

I picture pre-Sarah Len briefly. Losing her was like a weight, but inverse. Like there's a little less in him now of the stuff that anchors us.

"He is definitely a runner," Lacey finishes bluntly. "But still!

I think that if anyone can be the one to straighten him out . . ."

I open my mouth to ask what on earth *that* means, but Len comes back before I get the chance.

"What are we talking about?" he asks, putting a stack of photos down on the bench.

"How much we hate you," Lacey says sweetly. "Weren't we, Hamlet? We're actually thinking of starting a club."

We have sandwiches for lunch, and it's fine, though it feels like Lacey is watching us closely. My stomach is still churning over *runner*. And the fact that she knows at all. That anyone does.

John's meant to be getting home at six, so Len drops me home in the late afternoon. When we get to my place, he parks on the curb and cuts the engine, then folds his arms combatively.

"Out with it."

"Mmm?" I play dumb.

"What'd she say to you?"

"Nothing."

"Yes, she did. You've gone all weird."

"I haven't—"

He gives me a similar look to Lacey's: *cut the shit.*

I pause.

"You told her."

"And?"

"I guess I wasn't expecting that."

"I tell her everything. It's not a big deal."

When I don't respond, he adds, "Whatever she said, she was probably just trying to rile you up. She can't resist it. Ignore her. I do."

I swing open my door and step onto the pavement, which is still slick from morning rain.

He shuts his own door and stalks after me, confused. "Don't just walk away."

"Why?" I spin around. "It's what *you* do."

He stops. "Where'd that come from?"

"Just . . . she made me realize something. About this . . . whatever it is."

Len's eyes flare, but he waits.

"It's going to end eventually, isn't it? You're going to run."

He takes another step toward me. "Henry . . ."

"You always do—it's how it is with you. You don't commit."

He looks pained. I'm not sure how or why I've gone from zero to cling wrap in the space of a single afternoon, but I can't find the off switch.

"That's not *how it is* with me," he says. "And anyway, you're . . . different."

I tilt my head to the side, derisive. I hate myself for it. "Different, am I?"

"Yes," he says through his teeth.

"What does that—"

"Hen?" My mum's voice cuts across the tepid air. The veranda light clicks on, the fluorescent bulb poking intrusive fingers out at us. "Is that you?"

I shield my eyes. "Yeah! I'll be in in a sec."

Len is still staring at me. "Do you want me to go?"

"Yeah. I think I do."

He rubs his thumb over his bottom lip. "Whatever. Fine."

I'd call it our first fight, but we fight all the time. This just cuts deeper. My eyes burn watching him walk away. I will him to look back; he doesn't.

It's just Mum in the kitchen when I get inside.

190

She squints at my face, scrutinizing. "What's wrong?"

"Just hungry."

"There's lasagna in the fridge."

"Mmm. Maybe later." I start walking up the stairs.

"Hen—"

"I don't want to talk about it!" I slam my door.

Mum immediately knocks once and opens it a crack. "You sure you're okay?" she asks softly.

"Fine," I can barely get it out. This is too much, all of it.

"You're clearly upset, sweets. Talking helps. Is it . . . is it to do with the flu girl?"

(How can she know me this well but not?)

"I just need a minute, Mum! Okay?"

The concern on her face deepens, but she closes the door.

I cocoon myself, watching old *Friends* episodes without seeing them and trying (failing) to figure out the swirling in my chest.

Things have been good. Bizarre, but good. So why can't I breathe right? Lacey's knowing face flashes up again, like there's already a ticking clock, and . . .

I can't tell my mum.

Other people knowing is risk. *Fear.* I don't want it to be, but it is, is, is. The thought of them (anyone) touching this. Tainting it. Taking it.

And then there's Len. I've watched this play out from the sidelines too many times to have any delusions about how it goes. All the doubt I've been in too deep to feel is a paperweight on my chest.

My heart bashes away, sensing danger and wanting out. It's still going when I eventually traipse downstairs for lasagna before bed.

Mum watches me moving around the kitchen. I lean up against the bench for a minute, holding the bowl up under my chin.

"Sorry," I tell her with my mouth full.

She comes over and kisses my head. "You're really all right? Promise?"

I look away, shoveling pasta. "Yeah. Think I just need an early night."

I'm dozing off when a sound outside startles me awake an hour or two later. I jerk upright and look toward the window.

Nothing.

Possums, I decide. We have whole families of them living in our rain gutters, because Ham insists on feeding them illicit carbs whenever he gets the chance.

I hear it again and jump out of bed. Carefully, I lean toward the glass, peering out into the street-lit dark.

It's not a possum. Not unless one of them recently purchased a corduroy jacket.

I push the window open. "What the *actual* hell are you doing?"

"Oh, Hamlet," Len says. "Hey. Didn't see you there."

"You didn't see me when you were looming outside my window?"

"This your window? I just thought this tree looked particularly climbable."

I stare at him sullenly.

He wobbles a bit. "Let me in?"

I do, but only because he's straddling a branch I suspect is too thin to take his weight. He topples inside, wincing as he bangs his knee on the casement.

He straightens up and we stand facing each other. I can see

from the way his mouth is half-tilted into a smile that he's decided to disregard what happened.

"So," he says. "Are you finished being pissy?"

I don't respond.

"Come on. Get over it already."

"No."

His eyes are light, teasing. "Bet I could make you."

I take a step away. "Nein cigar."

We're quiet for a minute, arms folded, neither of us breaking rank.

He sighs. "Look. Lacey was out of line. I don't think she meant anything by it. She just doesn't have much faith in me, when it comes to this sort of stuff."

"What sort of stuff?"

"The stuff we've been doing."

"What *are* we doing, Len?" I snap. "Do you even know?"

He sighs again. "Jesus. You don't have to overanalyze everything."

"I haven't! That's the problem. I haven't thought, at all."

He sits down on the edge of my desk, leaning back and looking at the constellations on my ceiling we stuck up there when we were six.

"We're . . . I don't know. Exploring something," he says eventually. "It's normal."

"It's *normal* to hook up with your best mate, is it?"

"Sometimes, maybe."

We've avoided talking about any of this, and now the room is crowded to the brim with questions.

I sit on the bed, the springs giving like the extra weight in me is tangible.

"Do you have to be so bloody casual all the time?" I whine. "Have you even thought about any of this, or does none of it matter to you?"

His head snaps up; he looks hurt. "I've thought."

"*Really?*" I shoot back. "Because it doesn't seem like you have. And . . . I have, okay?"

He's watching me steadily.

"I . . . think. About you," I mumble. "I mean, I have done. A lot. For a bit."

I wait for him to say something, laugh, get up and leave. He doesn't do any of that. The ceiling fan clicks its slow rotation.

"I've thought about it," he says quietly.

"You have?"

"Yes. Not, like, seriously, or anything."

"Oh. Why?"

(Why didn't you tell me? Why didn't I know?)

"You're not exactly what I'd call uninhibited. I didn't think you'd *want* . . ." He breaks off, a slash of pink on both cheeks.

I look at him in shock. "Since when? Since when have you thought about it?"

He chews his index finger evasively. "I don't know."

"I'd say you do."

He looks at his jeans, pulling one leg down over his Docs. Looks out the window—everywhere but me. "A long time, all right?" he says. "Maybe always."

Four syllables like a hook in my chest.

"I don't understand any of this," I say.

Slowly—I don't know whether for my sake or his—he comes over and sits down beside me on the bed. I lean my head back against the wall. Our shoulders press together.

"I mean," I plough on, "up until a couple of months ago, I thought I'd probably be"—gulp—"straight, and you were too. Mostly, anyway. Now I don't know anything."

"Must be terrible for you," he says. "A smarmy school captain's worst nightmare."

"Be serious, please. We have to talk about this stuff eventually."

His mouth twitches. "So, talk."

"Okay. Well. Are you?"

"Am I what?"

My face burns. "You know what."

Len tilts his head toward me, eyes so direct I almost can't look. "It's never really been an either/or kind of thing for me."

"But like . . ." I suck in air. "What if it is for me? What if I am?"

"Okay," he says.

"Shouldn't I *know*?" I demand.

"I don't think it always works like that."

"It should."

"Should it?"

"Yes!"

"Why?"

"Because—*because*."

He picks up my hand and pulls gently, until I'm forced to look up properly.

"You don't have to have everything all figured out and put in a neat little box. Sometimes people do things just because they want to."

I sit there for a bit, running the words over in my head and wishing more than anything that I could view things the way he does.

"And then there's you," I continue.

He sits back against the wall. "What about me?"

"I realized, today, how high the stakes are," I whisper. "If Lacey knows, then everyone else will, and that's terrifying—"

"Why?"

I avert my eyes again. "Because . . . it just doesn't make sense, I guess."

"*What* doesn't?" he whisper-yells, exasperated.

"Shh, god. For you to want me . . . that way!" I burst out, my fingers twisting together between us. "I don't get it." I breathe in. This is the big one, the thing that's bothered me since the start. "Even more than the other stuff, I don't get . . . what I am, to you."

Len's face shifts, a rolling thunderstorm.

He leans in. Closer and closer, until he's got me pinned between him and the wall.

"You're half of me," he says, his voice soft and serious. "What else is there?"

And, yeah. There's not much need for talking, after that.

17

On the day of Len's eighteenth birthday, I jog up the front steps
of Scott's Corner with my biggest backpack (filled with food,
clothes, and five cans of bug spray) slung across my back and
my wrapped-and-rewrapped half-boyfriend present in my arms.

He opens the door before I knock, hair wet and no shirt on.

Smiles with his eyes first, then everywhere.

"Um," I say, shifting my feet on the mat. "Happy birthday."

"Thanks."

"You ready?"

"Yeah. Almost."

We head upstairs so he can throw things into a backpack
while I catch occasional stray items of bedding he hurls in my
direction.

"Remember to dress for the wilderness," I say.

He slips a green, black, and blue checked flannel shirt over
his head.

(I immediately think about taking it off.)

"Wilderness enough for you?"

I zip up the bag loudly.

Lacey's still in bed when we get downstairs, but John's sitting
at the kitchen table fully dressed, with a fancy filter coffee in
front of him.

"Henry. What brings you here?"

"Um. Just collecting this one for birthday shenanigans."

John's eyes run over the heavy bags and pillows in our arms, before coming to rest on Len. They're ice blue. Focused.

I wait for him to pick up on the birthday lead. Instead he sips coffee, then goes into the front sitting room.

I look at Len, but he's stuffing shoes into his bag. I go outside to dump some of the bigger items on the veranda, wrestling with the pillows until they sit one on top of the other.

When I come back the kitchen's empty. I think Len must've gone back upstairs, but then I hear voices coming from the sitting room.

"Give me the keys, Lennon. Richardson's borrowing it. He needed something with a tow bar. I'm sure I told you."

"I'm sure you didn't," Len insists.

"Yes, I did," John sounds irritated.

I feel like I'm peering through a window. I start to backtrack toward the entryway.

There's a serrated edge to Len's voice I don't recognize. "Right. It's not like we had *plans* today, or anything."

"Worried your little friends won't think you're so wonderful without the nice car?" John snaps.

Blood rushes to my head, flood-fast like when I'm about to be sick.

"No. But it's my car." Len.

"Oh. Did you pay for it?" John. "Was there a transaction of funds between us I'm unaware of?"

There's a metallic sound: keys being snatched from one hand into another.

"*My* car," John hisses.

He storms into the kitchen, keys in hand, and grabs his coffee without acknowledging me.

The heavy front door clicks shut softly behind him. I wish it would slam. That would make more sense.

I find Len in the sitting room. I want to talk, to run my fingers over that edge in his voice until I understand it, but he's already backing away too fast to chase.

"Let's take my car," I offer quietly instead. And we do.

———

Ged's dad was a pro football player in the early eighties, and the house in the hinterland is a vestige of that. A small cottage nestled into the side of a mountain, with shag carpet and dozens of big arch windows overlooking the valley, it's just over-the-top enough that I love it on sight when the Pissar miraculously delivers the silent two of us an hour later (after I kick the bumper, hard).

The Boiyss are blessedly on form, starting the ridiculousness as soon as we're inside. Ged claims the biggest bedroom, Harrison the second. Vince and I end up sharing one on the lower level, and Len gets the A-frame attic with the best view.

Vince leans on the doorframe of the master, arms folded, as Ged rolls around on the silky bedding.

"You know what I can't help but think, old bean?" Vince asks mischievously.

"What?" Ged looks up, out of breath.

"Your parents have had an awful lot of sex on that bed. Might have even been the exact spot you left the scrotal fold."

"Oh my god!" Ged jumps up with a start, wrinkling his face. "You're a sicko."

"I'm not the one sleeping in there, mate."

Ged glances at the now-tainted bedding, pained. "Trade?"

"Nope," Vince says. "Not a chance."

"Come on," Ged whines. "Somebody trade with me. Hamlet?"

Vince shoots me a look.

"Sorry, dude."

Ged stomps out of the room, throwing open the door to the back balcony. "Forget it, all of you!" He huffs. "I'll sleep outside."

"Isn't it supposed to rain tonight?" Len says. He's leaning against the wall with his hands behind him, relaxed now that we're here. I don't want to ruin it, but my mind's still overflowing from overhearing.

"Fuck!" Ged screams; it reverberates across the green expanse below, so loud that we laugh.

"Happy birthday," I tell Len again.

"'Tis," he responds.

———

Later, we order pizza and huddle by a firepit out the back. The sky is extra bright here. There's so much of it, and it's nice to get back to normal for a second. To be away from the city. Exam papers. Parents.

We eat with a chaser of Ged's home brew, which tastes like there's a very real possibility it's made from water stewed in an old boot. There's cake courtesy of Harrison's mum, and we all crowd around the Formica table in the dining room to sing "Happy Birthday."

"Make a wish!" Ged commands.

Len leans over to blow out the candles in one go.

"What'd you wish for?" I ask.

"Nothing."

"Vladimir Lennon!" Vince exclaims. "You must wish for *something*".

Len shrugs easily. "If I tell you, it won't come true."

"Presents," Harrison dictates. "Open mine first."

Len opens a copy of his favorite Led Zeppelin album on vinyl. Vince goes next, handing over a tiny package wrapped in tinfoil.

"Eyeliner." Len reads the packet.

"It's the sort Russell Brand uses," Vince explains proudly.

"Er, cheers, mate."

Ged produces a card with several scrunched vouchers to a steak restaurant haphazardly stuffed inside, and tickets to some big football game next year.

I pick up my present last. I bought it months ago and am secretly relieved nobody managed to top it.

Len looks at me suspiciously, undoing the masses of cork-colored wrapping paper. "Definitely a Hamlet present," he says, ripping through the last sticky-taped layer with his teeth. I always overdo it, wrapping and rewrapping until it's perfect.

Once it's finally free he flips it over in his hands, reading the cover. He pauses for a beat too long, then opens to the publication page.

It's an earlyish edition of *The Catcher in the Rye*. I've always found it a bit cliché that it's his favorite book, but then he made me read it a year ago. It suits him.

His eyes shoot up to meet mine. "You spent money."

"Yeah, well. Deal with it."

He stares at the book some more, running his finger over the dust cover.

"Thanks," he says.

"Just remember to mention, when you tell the story of this momentous occasion, that my present was the best."

Unexpectedly, he hugs me. He's careful to keep it sufficiently stiff and awkward-looking, but his arms are hot around my back. I catch sight of Vince standing off to the side, studying us, and pull away.

We disperse after that—Ged retreats to the den to set up an air mattress, Harrison goes for a shower, Vince skulks to our room to text a girl.

I clean up the kitchen while Len stands outside on the balcony, looking at the charcoal cluster of clouds covering the tip of the mountain. When I'm done, I join him, leaning against the timber railing and wishing I'd brought a coat.

He's smoking one of the cigarettes Vince passed around earlier. He coughs and holds it out toward me; I wave it away, watching for a bit as he exhales smoke rings.

"How's it feel, then?" I ask after a while. "The big one-eight."

He turns around, thoughtful. "Dunno. Ask me tomorrow."

"You don't feel a profound new sense of adulthood?" I press.

"Did you?"

I cast my mind back to my own birthday in January. We went to dinner in the city and everyone got so drunk that Gran ended up in a fight with one of the waitstaff.

"Hmm. Not really, I guess. We should, though, shouldn't we? It's supposed to be profound."

"You can't choose what's gonna be profound, Hamlet. It

surprises you. That's the point." He sucks in smoke, looking out over the valley, his eyes fiery and far away.

I take a breath. "Listen. Are you, like … okay? Your dad …"

I don't know if what's going on between us means I can't say it, or that I can.

"Is an arsehole," he finishes. "I'm aware."

I get the sick feeling again and drop my voice so it's barely audible. "You can talk to me, you know. You should talk to me. That's how this works."

His face is polished steel. "And if I said I hated him? What would you say?"

"Um." I'm thrown by the tone of his voice. "I'd say …"

"Exactly."

"But—"

"Look. I'm not you, okay? I don't need to sit and analyze every fucked-up thing." He gives me one last disappointed look. "Forget it. I'm going inside."

I try to catch his arm but he shakes me off, turning on his heel with smoke still dripping from his mouth.

I go to bed with a lump in my stomach.

———

Everybody leaves early the next day, loading cars with duffle bags (or trash bags, in Ged's case) under a cloud of fog.

"Let's wait a bit," Len says quietly when he comes to grab my stuff.

I'm lying on my made bed, tired but wired; Vince snored like a freight train the entire night.

I stare up at him, trying to read his face. I'm (very) aware that this is the only time we're likely to get *alone* alone for the foreseeable future, and so I nod.

We wave goodbye to Vince and Ged in his beaten-up BMW, then Harrison in his Swift. When they've all disappeared around the bend at the end of the road, he speaks with no preamble.

"Last night."

I take a deep breath. "It's okay."

"I . . ." He looks up at the downy gloom over our heads for what feels like a long time. "I'm not good at this."

"I shouldn't have pushed you—"

"It's not that. It's just—there's stuff I keep the lid on because I have to."

"I get it," I say, wanting to smooth out his conflicted face, even as internal Henry screams, *What stuff?* I want to keep him here, like this.

"I don't usually talk much, to people that I'm . . ."

"Well," I say slowly, sucking in gray sky. "That's fine. You don't need to."

Len lets out a breath. "Usually, I kind of . . . lose myself in them for a bit. And this is like the opposite. And—I'm *trying,* you know?" He's looking at me like he wants me to understand.

I walk over, my shoes crunching on the gravel, and wrap one arm around him. He hesitates, then presses his chin into my shoulder.

"You are very trying," I say to make him laugh, and he does. Soft as the trees.

———

The mist sticks around all day, a filmy coating on everything like magic. Len insists on taking hundreds of pictures, some of which I reluctantly star in. There's one he shows me that I actually like, where it looks like I'm wearing the weather.

I watch him, with his camera and his hair falling over his forehead, pale and drawn in wind. All the world slow. It's just now, here, this.

Night falls in fast peach-tinged stages, as though it knows as well as we do what we're going to do with it.

We sit next to each other watching TV for a bit—a rerun of *The O.C.* There's a kissing booth and much colorful clothing. Everyone's favorite emo nerd, Seth, is upset his girlfriend won't publicly acknowledge their love.

When the episode reaches its crescendo, he stands on top of the booth, and declares himself in front of everyone. Emilia has issues with shows like this—she always says the portrayed teenage experiences are unrealistic.

They seal it with a kiss, and it's . . . surprisingly unbearable. Len snorts softly at Seth Cohen's use of tongue, but the line where our legs touch feels more like it's covered in embers than denim.

"You hungry?" he asks once it's dark, snapping me back to the present.

I swallow. "I could eat."

He heads to the kitchen and opens a pizza box. "Ah, the continental option."

"Shut up. I don't see you contributing anything."

We set about preparing our meager meal, both of us quiet. Len reheats pizza and cuts up the last bits of cake. I source ice cream from the freezer to go with it, spooning it into Ged's mum's weird glass bowls.

It feels oddly domestic, bumping shoulders in the kitchen like this. Not that we haven't hundreds of times—but there were always other people in the background. Being alone makes everything charged.

Also, he keeps brushing his fingers maddeningly across every part of me he can reach. Even the skin of my forearm has become an erogenous zone. (Much more of this, and I'll actually catch fire.)

We make the mutual decision not to chance it with Ged's brew. Len finds some Coke with a questionable use-by date, which he pours into two tall mugs emblazoned with the logo of Ged's dad's football team.

We clink.

Dinner is good in a way it only ever is when you're starving, so we finish quickly, then throw our plates in the sink to deal with in the morning.

"I can't believe we actually still have to go to school in a week." I groan. "I'm not ready."

Len is silent, swishing a tea towel across the bench. I've broken the unspoken rule we've been operating under: don't mention what happens *after*. When things go back to normal, back to the way they were before.

(But they won't, surely? They can't.)

He finishes drying the bench and hangs the towel on the oven handle.

I screw up my courage. "If—"

He kisses me, pressing me up against the bench. My body responds immediately, like always; I push back, grasping his face between my hands. His mouth is urgent on mine.

"Whoa," I gasp between kisses. I try to wrench myself free,

to hide the effect this is having, but he holds me in place with his hips.

"What?" he breathes right in my ear.

The charge sparks, explosive.

I stare at him with my breath stuck in my throat, and then push him sideways, toward the bedroom.

"Are you s—"

I cut him off with a kiss of my own. It doesn't match the skill of his, but we're neck and neck for force.

Maybe it's last night, or the fact that reality is flexing its jaw, but for the first time this year I know exactly what I want.

I'm vaguely aware of the door being opened and closed. I hold him against it, and he makes a sound against my cheek.

I don't know what we're doing.

I don't want to stop.

Len guides me backwards, onto the bed. We line up perfectly, every inch of me arching toward him like he's the sun.

He presses against me, and it feels—god, so good, like light on the other side of my skin. It's just us, here. I can do what I want with him (to him), all the desires that've been stacked in my head blurring together.

I try to memorize each moment, but there's too much to be distracted by. He's holding himself up on his hands. My thumbs graze his hipbones and the belt loops on his jeans. I grab those and pull. Closer, not close enough.

He reaches for the hem of my T-shirt and yanks it up over my head. I do the same with his, and then it's all of us pressed against each other. Every drop of blood in me rushes to the surface. My fingers ghost over his back, his shoulders, the hollow of his stomach.

There's a hurried unbuttoning of jeans; I kick mine away clumsily. It's like my skin's come off. It's there again, the pull in my stomach: strong as home. He stares at me so hard I have to look away.

His mouth makes its way down my neck to the spot where it meets my shoulder. I feel the imprint of his lips on my skin like a brand. I feel it *everywhere*. I try not to make any embarrassing noises and fail.

He's better at some parts than me—the, er, French-derived parts. Expert, really. I keep getting tripped up by my teeth. But when I thread one leg through both of his, he shivers and whispers "*shit*" into my hair.

Is this normal? I don't know. I just know I'm dissolving, as though my atoms might split on the spot and burst me apart.

I wonder if it's the same for him. I don't have much time to wonder anything, though, because his hand slips down between us, warm and insistent and trembling slightly.

My eyes fly open.

He smiles breathlessly, teeth a flash of white in the dark.

"Do . . . do you want . . . ?" His voice is rough.

I'm already nodding.

Now. Here. "Yes."

18

I wake to birds chirping outside the window, and the cold of alone. I sit up and look at the indent in the left side of the bed.

This is it, then: the running. I try to breathe evenly, calculating whether I've got enough cash for a cab ride back.

"You're awake." He's standing in the doorway wearing yester-day's clothes and my Converse. "I thought you'd gone comatose."

"Hey." My voice cracks. It makes my whole neck flush, remembering why.

"Come on." He throws a T-shirt at me, smirking. "Breakfast."

I find my jeans balled up under the bed and pull them on. There's embarrassment curled hot on my chest like a cat, purring in wait.

(I can't believe I did those things. We did those things.)

I make my way into the kitchen and sit down at the table. Insecurity skitters through me. I run back over everything, looking for the moment. (I did something wrong—I must have.) There's a mark where I think I bit him, but that didn't feel like a misjudgment at the time—it made him say, "Hen-ry."

I jump when the toast pops. He spins around and puts two eggs onto a plate, then grabs the toast and plates it up too.

He puts the food in front of me and I stare, confused. "What?"

I clear my throat. It's scratchy, like I'm hungover. "I thought, when you were gone . . ."

He laughs. "Oh, man. You thought I left?"

I pick up my toast and chew.

"I'd never just strand you here."

I can feel myself going red. "I mean. Maybe, if you regretted . . ."

"Get over yourself." He rolls his eyes, then looks at me quickly. "Do you?"

The fear prickles again. But . . . "No. You?"

"I really, really don't."

———

We drive back at lunchtime, the fog cleared and the offensively bright sunlight back in all its glory. Len still drives too fast; the Pissar cries in protest, stalling twice. I clutch the safety handle so hard the whole way down the mountain that my fingers cramp.

When we get to his place, Lacey's watering plants out the front. She gives me a knowing wave.

Len touches my shoulder when I walk around to swap to the driver's seat. It's quick, but I still think maybe there'll be a hole in my jumper when I check later.

"Good game." He tips his chin.

"Did you just—"

His face is brilliant under the sun, grinning.

———

As soon as I get home, Dad shouts, "Henricus Rex! That you, mate?"

I walk through the empty house, out to the studio. "Yeah."

"How was it?"

(*Hen-ry.*)

"Um. Pretty good."

"What'd you get up to?"

(Can't you tell? From my face? Can't everyone?)

"Oh, you know. Same as always."

I dump my backpack and toe off my shoes: Len's Vans, because he's holding my mustard Converse hostage. They're tight in the toes, but I kind of like it.

Mum's at work, so it's just Ham and Dad in the studio. Ham's brown eyes are looking through me with that laser-beam vision kids have that sees into your frigging soul. "You look happy!"

"Mmm. I think I am."

"Then I am as well!"

I'm also drenched in sweat—whatever cool change we had has well and truly dissipated, and we're now living in a furnace. I wrench the studio window open and a paltry afternoon breeze pants against my forehead like a senile dog.

I can't even turn the air conditioner on—Reuben "environmentalist" Hamlet is morally opposed (not opposed enough to have them *removed*, though, because it's Queensland).

I give Ham a bit of "special sculpture" clay to play with and spend the rest of the day helping Dad pack his real sculptures into the van, carefully wrapping them in plastic and insulation.

The lifting and packing feels routine after a while, and the physical exercise further increases the rush that's still running through me.

I used to relish these times: when I'd get Dad all to myself and it was just us for hours, not saying anything but still being together.

"Can I tell you something?" I ask.

Dad looks up, his glasses fogged by sweat, and pulls his headphones out of his ears. "Eh? What'd you say?"

I lose my nerve. "Nothing."

I don't know why this is so hard. It doesn't make sense, but telling Dad feels like an admission to . . . myself. More than anything else.

Doing and being and saying are a hot tangle in my head. I can't make last night fit with this yet. I focus instead on my hands, bubble-wrapping and taping, lugging stone into the van. This series is all mostly human, and mostly to scale—several are over six feet.

"You still coming with me tonight?" Dad pants, sliding the last statue into place and pulling the rope tight.

I try to wipe my forehead on my arm, but that just transfers arm-sweat into my hair.

Crap. I forgot that tonight's the opening of his exhibition. I always go; it's our thing. How did I miss that? There's been too many *other things* crowding my head.

"Um," I hedge. "I mean, I just got back, and everything . . ."

"Oh, that wasn't actually a question." Dad laughs. "I just wanted you to feel like you had autonomy. You're coming."

I bite down on my lip; he talks a big game, but he'll be upset if I don't go. Plus, an injection of everyday routine probably wouldn't hurt, at this point.

"Okay," I agree. "But I'm going for a shower first."

"Make sure you keep it to four minutes—"

I gape at him through my curtain of dripping fringe. "Are you serious? It's a hundred and fifty degrees out here."

"Oh, please. More like ninety. I'm not even hot."

"If you insist on the disgrace that is only turning on the air conditioner at Christmas, I reserve the right to have the shower to end all showers."

He shakes his head in pretend disappointment. "Dude. I thought you were cool."

———

Dad's exhibition is in his usual space up on Mt. Coot-tha, twenty minutes of traffic and then a tree-hugged winding road out of the city. As soon as we get in the car he puts on *The Very Best of Prince* and starts singing along.

I draft and redraft a quick text to Len: **Gonna b MIA 2nite. 1 of Dad's bonding things. Sorry!!**

At the cemetery roundabout I look out the window at the steep sloping hill of headstones, half-moons glowing blue in the dark, simultaneously stretching to the sky and slipping under the dirt. I haven't been alone in my head for what seems like ages. It's messy. A deep well that I drop right down into.

I think maybe I'm disappearing. I don't know if it's all the *togetherness* of the last few days, or what.

(I do know I already regret the jaunty exclamation points. A lot.)

I try to absorb some of Dad's enthusiasm. He insisted we wear matching tie-dyed jackets.

"Is this really necessary?" I say when we park and get out.

Said jacket feels like it's made of chafe.

213

"Yes! It's a momentous occasion!" Dad booms, hugging me around the shoulders to steer me forward.

We approach the gallery through the yellow picket gate. It's a fairy house made of mountain, lit up and blinking warmly at us, already filled with the creatures Dad pulled straight out of his head. I'm sweepingly proud of him.

Then he whispers, "My butt's sweating."

"Can you not talk about your extremities in public, please?"

I stand back while Dad goes to greet everyone, then I meander outside into the garden. It's hot even in the dark when I stop and prop my foot against a tree.

I whip out my phone. Len may be rightfully ignoring exclamation-gate, but I am who I am—damned if that stops me from a rapid punch-and-send.

Feel crazy not seeing u.

Within a few seconds after it's sent, I start to think it looks desperate.

I stuff my phone back away and cringe-cover one eye, breeze licking the gaps in my fingers.

Then my hip buzzes. I flip my phone open so fast I lose my balance and leave a shoe skid on the tree.

He's sending a multimedia message, but the reception's so crap it's loading in wibbly thirds.

"Henry! You all right, mate?" Dad calls from the side door.

I walk back the way I came, hunting for reception. "Yeah! Be back in a sec."

I hold my phone in the air, searching for more bars. Dad watches me from the doorway for a beat longer, before retreating inside.

Two bars. Two and a half.

The picture pops up, finally: his face framed in messy gold hair with one arm propped behind his ear. He's giving me the finger with his other hand.

Now you do, it says underneath.

I do. My eyes get very stuck on the soft milk of his bicep for—longer than I'm willing to admit.

I look toward the laughter and voices inside, then down at Len again, and quickly type: **O_o O_o O_o**

He texts back straightaway. He never does that.

¯_(:))_/¯

ASDSDSDSHHSS&%#$

(Grip, Hamlet. As in get one.)

I snap the phone shut and leg it back up the path.

The gallery opening is a rushing success. I throw myself into it as best I can, standing among the statues and aggressively pitching big pieces to every baby boomer in a well-cut suit. Dad sells all of the works except two, in record time.

Everything goes so smoothly that we're done by seven with time to spare to go for dinner, since gallery food is notoriously inedible.

Dad finds me waiting by the door, sitting on a table with my legs dangling. I'm checking my phone again. (Haven't stopped checking it—whatever.)

"Lads' night!" Dad says with emphasis, handing me a drink. "We've tasted professional success, now let's go get dinner."

"Mmm?"

Len's replied to my gibberish. Properly. With: **Yeah. Same.**

"Henry?"

I'm half-texting back, letters glowing as I punch them in.

"What are you doing?"

"What? Nothing."

"*Mate*." There's genuine hurt in his face. "I feel like you've put all these walls up lately, and you won't even tell us why. I thought tonight we could reconnect. Bond. Like old times."

God. I close my phone, pick up the drink and grind ice between my teeth. "We're already bonded. We are one."

"Is it a girl?" he asks suggestively.

"Dad." I grimace. "No."

"Because, you can tell me about girls. I used to be pretty good at girls. Very good, some might say."

"*Dad*."

I crunch more ice savagely, staring again at my phone.

"We could start with: who is it you've been texting all night that's got you blushing this hard?" Dad prompts a beat later.

"Len!" I snap without thinking about it, just because his name flashes up on the screen with another text.

Oh.

Shit.

Dad's Hamlet-brown eyes lock on mine and go very wide. Searching.

Trust me to Freudian slip when we're trapped up a mountain together.

He knows. I can see it.

I set my drink back down shakily—a bit sloshes onto my shoe.

"Okay. If I tell you a thing, you . . . you have to *swear* you won't cry."

"Swear," Dad lies immediately.

"Okay," I say again, light-headed all of a sudden. "Crap. God. Okay. We're really doing this."

He waits.

I press my palm against my forehead and let it out in a rush. "Lately, I've ... sort of ... *kind of,* been with Len. Like, um ... with him with him."

Dad blinks. "Len. As in ..."

"I ... yeah."

Saying it out loud feels good in the way too much air in my lungs does.

Dad's careful expression starts to shift. "But you ... you can't be. I would've known. I wouldn't have missed that."

He doesn't look surprised, exactly, but he is rubbing his jaw pretty vigorously. I can see the rapid moving clouds of his thoughts behind his glasses.

And I'm angry.

"Well, I'm not a freaking artwork you made up in your head, okay?" I jump up. "I'm a person. And I'm sorry if the final product doesn't match your initial vision, but—"

"Henry." He catches my sleeve before I can get away. "Wait."

"Why? So you can tell me why I *can't be?*"

"I didn't mean that!" he exclaims. "Please, sit down."

"No! I'm sick of trying to be the person everyone else thinks I should be!"

"*Sit,*" Dad pleads. "Stop prejudging what you think I'm going to say, okay? It hurts. You think you're the only one who feels things deeply?"

I reluctantly do as I'm told, falling back down with a huff.

Dad takes a breath. "I am ... upset. Upset that you felt like you couldn't tell me this earlier. Which is on me."

My eyes flash up.

"Len, though," he says after a while, earnest and emphatic. "That's ... that makes ... yeah. I see."

He's looking dead at me. Sweaty. Anxious. Loving. My dad.

"So you don't think it's, like, a really bad idea?" I blurt out, needing to know. "That I never . . . and because he's *him*, and I'm just . . ." (Not good enough, maybe. Not enough.)

Dad watches me for another long minute. "Did you hear how I introduced you to everyone tonight?" he asks.

I shake my head. My brain sloshes around, matching the hard *da-dum* in my chest.

"That's my son—best person I know."

I rest my chin on the heel of my hand, wincing.

"But you don't think—"

"I *think*," he says, "life is so short, champ. It probably seems long now, but really it's a handful of shots in the dark, and then you're done. Anything that makes you happy is great. Both of you. I also think *you're* great, and I love you. For telling me. And for many other reasons."

"No crying," I remind him, not entirely steadily. "You promised."

Dad lets tears roll down his cheeks. They're turning the studio lights off, but neither of us moves. Not for the longest time.

When we're home, and I tell Mum, she doesn't say anything at all. She just studies me as if I'm a house she built, and the lights are switched on at night while she's standing on the street outside. Watching it be.

There's a lot of hugging. I confirm that she is not, under any circumstances, to ask him about it when he comes over. Then Ham screams, hugs my legs, and asks if we can get KFC.

19

On Sunday, I'm in a bone-chillingly cold shower when Ham
calls, "Henry!"

I switch off the tap and wrap a towel around my waist.
"What?"

"Len's here!"

"Okay!" I call, throwing open the bathroom door. "I'll be
down in a minute."

"No need," a voice to my left says.

He's standing at the top of the stairs wearing *jeans* without
a drop of sweat on him, his hair immaculate. I'm aware mine
is plastered into noodles on my forehead.

"Déjà vu," Len says softly, leaning back against the banister.

"Yeah. It's like I think I have a good body, or something,"
I joke, pulling the towel tighter at my hip. "I don't think that,"
I feel the need to add.

Len rolls his eyes.

"Team Hamlet," he says after a while. "Downstairs, they
were . . . they know, right?"

I am going to kill them so dead. "Um . . . totally. That okay?"

There's a kind of wistful look on his face. He reaches across
and pushes my hair back from my forehead. He arranges it for

a bit—until I stop breathing and it looks, presumably, less like an outward expression of the mess that I am.

"Yeah," he says, and his mouth quirks right up.

I told Emilia to meet us at South Bank, which feels like a safe distance, and then not, once we're actually driving there.

We're both nervous. I reach out to touch his hand and then stop. I don't know whether he wants to tell Ems—he's dead quiet. He doesn't even complain about the hourly rate for parking.

Ems is sitting on the grass when we walk toward the river. She's wearing a yellow skirt and a smile that ripples like the water behind her. She stands up and hugs Len first, then me.

"Happy birthday to you!" she sings at him, handing over a card. "I panicked and just got you money."

Len squeezes her around the middle. "You know you didn't have to get me anything."

Ems taps the dimple on her chin. "Oh, please. I'm celebrating! We are all, officially, standing on the *literal cusp* of adulthood."

"*Literally*," I tease.

"And you guys look like you're finally ready to admit you're cheating on me with each other."

I start to cough like I'm choking. Len stuffs his hands into his pockets.

Ems scans our faces for a minute, then screams. "*What?* I was fishing! I mean, I was pretty sure, but . . . oh my god. Oh my god!"

"You're the worst." I shake my head at her, blushing for gold. "The best," I qualify. "But also, the worst."

Emilia screams again and squishes us both into another hug. "*This* is the best! It's the best news I've had all holidays—nay, all *year*. I want to know everything. No wait—I don't. Actually, yes. I do."

Things are odd and cringey at first, but also pretty much just like always, except Ems stares at us when she thinks we're not looking a few times and trills, "You guys!" when she gets caught. Len's hand is resting right next to my leg, palm up.

I can touch it (that hand near mine) if I want (I do) and it's okay. More than okay.

Ems goes to get us ice creams after a while and insists on paying.

"How are we feeling re: the countdown to graduation? Pumped as a skunk?" she asks once she's back, nibbling a cone dipped in sprinkles.

"Ergh." Chocolate gelato drips onto my shorts.

Len tips his head back. "Don't listen to him—he's already made flashcards."

She giggles. "Hey, now. Not all of us plebs have photographic memories."

"Exactly." I shove him a bit, until he topples backwards onto the grass in a blur of jeans and bare arms.

"Or *lurve* feelings to keep away the dread," Ems continues, mock-despondently, looking at us. "Only . . . sugar, and regret."

I freeze, waiting for Len to balk, move away from me, but he smiles.

"Chin up, Captain Studypants," he says. "Eamon Matthews is ready to fall on his sword for you."

Ems rips up a handful of grass savagely. "Yes, well—I'm a career woman. Or at least I will be, if things go to plan."

"You will be," I tell her.

"And what'll you be?"

"God knows," I joke. (But I kind of wish I did.)

We accidentally stay out late, until the sky spits pink and Emilia has to go. She hugs us again, me first this time while she whispers, "Yes yes yes!" in my ear.

I don't want to go.

"Should we walk a bit?" I ask him.

"Yeah."

Len pulls me silently along the path. Not quite holding my hand but not quite not.

We don't rush. For once the arbor *feels* grand—purple flowers canopied above our heads and lights switching on in strips as if just for us.

His eyes are pools reflecting everything back.

(*Mine* is the word I think in a flare.)

We get chips for dinner but take them away, him driving while I stare across the water at yellow-and-black Rubik's cube buildings.

Len watches me watching and winds all four windows down, wind-blasting the city through us.

Lacey is out with school friends when we get back to his place and eat. Scott's Corner empty—ours.

After, I clean up the plates while Len showers.

A pointed edge of something sticks up from the bin and pokes me in the wrist. I put down my fork and pluck it out.

It's ripped a bit and covered in cold coffee grounds. They stick in coarse lumps to my fingers when I smooth it out.

A photo. Landscape of the riverfront, in black and white.

Len is a minimalist about most things, but he never throws his photos away. Ever. There's a dozen portfolios stuffed full of them upstairs.

I push more rubbish out of the way. There's a stack of them, from different days and locations, shove-scrunched so deep and covered in enough goo it's like someone doused them deliberately. The artist's son in me recoils.

I pull one out that's *my* face, pissed off and covered in sun. The back of my neck prickles. I stare at it for several shock-cold seconds.

I don't realize Len's in the room until he's standing in front of me, wet-haired and frowning. "What're you doing?"

I look with wide eyes, from him to the bin and back again. "What are you doing?"

He's stricken for a minute. Then his face smooths. "Calm down."

"You're throwing your stuff away?" I say. "Wrecking it? Why?"

"I didn't."

I tilt my head to the side. "Even you can't spin the evidence while I'm actually holding it."

"They're . . ." Pause, shrug. "Rejects, I don't know."

He's so casual it makes me almost furious.

"What is going on with you?"

Len's pupils dilate. He's wearing fresh navy tracksuit pants with pockets, into which he plunges both hands. "Nothing."

"If you're gonna bullshit me," I spit, "at least do it well."

I'm not aware until it's already coming out that I'm actually upset. The thought that I'm not inside, not special, is bigger than I can hold.

He rubs his collarbone, thumb on the side of his neck. "This is not a thing."

"Except it is, though."

"Don't be so dramat—"

"Yeah, that's me," I cut him off savagely. "Dramatic as usual. Stupid, too, for thinking you'd actually let me *in*."

He responds to my waking anger like clockwork, eyes bright and arms folding across his chest. "Right now? Yes. You are being stupid."

I drop the sopping pile of ruined photos on the bench. "Right. Well maybe I should go be stupid elsewhere, and you can call one of the many other people you've been Not a Thing with to talk about Things That Aren't a Thing."

Len unravels that for a second. "What other people?" he demands.

I throw up my hands. "Oh, I don't know. Random chicks from debating. Guys from interschool sport. Willa freaking Stacy."

We stand in stalemate, breathing heavily.

Then I'm abruptly, blisteringly self-conscious; I yank my sleeves down hard over my knuckles.

"Don't," Len says finally.

"Don't what?"

"Don't go." He pushes hair back from his eyes. "I don't understand what's happening."

"You don't?"

"No!" he insists. "There's nothing here you need to fix, okay? Just forget it."

Len steps around me and swiftly sweeps the photos back into the bin. Then he pulls himself up onto the counter so we're facing each other.

"The Willa thing . . ." His voice is low.

"Don't—"

"I *was* with her."

"*Very* with her—"

"Right. And now I'm here."

My face burns.

"Okay?" he asks.

I stare at him for a long minute, then release all the air in me, hoping it's true. "Okay."

———

The next morning, I have to rush home to throw on my uniform. We fell asleep talking (and not talking).

I'm tired and also buzzing—with last night, and a heavy fear that's equal parts *what are we when we're back at school?* and *how are we already back at school?*

Thank god Mum and Dad think I'm responsible, I think as I shovel toast into my mouth and tie my shoes in our empty kitchen before driving back to his house.

Len jogs down the Scott's Corner front steps pulling his pant legs down over blue-and-pink striped socks. He slides into the passenger seat, out of breath and with his tie undone.

I pick up the end of it, accidentally brushing his hip, then start to thread the knot at his throat, red silk slippery in my hands.

He grabs my fingers to still them, leans in, and kisses me.

Soft but with purpose. Fearless.

"What was that for?" I ask.

"Cause."

"That's cute," I say without thinking, then want to hide in my hands. Forever.

Len raises one eyebrow. "That might be the most offensive thing you've ever said to me."

"Whatever," I say, but feel slightly better.

I let Martin do most of the talking in assembly, and it drags. He gives a long spiel about last term, upcoming final assignments, and how much he's going to "miss these days." I say a sentence or two before handing the mic straight back. I'm in no mood for performing; I'm doing enough of that already, pretending not to be searching the seats for Len.

Classes roll by in tepid drips, the teachers still just as half-asleep from holidays as we are. The grades I get back are fine, but school is uncomfortably bright, a black-and-white film that's been colored over with a heavy brush. I watch the shapes move—it just doesn't feel real.

"Are you okay, Henry?" Ms. Hartnett asks in English. "You look far away."

I look up. "Fine."

"Penny for your thoughts," she says in an exaggerated British accent.

I smile tightly. "It's nothing."

"Was that meant to be British, Miss?" Vince cuts in with a filthy look on his face. "Because—no."

Ms. H. laughs. "My apologies, Vincent. Acting school was a long time ago—my voices are pretty rusty."

"Acting school?" I ask.

"Yeah! Before my teaching degree. It was fun, just not really for me."

"You mean you could have, like, been on *Home and Away?*" Ged asks. "And instead you chose to come here and spend every day with us?"

Ms. H. shrugs. "I thought acting was what I wanted, when I

was your age. But life has a way of pushing you toward the path you're meant to walk. Whether you know it or not."

Ged stares at her disbelievingly. "That's fuc—shocking, Miss."

She laughs again. "You'll see, soon enough. I know everyone's telling you to decide, saying that you have to *know* everything— but you don't, really. That's part of the fun." She winks at me.

At the end of the class we get our *Gatsby* monologues back. Vince and I get an A+, which he takes full credit for.

"Hamlet wasn't sure about the homoerotic stuff," he tells Ged. "But I insisted on it, for the sake of our art."

———

The day isn't real until we're away from school, back in his bedroom with the door closed, *bodies words thoughts* tangled around each other. Until I whisper, "Len" up into the warm air and he says, "Yeah?" like we were already talking.

"I was just thinking, today . . ."

"What?"

"I don't understand how I can be all these Henrys at once."

"Mmm. I feel like maybe everyone feels that way, a bit."

"But which one's *true*, though? This one? And what if I forget him—me, this me—without . . . this?"

"You won't."

"How do you know?"

"Because people aren't like ideas."

"What do you mean?"

"They don't change based on who's looking at them. People just exist, as they are—it's what makes them human. You couldn't love an idea."

"Hamlet?" he says after a while.

"...Yeah?"

"Nothing."

20

School takes over us again. Even though these grades won't change much in terms of our final results, I hear the word "maintain" so much it makes my ears bleed. When I tell Mum I'm going over to Scott's Corner to study, it's usually the truth (usually).

English this term is a film study of *1984*, and modern history is pre-1940s Germanic political structures, so I'm bogged down in reading. Len's juggling his art project and trying to stay on top of two sciences. Even Ged knuckles down, because he's sitting on a C– in several subjects so this term is make or break.

Preparation for Gran's wedding starts to mount too. It's not until November, nor is there that much to actually *do*, but that doesn't stop her and Mum from letting it consume our lives.

Don't get me wrong—it's exciting and everything. But the two of them, to use a Gedism, "fight like dogs on the roof" every time they have to make a decision.

The latest is the cake. Third week back at school is all about it. To fruit or not to fruit?

"Bill, I'm telling you—fruitcake tastes like frozen sick. Everyone loves brownies."

"But, Mum, it's tradition! Goldie and I just thought *some* might be good. For older relatives, et cetera."

"It's not your wedding!"

"It is hers, though!"

"Whose?"

"Goldie's? Your future wife?"

"Hmph. Well, she knows what she's getting into. I want brownies. Brownies, or nothing."

And on it goes.

Len and I mostly stay out of the prep stuff. He's quiet the next few weeks. Sarah-distant.

(It's coming up to three years. Last year it was worse—he went away, and I didn't see him for ages.)

(I understand—that I *can't* understand. But I try.)

I ask him to go through Gran's Rilke with me, reciting words I don't know out loud to test them for romance factor. Len follows it better than I do, never rushing or stumbling over phrases to try and force meaning.

He comes back briefly, for those afternoons. Laying with his head in my lap and the book held up, refusing to let me just settle on one of the first bits I find.

"There." He points to a passage eventually.

"Really?" I lean down, wrinkling my nose. "Isn't that a bit corny? Or—a lot corny."

Len looks up at me brightly. "Yeah. Perfect for you. It *is* you."

I knee him in the back of the head.

He's gone again the next day, here-but-not-here in homeroom.

I follow him silently to the lockers. His shoulders are rigid with more than just blazer.

"Hey," I say quietly.

230

Len slams his locker shut. "Hey."

"I'm—I'm here, okay?"

His eyes slip away, down the hallway. "I know."

But when I text him—every afternoon, when we're in the same room, right before bed—he doesn't reply.

─────────

That Friday night, he picks me up at dusk with a weird look on his face.

"Where are we going?" I ask as he turns right at the end of my street instead of left.

He doesn't answer, just drives toward the city with his eyes on the road, accelerating so fast down the big hill that my insides jolt.

It's just before six and traffic's banked up. He swings around angrily, taking a shortcut through the factory district until we hit the deserted showgrounds.

The redbrick old museum stretches up to a white sky; he pulls to a sudden stop across from it, jerking the handbrake up.

Len steps out of the car, slamming the door behind him and leaning against it.

I do the same and try to read his face. "What's up?" I ask, worried now.

"Nothing," he says, tapping his foot. "Can't I just want to see you?"

"Yeah. But . . . you seem preoccupied."

Len inhales, and I look out at the city for a bit.

"Lacey is up again for the weekend." He looks at me. "She

wants to do a dinner tomorrow night, for . . . Mum. She wants you to come."

"Oh." I keep my mouth in its shape after I finish the word, head swimming. "Um. Should I?"

Len's eyes flick down. "You don't have to."

"No, it's not . . . I just mean, will your dad want me there, if it's like a family thing?"

Len shrugs, face closed off but blazing like the sunset on top of us.

"Um. You don't need to invite me just because Lacey did," I offer. "Like, if you don't . . ."

"Hamlet," he says. "I want you there. But it's your choice."

"Right. So then I'll come," I say, still feeling uneasy. There's something vibrating in him.

"Okay."

We drive back to my place.

I get him alone in my room—to try and talk to him. But he's very good at *distracting* me from the fact he won't talk back.

———

When I get to Scott's Corner on Saturday all the lights are on, spilling sickly white across the front lawn. Len opens the door with one hand and takes mine with the other, pulling me through the kitchen to the formal dining room.

John is front and center in a white-blue shirt, plucking ornate glasses out of the liquor cabinet in the hall and setting them on a tray.

"Henry," he greets me, gold cufflinks catching the chandelier light. "Wonderful."

I can't tell from his tone whether it is or not, but I accept the drink he pours me.

"Grandma's tumblers?" Len questions.

John turns around exaggeratedly. "Problem?"

"Mum never used those."

"Yes, she did," John says, his voice as close to impatient as it gets. "She used them all the time."

"No, she didn't. She never used them. They're the special ones."

John turns his back again and pours more liquid into his glass, then faces us and does a long sip-and-*ah* routine. "It's an occasion, isn't it? Saintly Grandma Hazel's hardly going to materialize to chastise us, is she?"

"Dad," Lacey calls from the kitchen, "I need you to carve for me."

John knocks back the rest of his drink and walks out.

I touch Len's back, unsure of what else to do. He leans into it for a minute, before shaking me off and snapping the cap off one of the beers on the side table.

"Are you sure I should be—"

He gives me a look, and I drop it.

"Never mind."

We sit down spaced apart. The lamb is underdone. We bravely hack into hunks of angry pink and slip mint sauce over the top. There's a giant flickering candle nearby that smells thickly of blackberry and bay leaves and salt.

Things get a bit better while we're eating, mostly because of Lacey. She talks a mile a minute about uni, friends, boys, politics. She occasionally throws the ball to me, and between us we get most of the silences filled.

"What about you, Lenniekins?" she teases over a glass of wine before dessert. "What'd you end up putting for preferences?"

Uh-oh. Danger zone.

Abort mission, I try to tell her telepathically. *Turn back*. But it's too late.

Len stretches his legs out, slipping down in his chair. Delaying.

"Fine arts," he says flatly after a minute. "Photography."

"Oh! That's good," Lacey says, neatly hiding her surprise. "Isn't it, Dad?"

John reaches for a toothpick, and chips away at the space between his front incisors before answering. "Is it?"

Lacey widens warning eyes at him. "*Yes*, because it's what he wants. More people should take the time to figure out what they're actually good at, I say. The world would be a much better place."

Len's expressionless, but his cheeks are flushed.

I put my open hand on his knee under the table. He takes it softly.

"And I suppose practical considerations don't factor, then?" John asks smoothly, still addressing Lacey. "In this utopia of yours?"

Lacey exhales. "Meaning?"

John drums the tips of his fingers on the table. They're long like Len's, but ghostly pale.

"Money," he says. "Security. Of course, those things *can* happen, if the artist is actually any good. But generally . . ."

"Dad!" Lacey admonishes.

"I'm just saying," John continues, and sips his scotch. "If he wants to fart-arse around looking through a lens his whole life, that's his prerogative. I just prefer the notion of actually *contributing* to society."

There's a spot of sauce stuck to the stubble on his chin. I stare at it and think about punching him in the face.

"Sure." Len comes to life beside me, tilting his head. His eyes are bright fires. All or nothing. "Ripping people off every day so you can drive a wanker car and feel like a man is so useful."

"Oh, that's it," John says. "Tell us how you really feel."

"What's it?" Len demands. He sits up straighter and squares his shoulders, chair squeaking on the wooden floor.

I squeeze his hand, but he doesn't squeeze back. Gran says grief makes people crazy, but this is something else. I'm watching everything that's been buried between them get dug up and flung like knives around a twelve-piece oak dining set.

John tops up his drink. "Let's see. Wrecking your mother's family dinner." He lists it off on his fingers. "Making a scene. Making everything about you—just like it always was. Because you're a spoiled, selfish *child*."

"Dad!" Lacey says again, her eyes filling with tears.

Len tips up his chin. "Don't pretend you ever cared about family, John. Or anyone. You'll just embarrass yourself."

Lacey scrapes her chair back hard. "I'm going to get dessert, and then we are going to stop talking about this."

I stare after her, trapped.

"What did you just say to me?" John hisses at Len when she's gone, his eyes narrowing into slits.

Len downs his beer. I want to tell him to slow down, but he pulls his hand out of mine just as I notice it's shaking.

"Do you need me to repeat it?" he throws at John. "Seeing as you never actually went to university."

John is . . . very drunk. I realize when he tries to stand up and can't. He's just been holding it well.

He and Len glower at each other.

It's a speeding conductorless train I can't stop.

"And how would this little artist lifestyle play out for you without my money? Should I cut it off, and we can see?" John asks.

Len hisses, unfazed, "I don't need you."

Everything slips into slow motion. One minute we're all sitting opposite one another and the next John's standing huge and straight. He staggers, knocking the drinks tray so hard across the table that it flies off and hits the wall behind Len.

Glass shatters and sprays everywhere; the tumblers scream as they break apart. Their pieces splash, shrapnel-like, all over the floor. Scotch drips down the wall in the cruel quiet that follows.

Lacey comes back into the room, running and sheet-white.

John looks at her briefly, then leaves.

Len stares down at the fractured shards of glass under his feet.

21

Lacey and I clean up the mess.

Her phone buzzes on and on, insistent.

After a while she checks it. "Hotel," she says. "He's meant to be flying to Singapore tomorrow anyway. So . . ." She's still crying.

I don't know what to say, so I scrub harder at the wall.

Once we're done, I find Len in his room looking out the window.

I put a hand on his shoulder and he jumps.

"Hey," I say, trying to imitate the voice he uses with me when I'm freaking out. Not that I've ever had as good a reason to do so as he does right now.

He's not crying. It's worse than that; his face is completely blank.

There's a cut on his cheek, a tiny slashed half-moon that twists my stomach into a fist. I run the tip of my finger over it slowly, checking there's no glass.

Len's hand comes up to grip mine. His eyes are tight. I want to unwind him, but I don't know how.

"It's fine," he says woodenly. "I just . . . shouldn't have done that."

It's only years of knowing him that lets me hear the falter in his voice. Nothing about any of this is remotely *fine*.

When I can speak I choose my words carefully. "Of course you should've."

I manage to get him to sit on the edge of the bed, then I lead him down slowly until we're lying side by side, arms folded over our stomachs. Neither of us speak for a long time.

My mind is hectically running over what happened. Trying to fit it with everything else when the puzzle pieces don't match. Trying to figure out how it is that the person hiding behind a shiny middle-class veneer can be *that*: seen by everyone, and not at all.

Len's quiet. I think maybe he's asleep.

Then he says, "It wasn't always like this. When Mum was still here, he just wasn't interested, but now, when he *is* . . ." His face screws up. "And she's *not here*, and . . ."

I inhale deeply and hold it. Usually, I do the talking for both of us, but I wait. It kills me to stay silent, but I do.

"It's stopped even making sense," he whispers like a confession. "It'll just be random things that set him off, and then he stands there and says—"

"What?"

He looks up at the ceiling, his face still blank. "That I'm useless. I'll never do anything. My photos are never going to get me anywhere."

My brain keeps processing, trying to think of something to say.

"He's *wrong!*" I burst out finally.

Len just sighs, one hand hovering up near his forehead.

"Whatever the hell that was," I say with as much conviction as I can, "he's wrong. You're so far from useless, it's not even funny. You are nothing like that. You're, like—brilliant. *Golden.*"

238

"I'm not," he tells the ceiling.

"You are," I insist, thinking, *How can you not know that?* "You're ..."

The one time I really need them, I can't think of the words. I'm so out of my depth here I can physically feel it.

"Len?" I try again. "This isn't on you, okay? It's just not."

He rolls over and looks at me kind of quizzically, then he grabs the back of my neck and starts kissing me hard.

I kiss back for a minute, until I start to really feel it—but I can feel what's behind it too: him shutting down. I push away.

"*Stop*," he grunts.

I pull him in with all the force I've got. I don't know what could possibly make this better, so I just wrap my arms around him and hold.

Len's totally still, for a minute. Then he hugs back all at once, his chin digging into my shoulder and his rough sounds against my throat.

"It's okay," I say, like a prayer.

I just keep saying it. Over and over.

For an immeasurable stretch of time, we're not Lennon and Hamlet, or two people who want each other, or two people at all.

There's never been a proper membrane separating us the way it does other people; we're connected, and it runs so deep. I know, from how much this hurts.

I want to give him all my energy to borrow. To keep. To burn.

I give him whatever he lets me. Let him take whatever he needs.

He's already awake when I open my eyes in the morning.

I prop myself up on my elbow, and clumsily brush the back of my hand across his cheek. His eyes close, so I do it again, letting my fingers push through his hair where it's fallen loose from its careful style.

He leans into it for a moment, then seems to collect himself, opening his eyes.

I start with, "Hey."

"Hi," he says. His voice is tight, the words bitten out through clenched teeth.

His face is tight too: jaw taut and skin blanched white.

"What's wrong?"

His forehead furrows deeply.

I touch it. "Stop."

"Stop what?"

"Thinking whatever you are."

His eyes are dilated, but it's different to last night. They're not wide with need—it looks like fear.

"Look. I'm not gonna pretend this isn't . . ." He swallows, changes tack. "These last few weeks have been like . . ."

I wait, confused.

"Like something from a book," he finishes. "Something that happens to other people."

"I'm that good?"

He doesn't take the joke. His face is pained. "Yes. But . . ."

But. That's not good. It comes before—

"I don't think we should do this anymore."

The light in me blows out.

He keeps going, like he's afraid of what will happen if he stops.

"The way I stay sane here is to keep away from stuff like this," he says. "I just . . . We have to stop, okay."

Stuff like what? I want to ask.

"Why?" is what I ask instead. I'm fully awake now. I can feel my cheeks heating up, anger and shame and disappointment rolling through me. "I don't understand."

He sits up so that he's looking down at me. "Jesus, of course you don't! The world's so simple to you. Life isn't like a book, okay? It's not a dream, and people don't always just get what they want. They don't get happy endings. And we won't get anything we want if—if people find out."

"You don't believe that," I say, hurt poking through me.

Len tugs at his hair. "Everything's . . . I can't think straight."

"*Len.*" I reach out to touch his arm, but he stands up.

"I need . . . space. I can't be here with you like this."

I see it, then: I'm losing him.

The magic bubble of the last few weeks is dissipating before my eyes, and there's nothing I can do but scrabble for the pieces.

It feels like drowning in reverse.

"Hang on." I grab his arm. "Whatever this is, we can sort through it together. Talk, or . . ."

I wish my voice didn't sound so desperate. I feel desperate: everything I never knew I wanted but *need* is slipping through my fingers.

"What is there to talk about? We were probably stupid doing this anyway," he says flatly, all color gone from his voice. "We messed up, letting it go this far."

"Don't say that! Don't be such a dickhead."

His eyes shoot over to mine. "It wasn't meant to be like this. I should've just left it alone. You're meant for big things. Not"—he gestures to the room around us and down the stairs—"this. Me."

"Stop it!" I snap, livid all of a sudden. "Don't tell me what I'm supposed to do. Do you really think I'm that weak? That I'd just drop you if things got a tiny bit difficult? Because I won't."

His jaw is set—the way it does when he's decided.

I need something drastic. I take a deep, heart-thudding breath.

"I'm not going anywhere. Len, listen. I think I lov—"

"*Don't.*"

The back of my throat burns. I will not let myself cry, but my face is beet red at this point. I curse my Celtic genes for giving me away so clearly.

"I don't get why you're doing this," I say, thickly. "We're happy like this. It's . . . *ours.* It's not like anyone's gonna know—I wouldn't give a shit if they did!"

"As if, Hamlet!" he snaps. "This kind of stuff always comes out. And he'd find a way to wreck it. Or I will, and I couldn't come back fr—it'd be the end, okay."

"So you'd rather just end you and me. Us." My voice shakes. I don't care; let him hear it.

"We can be friends," he says hollowly. "We'll always be friends."

"I don't want to just be your friend! We're more than that. I'm more than that!"

He lets me in again, just for a second. Leans in close and brushes my hair back from my forehead, holding onto my cheek, breath hitching, eyes black. I have never seen him like this.

"I just really have to go," he repeats.

"Go where?"

"Out. When I get back, I need to . . . not see you for a bit."

"This is insane!" I protest. My heart's hammering so hard it feels like I might throw it up. "We don't have to . . . we can . . . we'll figure this out. We always figure it out."

I try to reach him with my eyes, but he's as far away as he's ever been. He starts shoving things haphazardly into a backpack. When he turns to look at me, his features are stone.

"I started it. It's my fault. I made a mistake, and . . . I'm sorry." His face falters on the word *mistake*. That one hurts.

"I get that you're scared," I persevere. "And, I don't know, maybe you don't think you deserve good things—or things you want, or whatever—but you do."

"*I don't want this!*" He hurls the words at me like acid. Then he walks out the door and down the stairs.

I watch him in the garden, morning sun drenching his hair like a spotlight. It follows even when he slams the gate and exits onto the street, as though it knows: he's taking it with him.

Part III

You are so young, so much before all beginning, and I would like to beg you, dear Sir, as well as I can, to have patience with everything unresolved in your heart and to try to love the questions themselves as if they were locked rooms or books written in a very foreign language. Don't search for the answers, which could not be given to you now, because you would not be able to live them. And the point is, to live everything. Live the questions now. Perhaps then, someday far in the future, you will gradually, without even noticing it, live your way into the answer.

—Rainer Maria Rilke

22

For days, I don't sleep.

I go through the motions of life: eating, cleaning, answering basic questions. But I don't sleep.

I just lie there. For hours. Thinking about everything and nothing, the monotonous silence broken only by the hammering in my chest that never lets up. I can't stop hearing it—obsessively counting the too-fast beat.

Lacey texts that she's staying indefinitely. He doesn't call. Neither do I.

I type: **just tell me if ur ok** and backspace it, approximately eighteen times.

I wonder too. Years of constant proximity have instilled in me an innate need to know where he is, what he's doing, if he's safe, if he's happy. I'm used to knowing. I'm not used to needing to.

I'm not used to missing him like this.

It's so bad, I wantonly skip school for the first time ever.

On the third day, Mum and Dad stage an intervention.

I haven't told them the specifics. I'm loyal enough to Len not to say anything, for better or worse.

They know something's up, though, and they bulldoze into my room on Tuesday morning armed for a fight.

Mum sits down on the bed beside me and hands me a takeaway coffee. I spin it around, see the café logo, and feel sick.

Her face puckers with concern. "What's wrong, Hen? You look like someone's died."

It feels like they did. (Like I did.)

"You know you can always talk to us," Dad says.

I don't know where to start, and I'm exhausted, so I do something I can't remember doing before: I lie to their faces.

"Just stressed about exams."

Mum pouts. "You said you felt like you'd done all right."

"You know we don't care about that shit," Dad says. "With us as parents, we're just lucky you're not a drug addict."

I can feel both of them wanting to ask about the elephant in the room but knowing to hold back. I'm abruptly, incredibly glad these people are my parental units.

"I've just fucked everything up," I murmur. "All of it."

Dad *tsks.* "You're eighteen! All of it hasn't happened yet. What's this really about, champ?"

I push myself upright. "I appreciate the pep talk, guys, but I'm fine. I just need to get out of the house for a bit. Thanks for the coffee."

Mum scrutinizes my face, but then they leave me to it.

I throw on some clothes and grab my keys. I do need to get out of here—that part wasn't a lie.

Today is drawn in gray; it cloaks me when I step out into it. It's drizzling but only slightly, the rain clouds almost as lethargic as I am.

I don't know where I'm going. I just drive aimlessly through the neighboring suburbs and then onto the highway, until I'm headed toward the coast with all the windows down. Wind bites my hair and face, and I turn the radio up to blasting.

I reach the turnoff for the coast road but hesitate, blinker clicking, the Pissar wheezing.

Someone honks from behind me. I swing around through a divider and turn back the way I came, ignoring the shouted expletives. The city springs up ahead of me, a blue-gray coconspirator of misery. I decide to drive into the heart of it, since mine's a shredded pulp.

I end up at the old bookstore in the city center that Mum and I used to go to. I reverse in, only slightly nicking the curb, and put my money in the meter.

It's quiet at this time of day, not quite breakfast or lunch.

I order another coffee from the counter at the back and then browse the shelves half-heartedly until I land on a thick-looking academic examination of Caligula's mental state. Perfect.

I'm several pages into the chapter about him making his horse a consul when my phone pings with a text. I flip it open, clicking on the message without reading who it's from.

Emilia: <33333

She's attached an image. I open it, expecting to find a picture of a dog doing something funny or her pulling a face. Instead, it's the photo Willa posted of us at the Party at the start of last term. That feels like years ago now.

I'm lying on the couch, my head propped on a pillow on Len's stomach. His black-clad legs are dangling in front of him and his arms are around me loosely, one hand resting on my chest and one on the opposite shoulder. Our heads are bent together, cheeks touching, eyes closed and mouths parted, asleep.

I stare at them for a long time, these versions of us; they look so peaceful. I want to rewind.

I keep staring until the bottom half of my coffee is cold.

———

I go back to school on Wednesday, nerd that I am. My personal apocalypse takes place, and I'm still sitting in homeroom at 7:56 with my religion book ready for first period, three days later.

The first time I see him cuts like a knife.

The second time is duller, but still bladelike—a fifteenth-century practice sword, maybe. I watch him walk through the quad, shoulders square, and the splinters twist in my chest.

I want to talk to him (so much) but decide to take the high road.

Vince corners me in math when it's just the two of us. "What in the ever-loving shit is going on?" he demands. "Why've you and Citizen Cane gone full Stalin and Lenin?"

"Top historical reference," I compliment blandly, stalling for time.

"Been studying your flashcards, haven't I?" he responds impatiently. "Don't try to change the subject."

"We had a fight," I say. "It was nothing." Even to me, it sounds weak.

Vince gives me the evil eye. "That's a bloody understatement. When I asked him where you were the other day, he went off like a frog in a sock. What'd you fight about?"

I'm spent by this day, and it's not even lunch. "Just leave it, okay?"

To my surprise, he does.

250

Harrison and Ged have similar reactions when I tell them I'm going to the library at lunch. I can tell the latter wants to shake the truth out of me (by brute force if necessary), but Harrison holds him back.

They probably assume I'll crack eventually. It's usually a safe bet, but not this time. I'll take this secret to the frigging grave.

Between library exile lunches and it mostly being an elective classes week, I make it through two days and see Len only in passing.

Our lockers are still a problem, though.

On Friday afternoon before our last debate club meeting, I bodily run into him while I'm pulling party food out of my locker, books and chips hitting the floor.

We both stop for a minute in the harsh-lit hallway. Habit. Gravity.

Len opens his mouth, then closes it again, and stalks away.

(Seriously?)

I snatch up my stuff off the floor and set off after him.

Martin's already waiting outside shit block with three bottles of Coke Zero. Harrison, Eamon, and Ben are there too, with various baked goods. Len leans against the bubblers.

I regret deciding to make this a party. My mood's about as celebratory as a sugarless soft drink.

Once we're all inside, Len sits right at the back.

We divvy up the food quickly, crunching chips. It's so quiet it would be awkward, but there's always Martin Finch. "Is anybody else finding all these extra study periods counterproductive?" he asks.

"You're kidding, right?" Ben looks horrified.

The Fincharoo is not kidding. "Research shows that dedicated individual study time is best! We should be doing it at home, away from distraction."

"Christ, Finch," says Eamon.

"*What?*"

Harrison laughs politely. I don't, and neither does Len.

Something's brewing in me, watching him sitting there silently when there's still so much to say.

"Hey, everyone. You know what I think we should do?" I say without fully knowing I'm going to beforehand. "Have one last mini-debate! For old time's sake."

Even Martin looks disdainful.

"God's sake, Hamlet," Ben says. "Are you actually allergic to fun?"

"This is fun," I insist.

"What would we even debate about?" Harrison asks.

I rack my brain for topics from over the years for what I need—and then I have it. "What about: should Australia break from Britain?"

"Didn't we do that already?" Eamon asks.

"Nope. Let's do it now." I pull myself up with shaky hands to sit on a desk, flicking a quick glance at the back corner. Len's face is tightly resigned.

Of course he'd figure it out straightaway.

"So, let's just discuss it objectively, first." I'm talking fast. "We've got these two countries—*allies*—with masses of history together. Why would they end it?"

Silence. I think: *it's not going to work.*

Then he says, "Because it's what's *best.*"

"Who gets to decide that, though?" I counter, fury coursing through me sudden and bright. "What's best?"

Len shrugs, casual, but his gaze doesn't drop from mine. "Britain should have already, really, seeing as the whole situation was their fault."

I stare down the gray-green. "*If* that were true, is it a good enough excuse for ruining a good thing?"

"Wait. Since when are you a monarchist?" Harrison asks.

"They wouldn't do it because they want to *ruin* it," Len says forcefully. "They'd do it for the opposite reason."

I lick my lips. "Right. Which is?"

"That they couldn't give . . . Australia what it deserves."

"Britain thinks their shit doesn't stink, though," Ben Cunningham cuts in, and I could club him over the head. "They wouldn't think that, would they?"

Len tears his eyes off mine to glare at Ben. "Britain's not that narcissistic."

I shake my head, refusing to let him off the hook. "Maybe they are, if you think they should leave Australia in the lurch like that."

"A republic is freedom. You're being pretty narrow-minded, captain," Len says. He looks as riled up as I feel.

"Shots fired," murmurs Eamon, raising his eyebrows.

"How do you even end a relationship that long, second speaker?" I hiss. "Just: thanks for the memories? Here's some freedom, that's it, goodbye?"

"Hamlet."

I wish he'd say Henry, but the walls are up, higher than ever.

"And what if Australia *needs* . . . Britain?" I know I'm reaching, but I can't stop. "What then?"

"Then maybe Britain has to let them go."

"Bullshit!" I burst out, standing up. "That's such *bullshit*."

Len chews his lip. He looks so sorry.

The others are all watching us wide-eyed, unsure of what they've just witnessed.

"Guys . . ." Harrison starts uneasily.

"Just forget it," I snap, picking up my stuff. "Enjoy the party everyone."

When I get to my car, the last shred of hope falls out of me and rolls under the seat.

It's worse than I thought, even with days of prep time. I wipe my face on my sleeve and hit the accelerator hard.

I drive until I'm lost in the tangled streets of the city again, but it's not far enough.

He's there in old house fronts and tired trees poking up from cement. He's the bridge and the river. Each towering building. The burnished sky.

How do you un-know someone if you only know most of *you* because of *them*?

How do you even try?

23

We don't speak after debate-gate. Things shift into a new gear, until we're actively avoiding one another.

I take every possible shortcut at school, kicking my way through the spiky bushes behind shit block so I don't even have to see him in the quad.

We keep amicable shared custody of the Boiyss.

I tell Mum and Dad a version of things, careful not to leave room for further discussion. Mum argues at first and follows me around a lot, face pinched in concern. I catch them out at least twice sitting in tense discussion on the veranda, but they leave me be.

Weekends are the worst; aimless hours spent overthinking, trying to read, almost-texting. I confine myself to my bedroom.

It's always been my sanctuary, but there's no hiding even up here—not with glow-in-the-dark stars and newspaper letters reminding me.

I have a tired crack at writing, but nothing comes. I just stare at the blank page, writing and crossing out bits of him over and over.

MISS

I   YOU; IT'S KILLING ME.

KISSED

At the end of the next week, I can't face Mum's pinched face or Dad awkwardly patting me like a dog a moment longer. There are only so many times one can say, "I'm fine" before it starts to sound like "fuck off."

I escape to my car and plug my iPod into the ancient aux chord Dad fitted into the stereo with one hand, then turn the key in the ignition with the other.

The Pissar gives an almighty sputter.

"No," I tell her firmly. "Come on. We've been going so good."

She revs sadly in response, then peters out.

"Come *on*," I say again. "You made it all the way to the hinterland. Remember that?"

I twist the key and the sputter is louder this time: squeak-clank-grind.

"Just start, Piss—noble steed!" I beg. "This is not how it ends. *Please*. For me."

I smell smoke.

I rip out the key and yell into my fist. I'm so tired all of a sudden. Tired of listening to shitty music and shitty cars and swimming in all the thoughts of him all the time.

I let my head rest on the steering wheel and pull in a few shallow breaths. After a while I roll the window down, the breeze hissing through my ears a reprieve.

"Henry!"

I look up and see Emilia getting out of her car across the street.

"Hey!" I wipe my eyes quickly. "What're you doing here?"

She peers into my car, which is strewn with melancholy

256

McDonald's wrappers and half-empty coffee cups. "You texted me an analysis of a Jordin Sparks song last night—of course I'm here."

"It was on the radio," I lie.

Emilia just looks at me.

"I'm fine," I say flatly. "You don't have to—"

"We are going to have breakfast, right now."

I don't have time to answer before she's dragging me toward her passenger seat.

We end up outside an old Queenslander three suburbs over that's painted stark white and has climbing roses on its face. It looks like the other houses on the street, except for the dozen people sitting at rickety tables out front.

We head inside where it's quieter and walk between green velvet chairs with their frays spun gold by morning light.

Emilia instructs me to sit by the window while she orders iced lattes and a piece of carrot cake bigger than my future.

"Entrée," she informs me, setting the cake down between us and sliding me the spoon. "There's eggs coming."

"Okay. Thanks."

She shifts in her seat restlessly before settling with her elbows on the table and her cheeks in her hands. "So."

I take a giant spoonful of cake.

"*You're* doing great, obviously," she jokes. "Let's talk about me."

I chew the cake with deliberate slowness. "I'm fine."

"Oh, absolutely. You seem it. Crying in your car, listening to 'Tattoo' at midnight."

"It was on the radio," I lie again.

"Uh-huh," she says. "Just tell me. Whatever it is."

Our drinks arrive. I sip mine semi-aggressively.

"*Fine.*" I crack before Ems does. "There was a Cane family dinner. And it . . . did not go well."

"Uh-oh," Ems says.

"It was okay at first. But then it escalated into this completely massive fight."

"With his dad?"

I wince at the memory. "It was bad, Ems. He was so drunk—ripping into Len, attacking his art—and then they were just going at each other, the two of them, and it was awful, and I couldn't *do* anything. I couldn't stop it."

Emilia's eyes are cry-shiny. "How did it end?"

"John smashed a bunch of these glass tumblers of Sarah's mum's into the wall. Then he left."

"Oh my god!"

"He's gone now—I've been checking for his car. And Lacey is there. But. Yeah."

"Oh my god," she says again, eyes huge. "Is Len . . . is he okay?"

I shrug; thinking about it hurts. "Vince says he thinks so. He's not speaking to me."

Emilia's forehead wrinkles. "Well, he's going to speak to me. Wait. Why isn't he speaking to you?"

I cover one side of my face with sweaty fingers. "Because he dumped me."

Now she looks horrified. "He *what?*"

"Yeah." I pick up my drink just for something else to do with my other hand. "Record time, hey."

Ems pushes her glasses up into her hair. "So that's just it?"

"Um. Yes?"

"But why?"

"I guess he just realized he was better off."

She slaps my wrist. "Henry Hamlet. Don't even. He . . . you guys are—"

"*Don't*, Ems," I beg. "Please."

She furiously sips her own drink, eyes darting across thoughts she doesn't voice for a good few minutes.

"Fools," she pronounces finally. "Both of you."

"Ems!"

"Nope. That's my official ruling." She drops her voice. "You *love* him, don't you?"

I slump in my seat and look into the distance darkly.

She throws up her hands. "So then, fight for him! Maybe he needs that."

"I did," I murmur. "He hasn't really given me much of a choice."

"That's just Len being Len—"

"You can't fight for anything if the other person won't even try!" I slump down further. "Sorry, it's just . . . it's been a rough few weeks. Between exams, family stuff, and—" (Losing the potential love of my life . . .)

Her face softens. "I know, babes. This is a lot to have on your plate. I'm here, okay?"

I look into the distance again, trying to remember what you're meant to think of to stop yourself from crying. "Yeah."

A dapper waiter sets eggs, sourdough toast, and a boat of hollandaise sauce between us. Ems divides everything up neatly, ladling sauce all over my eggs and pushing them toward me.

"I've got a lot on my plate," I say, in an effort to lighten the mood.

She pity-laughs. "Corn."

I pick at my eggs for a bit, hiding my eyes. "I miss him."

Ems pouts sympathetically. "I know."

"I'd say he misses you back," she says when we're mopping up sauce with our crusts.

I pause mid-mouthful, teeth gritting together. "Doubt it."

Ems stirs ice in her glass. "Please. You're like his cornerstone. Why else does a football player do debate club? Think about it."

I look up.

"Because he wanted to spend time with you, Hen. He cares about you too."

"Maybe," I allow. "Just not enough."

She shakes her head, thoughtful. "Maybe *too* much. He's always kind of had this way, with you—like you were his. I think losing you terrifies him. So he's pushing you away."

I consider this for a second. She's describing it the wrong way around, but I don't have the energy to push it.

"Can we change the subject, now that I've done my time?" I ask faux-brightly, desperately scanning my brain for Myspace gossip. "What's this I hear about you being seen on the lam with Eamon Matthews?"

Her cheeks immediately flush a delicate pink.

I stare at her in surprise. "Emilia Elizabeth Eastly," I chastise. "Emilio Estevez. *Mon petit* triple E. Have you been holding out on me?"

"Oh, I don't want to talk about this—not now."

"Now is the *perfect* time. I'm an emotional vampire. I dine exclusively on other people's drama."

She laughs and fiddles with the lace collar of her shirt.

"Come on," I press. "Let me live through you."

Ems sighs. "I'd like it to be put on the record that it wasn't my idea to tell you this in your hour of need."

"I'll adjust the record accordingly. Spill."

260

"Eamon and I . . ."

"Mmm?"

"We've been . . . seeing each other. A little."

I raise my eyebrows. "*Seeing* each other seeing each other?"

She nods. "It's actually going really well." Ems searches my face for signs I'm about to collapse in a heap.

"Relax," I say. "I'm happy for you. If you're happy," I qualify.

She still looks guilty, but there's a gleam in her eyes. "I am."

"Great! Eamon's cool. I never understood why you didn't give him a shot."

She hesitates, like she's deciding something. "I guess I can tell you, now you've made a mess of your own love life."

"Hey now."

"Oh, sorry! You know I didn't mean it like that—"

"It's fine," I cut her off. "It's true. Tell me what?"

She takes a deep breath. "The reason Eamon and I went our separate ways, at the start of the year."

"Yeah?"

"Was because I . . ."

"What?"

"This is so embarrassing!" She scrunches up her face. "I slept with him."

I lean forward with my chin on my hands, waiting for the rest.

"On the first date," Ems adds.

"And?"

"That's it! It wasn't even a first date—it was the first time we ever hung out. And after that I realized I really liked him, and I'd ruined it before it even started."

She's wringing her hands on the tabletop like she's just confessed to a white-collar crime.

"Wait. *That's* why you've avoided him like the Black Plague?"

"Is that not reason enough?" she asks.

"I thought it was something bad!"

"That *is* bad!" she whisper-yells. "I gave him the whole cow, or whatever. I threw the cow at him, actually—he wanted to wait. But I just wanted to get it over with before uni, and he was there, and he was nice, and . . . Why are you laughing?"

"I'm sorry." I cover my mouth. "I'm not."

She glares at me, sipping the last remnants of her drink. "You don't understand. The rules are different for boys—you can get away with stuff like that and it won't make anybody like you *less*."

"Ems, trust me when I say, categorically, that sleeping with a teenaged male is not going to make them like you less."

She's silent for a second. "You're probably right. But I was too embarrassed and awkward after that. I couldn't go near him."

"Aw. My poor little prude."

"Like you can talk!"

I tilt my head. "Actually . . ."

Em's mouth falls open. "*No!*" She throws a piece of toast at me. "Who's been holding out on who, hmm?"

I don't say anything.

She senses the shift in my mood, and rushes in with a distraction. "Anyway. He messaged me over the holidays and we talked it over. We talked a *lot*—he's actually got some really interesting opinions on things."

"I know." I agree. "I'm glad." And I am—it feels good to know there's still romance in the world, even if it's gone from mine. I might be a shriveled moth-like shell of a human, but I love her too much to begrudge her this.

"We should stop talking about this." She sighs. "I'm sorry."

"Are you kidding? This is the most cheering up I've had in weeks. Tell me again about throwing the cow at him."

24

Things get a bit better after I tell Ems, which makes it a bit worse. I don't want to get used to us being apart—but it happens, against all odds and against my will.

Our last assessments roll in at school. Ged gives up begging me not to make him a child of divorce in favor of stealing my study cards. Harrison and Vince are quietly disapproving, but neither push the point. Len keeps up his end of the bargain so faultlessly that I almost don't see him ever.

I stop asking about him, more out of necessity than altruism.

By the time I put my pen down at the end of the last English essay of my schooling life (*1984* and freedom of the individual), I'm . . . better. But not good.

It helps that the two weeks before Gran's wedding are a total frenzy. We're all in a flurry of preparation, running last-minute errands and double-checking the numbers for catering. Mum has two meltdowns; I have one. Dad and Ham steer clear.

It's not until we're a week out that I remember about the photos. I don't bring it up, hoping maybe if I don't, it'll just go away—but I'm not the only one who remembers.

"Henry!" Mum calls upstairs on Thursday night. "What time is Len getting to the ceremony?"

Thud thud thud.

"I don't know!" I yell back.

"Have you asked him yet?"

"We're not really—I mean . . ."

"*Henry!* You're going to have to talk to him eventually!"

I run through it rapidly in my head. Whether I can message him. What it would mean if I did.

"Hello?" Mum shouts. "*I* can ring him, if you want."

"No! I'll just text him."

"Too late, already dialed."

"*Mum!*"

I jump up and race downstairs.

Mum hands me the receiver with a meddling look in her eye. I frantically wave her away, then clear my throat. "Hello?"

Pause.

"Hey."

It's physical, what happens when I hear his voice. It sounds different, but also—exactly *exactly* the same. I squeeze my eyes shut for a second before plowing on.

"Um. Sorry about Mum ringing you—I was going to text."

"No, it's—"

"How are you?" I ask.

"Fine. You?"

"Yeah. Bit hectic at the moment."

"I bet. How's Iris going?"

"Bridezilla. She's driving Mum mad."

We're quiet for a moment.

Strangers.

"So, it's nine o'clock on Saturday?" he says after another pause.

"You're coming?"

I can almost hear him rolling his eyes. "I said I'd do the photos."

"I know, I just thought maybe—"

"I'll see you there, Hamlet," he says, and hangs up.

———

Gran gets ready at our place on the big day. After weeks of obsessing over each and every detail, she's uncharacteristically calm when the moment comes. She puts on a yellow dress and red lipstick, and piles her hair on top of her head.

"There," she says, surveying the final effect in the mirror. Her long sleeves trail along the floor. "Now for mimosas."

I mix the orange juice and champagne dutifully.

"Have one with me," she says. "Make it a double."

I make a second one for myself. Because he's going to be there today, I only add a dash of juice to the champagne.

We sit in the armchairs by the window in the front room, watching the day bloom clear and sunny. Nature's turning it on for Gran—color slashing across the flower bushes and light rubbing everything into high definition.

She downs her drink. "How you feeling?" I ask.

"Grand, love. Just grand."

"No second thoughts?"

"Not a one." Her champagne-y eyes home in on me. "You, though," she says, "are sad."

I lean forward and grab some chips off the table, shoveling them into my mouth. "I'm fine."

She tilts her head to the side, scanning my face for ages. "It was love, wasn't it?" she finally says. "You and him. It must have been."

I clench my chip-dusted fingers into a ball. "Me and who?"

Gran just reaches both hands up around her eyes and mimes holding a camera. *Click*.

(It's too hot in here. Why can't I have a father who believes in air conditioning?)

"Past tense being the operative," I say a few moments later. "It didn't work out."

Gran grabs my wrist. Her eyes go mistier and I prepare for the worst, but her voice is soft. "It's the greatest honor, you know, love. To have your heart broken."

I stare down at the familiar wrinkles of her hand, blinking hard. Her first wedding ring winks elegant gold.

"You reckon?"

She nods. "I do."

"Why?"

Gran's eyes are far away. "Broken-hearted people live the hardest."

I consider her words for a moment. I feel like maybe she's thinking about her own lost love, Pa. I'm thinking: *I hope she's right.*

"What are you two doing!?" Mum demands, crashing through the door with a bouquet in each hand. "We have to go— now. Henry, you're not even dressed!"

"I wish you'd relax, Bill," Gran says calmly. "You've done a wonderful job. All this flapping around is futile—what will be, will be. Have a mimosa."

"What—"

"You look really beautiful, Mum," I cut in, taking the bouquets off her.

"Thanks, Hen." She sighs, distracted but only just. She shoots one last exasperated look at Gran. "Five minutes, you two! I mean it."

———

I drive us to the church in Dad's car. Gran's quiet the whole way into the city. She just stares serenely out the tinted window while Mum worries aloud about every detail one last time.

We pull up outside the old church—a sandy brick number framed by fig trees with tall spires cutting into the sky.

Mum steps out of the car first, holding the hem of her pink dress off the ground. She really is beautiful. I open Gran's door and help her out; her hand is warm and dry in mine.

People are milling around outside—Gran's friends from bridge, neighbors, Marigold's relatives from Sweden. Gran lets go of my hand after a minute and walks fearlessly inside ahead of us.

Mum and I wait at the entrance for Dad and Marigold. Gran immediately starts chatting with the officiant, a balding guy in a three-piece suit who blushes under her attention.

I'm wearing the same navy-blue jacket and skinny tie I wore to Dad's gallery show last year. It's cool, but a little tight in the shoulders. I worry, for the thousandth time, that it makes my head look overly large.

"What time is it?" Mum asks anxiously.

I check my watch. "Five to nine."

She looks around, all stressed.

I peek ahead of us at her masterpiece. There's sheer material draped around the backs of the wooden pews, candles in candelabras at the end of each row. Roses in every color are bunched, woven, strewn and hung on every surface, draping the room in sweet.

Marigold should be here any minute.

Mum sucks in a breath. "I hope your father finds it okay."

He's only "my father" when Mum thinks he's poised to monumentally screw up.

"He was here yesterday for the rehearsal," I point out.

She ignores me. "What if he takes a wrong turn and goes over the bridge? What if he ends up in Coorparoo?"

"Then he'll turn around."

Mum looks aghast, as though a more appropriate response would have been, "Well, then we'll all die."

"Are you okay?" I ask. "You look kind of . . ."

She stares at the altar blankly. "I quit my job yesterday."

My eyes pop.

"Stepped down, technically," she clarifies, looking at me apprehensively. "But, yes."

"Wow. That's . . ." I chew my lip. "That's big."

Mum drops her shoulders and switches her bouquet to the other hand. "I love my work, Hen, you know I do, but lately I've just needed *balance*. Between it and the other three loves of my life. Dad and I have stuff we want to do, you know? And maybe I'm not cut out for being at home, maybe I'll miss work or be bored or realize I actually hate cooking. I at least want to remember who I am without it, just for a bit . . . Oh, what do you think?"

Mum's eyes are wide blue worlds, waiting for my opinion.

(When I was really small, I used to think you could see everything in them.)

"I think you're gonna be absolutely fine."

She drags me into a sudden fierce hug, rose thorns poking my shoulder.

"I knew there was a reason I love you."

"Yeah." I smile. "Just the one, though."

The others arrive exactly three minutes late. Mum looks about ready to go nuclear but takes her place up at the altar.

Marigold walks down the aisle in silver suit pants and a billowy blouse that's untucked at the back, with black shoes I want to borrow. She carries a big bouquet the same as Gran's.

I cry. We all do. Dad is the worst; the videographer has to lean over at one point and hiss for him to be quiet.

Gran talks of love and loss and the fluidity of life; Marigold makes good-natured jokes at Gran's expense before telling her she's the most beautiful thing she's ever seen.

I get up and shakily recite the Rilke quote. In the end, I went with the one he chose, about adjoining souls and love being an exercise in protecting each other's solitude. I've rehearsed the shit out of it, but I can still *feel* the words while I'm saying them.

I look for him, then. I can't help it.

My eyes scan the crowd, coming up empty at first . . . and then they snag on his.

He's wearing gabardine pants with a black jacket over the top, which makes his gold hair lucent in comparison.

(And I just . . . Why does he have to look like that in a suit?)

He holds my gaze for a moment too long and my throat aches. I swallow and look away.

When the simple ceremony is over, their glasses clink together on the kiss. Gran dips Marigold down so low she almost snaps her in half. Goldie blushes when she jolts back upright. She shakes her head reprovingly, but her smile is huge.

270

Outside, the sun is bright and fierce over our heads. Mum marshals us together in the small garden for family photos, pulling Len along behind her.

When he lifts up his camera, I grit my teeth, settling in for the worst.

Len snaps some pictures of the happy couple before waving us all in to stand fanned around them. Briskly and without making eye contact, he directs me to stand with Mum and Gran, Gran and Goldie, Dad and Ham.

He's careful and clinical, but being under his lens feels like touching. There's a ring on his index finger I haven't seen before. I'm trying so hard to not to stare at him again that I probably look constipated in every single shot.

We finally pile into the car to head to the reception, ferrying across to the riverside restaurant owned by an old friend of Marigold's.

It's sparsely decorated, filled with ornate light fixtures and long tables arranged around wide windows with a sweeping view of the bridge. The appetizers are already out by the time we arrive. Ham makes a beeline for them immediately, stuffing two sausage rolls in his cheeks.

I can feel Len in my periphery, taking candids of guests by the bar on the opposite wall. I follow Ham and load my plate with enough spring rolls to feed a small family.

I find my seat at the bridal table next to Mum and plant myself down, then commence eating my feelings.

At Gran's request, there aren't any speeches (she made the grave mistake of having an open mic at her first wedding).

The cake is cut early, and the bar tab runs for the entire party.

By four o'clock, everyone is *quite* merry, including Gran, who holds Goldie hostage waltzing for a solid hour. The dance floor quickly becomes packed—Mum and Dad break it down to "Greased Lightnin'," and Ham joins them for a hideously loud Nutbush.

I eat my fancy brownie dejectedly. I've always enjoyed weddings—the sense of promise that comes from them, witnessing lurve up colorful close. It used to give me hope that one day I'd understand what they were all going on about.

Turns out, weddings are intolerable when you actually are in love. Hopelessly unrequitedly so, anyway.

All the happy couples seem to be rubbing their joy in my face like proverbial sandpaper.

I bump into Len when I get up to get more cake. He's holding a rum and Coke and talking to a leggy graduate student of Gran's. I ignore both of them and the lightning bolt in my chest.

I sit back down, eat more chocolate buttercream, and chase it with wine.

I'm three glasses and another brownie deep before I notice he's still talking to her. They've floated outside, him smiling slow and pausing every now and then to take more candids.

After a while, I stand up and mill around the edge of the dance floor. The DJ's taking requests. I manage to walk straight toward him, looking over my shoulder again at the snap of Len's ringed finger on the shutter button.

I take a deep breath that's at severe risk of becoming a burp, and ask for "Lucky You" by The National, just to be a dick.

I regret it almost immediately, because: a) I remember with painful clarity the last time he and I listened to it, one earbud each; and b) Gran materializes out of the ether and shouts, "Young people music!"

272

She hurtles toward me before I can get away.

"My favorite grandson, the one who never has any fun," Gran slurs. "Come and dance, Henry!"

Goldie appears to still have her wits about her at least. She shushes Gran, squeezing her hand reproachfully. "Come on, Ris—how about we go and peek at the guest book?"

"Look—Lennon's fun." Gran points at him, eyes still on me and lit with mischief. "Dance with him."

The first verse rolls into being. I turn around; sure enough, he's standing by the cake table changing lenses. His face tells me he's heard every word.

I will the floor to open up underneath me. "Gran, I don't—"

"Dance!" she orders.

I widen my eyes at her—*I know what you're doing*—but she just giggles.

Marigold mouths *sorry* at me and pulls Gran away.

When I look up, Len's got one hand burrowed in his pocket, and he's holding the other out to me.

I glare at it, arms still folded. "What are you doing? No."

"Come on," he says in an echo of a hundred other times from another life. His gaze is tipsy. "Let's have some *fun*."

I roll my eyes but take his hand because I'm nothing if not pathetic.

We fumble for position, Matt Berninger singing us in, until I've got one claw-hand clamped awkwardly on his bicep. Len slides his hand to the small of my back. We're standing so far apart it's hard to move.

"You're gonna have to come closer," he murmurs.

I check if anyone's looking. It's getting late; just us and half-a-dozen elderly couples on the dance floor. The other guests at their gossamer tables are royally plastered. Mum and Ham are asleep in their chairs. I sigh and give in, closing the gap between us.

He brings our hands up gently, his left and my right.

When we touch, it's fireworks rattling in a cage even though there's no matches left. His face tightens like he feels it too.

"We don't have to," I say. "If you don't want. Gran's gone."

He tightens his grip. "Don't be dumb."

I can feel each of his fingers splayed out on my back. "I just meant—"

"Relax. I want to."

(What does *that* mean?)

The chorus crashes in, and then we're dancing.

He takes the lead easily, stepping us around in a square by the window. Somehow, he manages to keep me from getting tripped up by my feet. We move together, swaying gently.

His torso's warm against mine. I feel him take in a deep breath before he leans into me fully. I close my eyes and take his weight.

The last few weeks disappear. My world shrinks to a tinkling musical bridge. The lights on the Story Bridge switch from blue to red to green on the river outside.

After a while I let my cheek rest against his hair, because why not, if this is the only time I'll ever get to dance with him?

The song crescendos around us. I do my best to breathe unobtrusively, wanting to prolong the spell.

His nose nudges along my shirt collar and up to my neck.

He rests there, inhaling, and *what*?

This is seriously passing even my threshold for PDAs, but I don't move.

Len shifts slightly until his lips are pressed against my skin, just below my ear. Once. Twice. It's so soft I'm not sure it happened.

My hand tightens in his. I think: *bastard*. I think: *do it again*.

Then he steps back, gently setting my arms down by my sides.

He stares at me for so long I don't know how my face doesn't burst open. His eyes are foggy, like he's dreaming and unsure whether to wake up or see it through.

The song's over.

I reach out a hand to him. But he's walking away, and I'm watching him go. Wondering if either of us will even remember this in the morning.

25

Any delusions I've harbored about being over him disappear completely. I go into full Bella-Swan-in-*New-Moon* wallowing.

I look for him.

Constantly.

(Even more than before, now that our days of being in the same place are numbered.)

I don't talk to him, though.

From what I can tell, he's still spending most of his time in the art room working on his final project. I don't even see him at lunch, except occasionally just after the bell's rung, striding across the grass with a frame tucked under each arm.

I know he's gunning for the gallery show, but it feels like a worrying level of dedication for someone who's supposed to be "fine."

The countdown to graduation hits single digits in what seems the blink of an eye. People always say that, but it's true. I don't know where the last six months—or twelve years—have gone, but they are, and so are we. Almost.

We won't find out our final exam results until the holidays, and uni offers aren't until January, so we're all caught in this teetering limbo, staring over the edge at whatever's next.

The end comes nothing like I thought it would. I always pictured it differently when I thought of finishing school. I thought I'd be older, wiser, with the next ten years of my life planned out in meticulous detail.

(I pictured us together.)

───────

The last week is the fastest. It's stiflingly hot, the airplane-like hum of air conditioners a constant backing track while our teachers rack their brains for things for us to do.

There's a football scrimmage I don't go and see, because I'm not a masochist. They play dude movies about dudes playing various sports in the auditorium instead of math. Ms. H. makes us perform one last Shakespeare excerpt for her. I pick the tomb scene from *Romeo and Juliet*, because it feels most appropriate to summarize this year.

(Thus with a kiss I die.)

We clean the desks in our homerooms until there's barely a trace of us left.

The seniors have Leadership Day on the last day of the year. My entire grade is herded into an abandoned staff room above shit block. The Sniffer pulls out all the stops and hires a guy from some organization that specializes in team building to keep us occupied.

There's a lengthy video from the nineties to start, all about capital-V *values*. We do actual trust exercises for a while afterwards, Vince falling back heavily in my arms.

"Ow! Catch harder, Hamlet. God."

I grunt and shove him upright. "How does one *catch harder?*"

"Like this," says Ged, yanking Harrison sharply backwards by his blazer. Just before he hits the deck, Ged sticks his hands roughly through Harrison's armpits and his knee into the small of his back.

"Catching, not impaling!" Harrison snaps, rubbing his tailbone and glaring at Ged.

After that, things get serious. For the middle session, a projected boxy word art heading appears on the whiteboard that reads GOING DEEPER.

"Christ," Ged says under his breath.

The facilitator dims the lights and asks us to all sit cross-legged on the stained crimson carpet.

"What would you say," he opens once we're quiet, stroking his goatee pensively, "if I told you that you don't really know anybody in this room?"

No one answers him.

"The answer I was looking for was . . . enlighten me! Which will be our theme for this afternoon. *Enlightening* your peers about your freshly minted young-adult selves, before you step out into the rest of your lives."

The room is a groan.

"A theme within a theme," I whisper to Vince. "Excellent."

"Kill me." He shakes his head. "Seriously."

We split off into groups—the Boiyss gravitate together out of habit, save for one.

I (stealthily) find Len in my periphery. He's expressionless but very bright, sitting back on his hands with one leg crossed over the other two groups down from us. Green socks.

Goatee man hands out butcher paper. "I want you to reflect on how you've grown this year," he says, weaving through the groups and narrowly avoiding the several rogue legs attempting to trip him over. "Perhaps focus on writing down one thing you've learned, and one thing you regret."

The next communal groan has a lot of swear words in it, but we half-heartedly do as we're told. I grip my pen, unsure what to write.

Ged writes, *luv hurts but life doesnt always. Keep trak of ur illegal tackles.*

Vince writes, *Emo isn't a look, it's a feeling* and *not causing more anarchy* then grins when I pull a face.

Harrison puts, *productive/destructive.*

In the end, I go with, *take the path of least resistance,* purely because it fits both categories.

We sit looking down at our writing scratched into the crumpled yellow page. It's not much; it's a lot. The sum of this world that's about to be over. A full stop.

Then we watch the final scene from a football movie to round out the message of growth, and Goatee dismisses everyone for a quick lunch break.

I don't let myself look at Len again, but I do volunteer to stay back and clean up all the pieces of paper so I can perve-puzzle over his answer.

I roll the sheet from his group into my hands until I hit his familiar handwriting. All I can see without being totally conspicuous is *CORDIUM*.

(Huh?)

I stare at the letters until they blur, then give up being stealthy and twist the paper around so I can see what he's put next to it: *COR*.

Is that Latin? I recognize it but don't remember where from.

My brain sifts through memories haphazardly, until it lands on our term-one poetry unit: Percy Shelley's grave.

I scrunch the paper harder in my hands for a second. That's all he took away from this entire year? Really? The romantic stylings of Percy Bysshe Shelley?

I think we had an argument about Shelley and *cor cordium*. I put forth . . . what was it? That his friends just wanted something cool to whack on the headstone? That it was an overdramatic sainting of the dead.

Len totally took me down. He said it was meant to be a summary of the way Shelley lived, what he believed. Because it means . . . "heart of hearts."

Everyone starts filing back into the stuffy Trust Growth Sharing Room. I hastily shove the papers away in a cupboard.

"For this final hour," Goatee man intones, "I want you to share what you wrote in the last—what you've learned this year. Introduce yourself, your pre-adult self, to your peers."

I fidget, crossing and uncrossing my legs. My mind's spinning off the charts while everyone gets up on "stage" (a theatre block shoved against the wall) one by one.

Most guys take the piss, apart from Martin Finch, who makes such a go of congratulating himself he's lucky not to get laughed offstage.

Jake Clarkson's is a litany that ends with, "Yeah. I learned I'm a total legend, basically."

Harrison and Vince refuse to read theirs. Ged gives a brief spiel about football and girlfriends and passing biology, and then it's my turn.

Walking up to the front, I'm thinking about Percy Shelley.

I'm thinking about Len, and all these sweaty bodies between us.

I picture this week as a full stop.

I picture Seth Cohen.

A thought strikes me. I grab its rope, and then I'm climbing up on stage. Clambering, really. It's definitely more difficult at North than it looked in Orange County. I almost fall.

When I look out at my grade with their uniforms already half taken off, I think that Goatee man has it wrong. These aren't my peers. They're just people—most of whom don't matter and maybe never did.

"Ahem." I'm projecting my voice but it still cracks a bit, for the first time in my high school public speaking life. "Oi!"

"Go ahead, son," Goatee says encouragingly. "Tell us what you've learned."

"Um," I start. "I just, er, just wanted to address something."

"What'd he say?" someone hisses from a group near the front.

"I think he wants to do one of his captain speeches."

"Didn't they just elect the new one?"

"God. So far up himself he can't even see."

I take a deep, deep breath. Down to my feet. "Er, no," I say. "Not quite. I just want to share something I ..." Pause, swallow. "Learned."

I look out at the sea of faces for the one I need. Len's eyes meet mine. Green-blue-gray.

I take another breath. "We've been told a lot this year about figuring out who we are. And I still don't have any of the answers I wanted. I actually don't even think it's possible to *have* answers at this point. Only questions. But I learned this year that the thing about questions is we get to choose the ones we ask ourselves."

Most people in the crowd are either pissed off or amused.

A few guys nudge each other and laugh.

Len doesn't. After a beat, he inclines his head slightly. *Go on, then.*

I square my feet. "Um. I'm Henry Hamlet."

"We know that, dumb-arse!" someone shouts. Then it's dead quiet; everyone's listening.

"I'm a Capricorn," I say clearly. "I'm into writing, and debating, and . . ." (Oh god, Seth Cohen's elevator pitch had Death Cab for Cutie and mine's *debating*, but there's no turning back now.) "Kissing boys."

My heart is the only sound in the world.

"I mean, technically it's just the one, so far. Not that that's important. He is, though. Important. The important part is I liked—*like*—him, as more than a friend, by a lot. And the only bit about it I regret is keeping him in the back of my head for so long."

I look at Len again.

He's watching me so steadily.

"So—yeah." I let out a breath that's almost a laugh. "That's me. That's what I learned. Thanks, I guess."

When I brave another glance at the crowd, there's a collective domino effect of frowns and "whatthefucks," but it's peppered, unless I'm imagining things, with a sort of begrudging respect.

Eamon Matthews claps. Jake Clarkson's mouth is hanging wide open. Travis Burrell's too. Ged's standing up, Harrison trying to pull him down. Vince looks like he just won a bet. Goatee man is frozen.

Ms. Hartnett is by the door with her laptop poised on her knees. Her hands are cupped on both cheeks, as though she's trying to stop her smile from flying off into the popcorn ceiling.

Len hasn't moved.

My victory haze fans back like the Red Sea, awareness creeping in. Of how high up I am and the fact that I've just effectively outed myself, and like ... declared my feelings in front of all of grade twelve, *after we broke up.*

It's so silent you could hear a chicken nugget drop.

There's no sweet music, no fade-out to credits like Seth had. Just the twin realizations of how many eyes are on me, and the fact that someone is definitely going to have to help me get down.

There's movement at the back of the room. Len stands up and walks toward me. Purposefully, with his face set.

Everyone's unwillingly transfixed, like we're an amateur theatre performance that just got really good.

Len reaches up and takes my hand. Holds it. Then I'm back on the ground.

Ms. Hartnett jumps up. "All right everyone, off to period six! Come on—the bell's about to ring."

"But Miss!" Clarkson says.

"Out!" Ms. H. forcefully herds him and the rest of the boys away.

I look at Len. His jaw is tense, a hundred different things playing across his face. "Alarm" is probably the one I'd pick if I had to choose. Me too.

He's still holding my hand.

Then the bell rings, and he spins away to go to class.

I stare after him for a bit, my head humming humming humming.

Goatee man looks like he's about to talk to me so I walk out too. I have a study period next, so there's no one to miss me while I regather my wits in the corridor.

IsaiditIsaiditIsaidit.

It'sout.

The world didn't end.

But it's still taking my bones a while to snap back into place. Eventually I make it to the library. I slip into one of the far tables unnoticed, leaning against a bookshelf and breathing hard. There's a weight missing from my chest; I can't decide, yet, exactly how it feels.

I pull out my notebook and pretend to write. Then I check my phone for the time.

I don't let myself think about him.

What he must be thinking. What I said. The way I said it.

My hand burns dully where he touched it. Then someone else touches it, and I jump out of my seat.

"Aaah!"

"Henry," says Martin. He's standing behind me mottle-cheeked and urgent.

"*Finch?*"

"May I speak with you?" he asks, eyes intense.

"O . . . kay?"

We stare at each other in mutual unease, before shuffling over to the deserted nonfiction section. The librarian is watching us beadily, so we shift farther back, toward a banner reading *I Love Geo.*

I dig my hands into my pockets and cough. "Uh. Sup?"

If I had any adrenaline left, it'd join the party around now, but I feel like a deflated balloon. I want to go home. Whatever this shit show is going to entail, it had better be quick.

Martin pulls an atlas off the shelf. It's got a blown-up picture of an iceberg on the front, a tiny peaked white top sticking out of the water and masses of fluorescent blue underneath. He flips through it for a bit before sliding it back into place.

"I wanted to say . . ."

I tense and wait.

"I never knew you had that much *depth* to you," he says in a shocked rush. "Or any."

I raise my eyebrows as high as they'll go. "Are you joking right now?"

"No!"

"Or just . . . weirdly trying to insult me?"

"No. Sorry! That's not what I meant!" Martin looks as horrified by this situation as I feel.

"What I mean is," he pushes on, "it was really . . . brave, what you just said. Did. Out there. It was sort of incredible, actually. I mean, I've never felt that way about anyone, not even close. And I just wanted to come and tell you that."

"What?"

"I always thought you were just a pretentious, argumentative bastard," Martin continues, moving his head from side to side in disbelief. "And god, I'm . . . sorry, I suppose. That I didn't look harder for what was underneath."

I gape at him.

"You never do know the full extent of someone, huh?" he says. "We're all icebergs." Then he sticks out a hand so sincerely that his blazer sleeve slips and gets stuck to his chunky watch.

Martin Finch is extending the literal hand of friendship.

Maybe the world did end, after all.

Cautiously, I reach out and shake his hand. My palm is sweaty, and he doesn't even say anything.

"I mean, I *am* all those things you said," I stammer stiffly, trying to tether this back to some semblance of reality. "As well as . . . you know. Having depth or whatever."

Martin shrugs. "And I *am* an insufferable know-it-all."

"You heard that?"

"A few times. I have a bit of an eavesdropping problem."

"I'm sorry too. And sorry, you know—that I beat you for captain."

"Nah."

"You deserved it more."

He smiles a bit. "I think what you just did sort of disproves that."

"Um . . . thanks," I say.

"We're not going to be, like, *bros* now, are we?" Martin jokes.

I smile a bit too. "Definitely not."

He turns to go back to class, then stops. "It's been a pleasure hating you, Henry."

"Back at you, Fin—Martin."

26

"You're going."

"I'm not."

"You are!"

"I'm not! I don't need to."

"Yes, you bloody well are, and yes, you bloody well do."

"Billie," Dad interrupts. "I don't know if this is the most productive way to handle things."

I've decided, in retrospect and after sleep, that going to graduation is impossible. I'm sweltering in my bed underneath all the pillows in the house, a tiny breathing hole my only means of communication.

"What do you suggest?" Mum is whisper-yelling at Dad in the hallway. "Our son is graduating from high school today—we can't just allow him to not go."

"I agree," Dad says soothingly. "I just think a bit of sensitivity—"

"I am being sensitive!" She's whisper-shrieking now.

"Guys," I say. "You realize I can hear everything you're saying."

"Good!" Mum snaps. "Then you can—"

"I'll handle it," Dad cuts her off.

Mum makes a frustrated sound but retreats downstairs. "Hamish! Are you dressed?"

The bed creaks as Dad sits down. I stay under my pillows, which I plan to keep doing for the entire night.

(Possibly for the rest of my life.)

"Hen," he says tentatively. "Can you come out for a minute, mate?"

I heave a giant sigh and move the pillow covering my face aside. "I can't go, Dad."

Dad pats my foot. "Why not?"

I pull the pillow back over my face and stare into the cotton until it burns my eyes.

After intense deliberation, I mumble, "I don't want to see him."

"Who?"

"*Len.* Okay?"

Dad shifts at the end of the bed. "What's he done? I know you've had some kind of fight, but surely—"

I sit up, rogue pillows falling to the floor. "He didn't do anything! *I* did."

"You're gonna have to unpack that one a bit more."

I breathe out hard through my nose.

Dad folds his hands, the same hands as mine, under his chin. "Tell me."

"That your shirt is offensively bright for nightwear?" I stall.

He blinks, unaffected. Dad genuinely doesn't care what anyone thinks. It's why his art is so good.

"Give me something here, champ. I'm trying."

I look up at the stars on the ceiling.

"Len," he prompts quietly, and my gut twists. "Am I allowed to ask about it yet?"

I sit up straighter and rub my eyes under my glasses. "You can ask."

"Okay!" he says, rallying. "Okay. So . . . ?"

"Um . . . yesterday I sort of . . . told everyone. About me. About us."

Dad's eyebrows mash together. "Was it a secret?"

"Have you forgotten where I go to school?" I snap. "You can't just *be gay*. Especially if you're school captain, and about to deliver the keynote freaking speech. And it's over now anyway, for good I think, even though I said . . . So it doesn't even *matter*! Any of it."

Dad frowns deeper, but he doesn't interrupt my tirade.

"Sorry," I say, flopping back down on my pillows. "I'm a shit. It's just . . ." I trail off, and we sit there together for a while. When I can't stand it any longer, I slap my hands against the duvet.

"You see, right? I can't possibly go tonight."

I finally look at Dad, and he's making a face.

"But . . ."

"What?" I exclaim. "There's no 'but' here. You don't say things you wouldn't say to someone's face *publicly*, and then just rock up a day later."

Dad's got his Yoda look on now. "Don't you think that's exactly why you *should* go?"

"Um—no. I do not."

"If," Dad says, "you stay here holed up in your pillow fort, you won't see Len again. For who knows how long. What's *he* gonna think of that?"

(Don't start making sense *now* of all moments, old man.)

"You should show up," he finishes. "Whatever else has happened."

I exhale again. "I really can't."

"You really can," he says with certainty, leaning over to squeeze my shoulder. "You're the son of the Reubenator."

"I don't have my stuff ready," I protest.

Dad just points to my uniform hanging on the door. He's even polished my shoes.

"Billie!" he calls downstairs. "Start the car."

———

I rush to meet Martin outside the auditorium at four-thirty. It's still blaringly hot, the day showing no signs of ending. I haven't checked my messages, so I don't know if the Boiyss are here yet.

"Henry!" Martin calls when he sees me. "I knew you'd show."

"Er. Hey."

"Everything's pretty much set up." He gestures to the stage, the house banners backdrop, the rows of seating on the floor.

"Cool. Thanks."

(I think we're friends. How is that even possible?)

The Sniffer strides through the side entrance. Martin takes one look at his face and melts away, back through the stage curtains.

"Hamlet! Where in the name of the Christ child do you suppose you've been?"

"Sorry, sir, I—"

"Had an existential crisis about some personal matters," he says briskly. "I heard."

I freeze. "You did?"

He pulls a list and a pen from his pocket absently, checking things around the room and ticking them off. "Yes. I expect everybody did."

290

I'm going to kill Dad for making me come here.

I tap my foot rapidly inside my shoe. "Er, right. Do you not want me to speak tonight, then?"

The Sniffer's beady eyes snap up. After a couple of seconds, his brow furrows in understanding.

"Oh, for the love of god," he mutters wearily. "I confiscate your infernal telephones a few times and you all think I'm an ogre. No. Your private life is your business. You are the leader of the student body—you give the farewell address."

"But won't the parents and bigwigs, or—"

"Hamlet," he cuts me off. "Do you know how many years I've worked in boys' education?"

I shut my mouth and shake my head.

"Enough that nothing—and I do mean nothing—shocks me, or even touches the edges at this point. You *will* deliver the best speech of your life tonight, as planned. Capisce?"

"Was . . . was that a joke, sir?"

It feels like I've entered a parallel universe. The sky should be at our feet.

He actually winks. Sort of. "Now go and make sure Finch has everything in order!"

―――――――――

Mum, Gran, Marigold, Dad, and Ham are all sitting front row when I take my position onstage with the rest of 12C fifteen minutes later.

Everything *seems* normal. We're all supposed to sit here in silence, while the school song drones through the speakers on repeat. I search again for the Boiyss.

The ceremony is meant to kick off at five, if the teachers go by the timetable Martin drew up.

I don't let myself check if *everyone* from my homeroom is present until ten-to.

I scan the heads. He's not here.

I'm glad, really. Len's not the one under fire—people have known about him, at least in whispers, for years. He's dated enough girls that no one asks about the rest.

Ged must be sitting somewhere behind me, because I can't see him either. I'm extremely grateful Clarkson's in 12B. Everyone's definitely staring a bit.

At five minutes to five, the last few gray and red blazers trickle in through the side doors. I don't look up—I'm busy counting the cracks in the linoleum floor (fifty-seven) to stop my hands from shaking—but I feel it when someone sits down in the empty chair beside me.

I stiffen immediately, allowing myself a precautionary glance at his shoes.

Pointed, with nonregulation socks. I look up.

Len makes himself comfortable in the chair, not even bothering to stop his elbow from brushing mine.

The seating plan is alphabetical. He must have swapped with someone. This is calculated. I look behind us; about a third of the class is muttering to each other and watching us.

He shifts his arm so that it rests on the back of my chair. Not around me, exactly, or even romantic. Loose and best-friendly. He throws a corrugated-iron glance at the mutterers.

Not just calculated, I realize—it's a statement. He is, publicly, daring them to fuck with me. Which they won't, not if we're a package deal. Lennon and Hamlet, back for one last hurrah.

I love you, I think, louder than I've ever thought anything.

The Sniffer strides onstage, turning on the mic and commencing his opening address. It's the same, word for word, as the one he gave last year. (I know, because I proofed it for him then as one of my captaincy candidate acts of kiss-arsery.)

"And so," he finishes, finally going off script. "Let us celebrate this, our graduating class for 2008. May they go forth as world-shakers, leaders, iconoclasts, and above all, individuals of integrity, judgment, and merit."

The academic awards pass by in a blur—I get two, Len three. The cheers for us coming from the stage are pretty lackluster, but Gran hoots and hollers so loud it's almost imperceptible. Martin is valedictorian, and I'm genuinely happy for him.

As the bronze academic awards wind down, my hands are fists on my knees in anticipation of the speeches. Len looks down at them like he wants to unfurl them himself.

(Wishful thinking, Hamlet. Focus.)

Martin grabs the microphone from Mr. Schiffer and waits for me by the lectern. He's wearing his version of a steely look—ready to take over if need be, I expect. I shake my head slightly; I've made it this far.

He hands me the mic, and I position it under my chin, the way I have every week of the year. I breathe in, imagining it's one of those times—mundane and low stakes—and begin.

"Good evening parents, teachers, guests, and fellow NGS graduates."

(That wasn't so hard. Now what?)

I give the speech. I couldn't tell you afterwards what I spoke about, but speak I do, and pretty well at that. Generic stuff about the end of childhood, thanks to our parents and teachers, etc. Martin and I banter back and forth—genuinely, this time. There's polite tittering laughs throughout, and it ends before I have time to remember I wanted it to.

Mr. Schiffer gives me a brusque nod for a job well done, and I go back to my seat.

This is it. The end smells like polyester rugs and two hundred bodies under the hot breath of old studio lights.

The final item on the agenda is the big-ticket awards—for mateship, overall achievement, sport, and spirit. I'm so relieved nothing went wrong in the speech that I'm not even listening as they rattle off the nominees for each.

A guy I swear I've never seen before takes mateship. Martin gets overall achievement. I tense when they get to sport—Len won that last year.

"Lennon Cane."

There's a faint sprinkling of unsurprised applause when he gets up, sheepish, to grab the trophy. He looks at me, right as they're taking the posed picture of him and Mr. Schiffer. I throw him a thumbs up.

Spirit is last, because it's the most lucrative—awarded to the boy who best embodies the school motto. I slump in my seat a little. At the start of the year, which feels several planets away, I'd set my sights on this one. It's normally awarded to one of the captains as a kind of farewell gesture. *Normally.*

I half hope they'll let Martin have it, just for the irony. Or some other faceless person. As long as it's not Jake bloody Clarkson, I'll deal.

Mr. Schiffer unfurls the envelope, and squints down at the name. "Henry Hamlet," he says in my head.

Except everyone's sort of staring at me.

294

I look over at Mr. Schiffer. He's staring too.

Len, standing beside him, mouths *congrats.*

I stand up somehow, even though my legs feel like pad thai noodles plugged into the sockets. I walk over and take the trophy, the faux-gold almost slipping through my clammy fingers.

The auditorium is quiet—the click of the shutter when they take the picture reverberates through the entire room.

Mum and Dad stand up, clapping furiously. Gran whistles. Len and Martin join in, as do the faculty onstage. Slowly, it spreads down through the parents and alumni into ringing applause.

Officially, without a doubt, the weirdest twenty-four hours of my life.

Because this is Brisbane, and trees are dying, there's no paper diplomas to give the night a conclusion. We're all just loosely dismissed to the soupy air of the quad, where there's party pies and sausage rolls and sweaty parents checking their watches every few minutes.

I'm edgy and ready to quit while I'm ahead. To be done for good. Mum insists on staying for half an hour to say goodbye to people she hasn't spoken to for years.

"Proud of you," Dad says quietly, bumping my shoulder with his. "I mean it."

"I'm starving!" Ham announces, and they disappear in search of pies.

Ms. Hartnett catches me on her way out. She's in full academic regalia, complete with a consequent sheen of sweat. "Congratulations, Nick Carraway! I voted for you, you know."

"Oh! Er, thanks. I didn't think . . ."

She touches my shoulder lightly. "Your speech yesterday confirmed it was the right choice."

"You were my favorite teacher!" I tell her, realizing I might not get another chance. "Really. You're great."

"You were my favorite too." She winks. "Best luck, Henry. I hope you'll write more—you have it in you."

A parent grabs her elbow then, and she's gone.

I stand by the auditorium door, soaking it in. The last time I'll ever be here, in the snug hold of this itchy gray ensemble. It feels surreal.

Also, I have to pee.

I peel myself off the wall and head for the bathrooms by the art block, which are always slightly less like a scene from a horror movie than the rest. They're also more isolated.

"Hamlet!" someone calls from behind me.

I start, but it's only Ged.

Vince and Harrison run up behind him.

"We tried to find you today," Harrison says breathlessly.

At the same time, Vince says, "I figure if you were going to try and snog me, you'd have done it by now."

My chest squeezes.

I look at them, leaving Ged for last.

"It's shitty that you lied to us," he says. "And I don't really wanna watch you kiss dudes. But you can, and you're still my mate. Okay? Forevs."

Vince elbows him hard in the ribs.

"What?" Ged hisses at him. "I didn't say anything bad!"

"What the hell was that last bit?"

"We don't think you lied," Harrison tells me hastily, forever the peacekeeper.

"I kind of did." I shrug. "To myself, anyway."

Harrison frowns. "We're shit friends for not getting it."

My throat constricts. "Nah. It's—"

"It's not fine!" Vince exclaims. "We're meant to have your back. Be your—"

"Boiyss," Ged finishes quietly. "North strong all day long."

"Oh man," I say, laughing, and then I do cry a bit, but no one sees because they're huddling around me, and Vince and Harrison are patting me on the back hard and awkward.

Then Ged says, "You can kiss dudes in front of me if you want!"

I shove him away. "Yeah. I'm not gonna do that."

"You totally *could*, if that's what you—"

"Shut up, Ged," Vince cuts him off.

"Speaking of," Harrison says suddenly, looking over my shoulder.

I turn back toward the quad. The familial groups are dwindling, but there's one I recognize, standing spaced apart by the drinks table.

John looks different from the last time I saw him. He's not wearing a suit, for one—just a plain blue shirt rolled up over a gaudy silver watch. He's standing off to the side, glowering at Len and Lacey, but still talking to them. *At* them, his mouth shaping low rapid words.

"I'll be back," I say.

I walk across the manicured lawn, until the downlights of the quad roof wash me in white and I'm standing right behind them.

"I don't know what you're even doing here, if you're just going to be like this." Lacey sighs.

"Trying to figure out what exactly your *plan* is," John hisses, looking at Len.

"Move out, together," Len snaps, "like we've said. It's already done."

"Stop this—"

"Hey guys!" I cut John off brightly. Bolstered by the Boiyss, I feel giant.

John looks up at me. For a second he seems almost chagrined, then it passes, as quick as it came.

"Well done on your academic awards, Henri," Lacey says sincerely, drawing out a French accent.

"Yeah, well," I pipe up, my voice too loud. "Not as good as this one." I point at Len, adrenaline coursing.

Len shuffles his feet.

John doesn't say anything.

Fuck you, I think, and then I can't help it, no matter what else has happened.

I say even louder, staring hard at him so he can't look away, "Three awards is a few too many for it to be a fluke. *Far* too many for a 'no-hoper.' Don't you think, Mr. Cane?"

Lacey looks torn between amused and sad. Len looks . . . like I probably did, when he sat down beside me earlier.

John's face changes when he realizes I'm quoting him.

Caught.

"Do you really think—" he starts.

"I think you should go, Dad," Len cuts him off, so firmly that pride shoots through me. "Now."

John looks at Len as if noticing he's there for the first time. His forehead creases slowly, right down the middle. Something passes between them again. It's different this time, though. There's a different winner.

"I'm gonna bring the car around," Lacey says once he's gone.

She squeezes my arm as she leaves.

Then we stand there, just the two of us.

Looking at each other.

Len opens his mouth and closes it again, pulling one side of his lip into his teeth.

Our gazes stay locked (there should be a law against all the color in his eyes—it's greedy).

"Oi!" Ged calls from across the quad, the sound cutting through the night. "We're going to the bridge! You guys coming?"

27

I find Team Hamlet by the food table and ask if I can borrow Mum's car, ignoring Mum and Dad's not-so-subtle tag-team, "Are you going to talk to him?"

(Am I? I don't even know if he'll come.)

We meet on the bridge people used to live inside, because it's equidistant from all our houses, sitting on the railing at angles that vary in degrees of recklessness. The city blinks glittering awake in the thick dark behind us.

Vince drops something in the river as soon as we arrive.

"What was that?" Ged demands. "Cane and Harrison Ford aren't even here yet."

"It's fine," Vince says, leaning out to peer at the surface of the water, his legs swinging over the void. "Thought it might've been my phone, but it was just my wallet."

I stare up at him from where I'm sitting cross-legged on the ground. "Sorry, but—that's better how?"

"Empty, isn't it? But my phone has Matilda's number in it." Some things never change.

"Who's Matilda?" Harrison calls from behind us. He jumps over the road divider, then leans back against it with his arms folded, all cool.

Vince exhales sharply. "I met her at a gig. Remember?"

"Oh yeah." Harrison nods in faux-understanding. "All those gigs you go to."

"Wait. You mean the one from dinner at the club with your parents?" Ged says.

"What happened to kayak girl? That's what I want to know," I interrupt, catching the look on Vince's face. It's the wrong thing to say, though, because his hands ball into fists.

Boyfriend, Ged mouths, shaking his head in solidarity.

"You didn't think to maybe check that first, before you spun your great love fantasy around her?" Harrison puts in.

"It was not—" Vince starts hotly, nostrils flared. "I didn't—wait. Where's Cane?"

"Late," Ged says. "He texted that he'll defs be here, even though . . ." He looks at me very obviously. "Ah, shit."

They all eye me, tense.

I sigh. "Look, I don't want this to be weird. I can go, if you—"

"Go where?" says a smooth voice. "To hang out with all the other friends you don't have?"

Len's mouth quirks into a half-smile as he climbs up to sit beside Vince. His cheeks are red when our eyes catch, but like—maybe he had to park far away and then run here.

"*Finally*," Ged exclaims, visibly relieved to have escaped *dealing with emotion*.

"To be fair," Vince says to Len. "He's got Martin Fincharoo, now. He looked like he wanted to *hug* you when you spoke tonight, Hamlet."

"Martin's all right," Harrison and I say in unison.

Len laughs, looking at the sky and dangling black shoes over the railing.

We bicker about exams for a bit, before turning to more serious things. The things that are about to scatter us off in different directions.

Harrison's still waiting to see about his marks for engineering. Vince leaves in a week for his Euro gap year. Ged's single. The world awaits. Next time we're all together like this will be who and how knows when.

A sudden breeze whips up, concrete and river, mud and trees. "Smell that." Harrison Ford inhales.

"What—bird shit?" says Vince.

Harrison shoves his arm. "*Freedom.* I'm going to die Christmas camping on the coast for four whole weeks with my family."

"I'm your family!" Ged protests.

"Exactly."

"Still better than a year staying with my granny," Vince grumbles. "Dad's told her to straighten me out. Fuck knows what that's gonna look like."

Len and I are both quiet. Separately. Together. I'm achingly aware that it could be the last time I see him and am simultaneously not looking directly at him and memorizing his every move.

"I still can't believe it's actually over," I think, and say aloud.

"Right?" says Ged. "We did it. No more Sniffer. It's gonna be *loosey-goosey* from now on, lads."

"Speak for yourself," says Len.

I laugh by accident and turn it into a cough.

"Anyone for a cheeky vino?" Vince asks, passing around a bottle of something red and expensive-looking he pulls from his backpack.

I decline when it gets to me. I'm churned up enough inside as it is. Plus, there's been too many alcohol-related incidents in my life this year—heights and *cheeky vinos* don't strike me as a particularly winning combo.

The five of us sit under the sticky summer sky. There's a point, a few passes of the bottle later, where conversation tapers off completely.

I get this falling-feeling déjà vu. Like this moment's happened before. Already happening again. Already a memory.

A car drives past, horn blaring.

"Get off the bridge! Bloody *youths*!"

"Should we go?" Harrison asks after a beat, swinging back down onto the path.

Vince shifts his trousered legs unwillingly. "Probs."

Ged sips more wine. "Yeah."

We spend a long time saying goodbyes, punching shoulders, and promising to email, knowing we probably won't.

Harrison gets into his car first. Then Vince and Ged get into the BMW, arguing about the aux cord, and they spin away without looking back.

I stand there for a bit, holding my keys.

Len does too.

"Thanks," he says quietly. "For before."

"Oh!" I nod. "I mean, anytime."

I want to say "you too." Or "always." I don't, though. I just hope he knows.

"It was a very you way to end an argument," he continues.

I smile a bit despite myself. "Yeah. Apparently I'm dramatic. Who knew?"

He smiles too. "Crazy."

We slip into silence for a minute. His face gets the expression it did yesterday when the bell rang.

"Hamlet?" he asks.

(If you ask me about it. If you ask . . .)

"Yeah?"

"I, uh, got the gallery show thing. It's tomorrow."

"Awesome," I say, digging my hands into my pockets and trying not to look disappointed. "Congrats."

He stares at me for a stretching second, eyes fixed somewhere between the bottom of my nose and my mouth.

"Will you come?"

I blink in surprise. "To the show?"

He nods.

"Um—yeah. Okay."

They also say there's gold buried beneath this bridge. If there is, it must be directly under his feet.

"Cool. It starts at four. Vince knows where."

"Cool," I repeat. "Coolio. Um. So I'll see you there, then?"

(Coolio!?)

He gives me one last look. "See you."

———

When I get home, Mum and Dad are sitting at the table with a laptop in front of them. Dad's got his head on Mum's shoulder while she scrolls through pages. I'm not ready to be back yet, so I watch them for a bit, both of their faces bathed in baby-blue light.

"Go back to that one!" Dad says suddenly. "That's nice, Bills—we could go there."

Mum shifts to look at him. "Babe."

"What?"

"That's a nudist beach."

"And?"

She laughs. "We're meant to be looking at serious trip destinations!"

"I am," Dad says, deadpan. "I've always wanted to go no board shorts. They give me a rash because they make your balls get all sweat—"

"Oh my god." I kick the front door shut behind me. "Stop there."

Dad turns around. "Look out, it's the graduate! How'd you go with the guys?"

"Good." I pick up a chip from the bowl in front of them, ignoring Len's face in my head. "Better than I am now." I point to the screen.

Dad laughs. "There's nothing wrong with it, Hen—it's natural! Look at how free he is. *Everywhere.*"

"Do not," I warn.

"Those could be my balls," Dad continues sadly.

Mum snorts and pushes his head away, clicking the mouse to a new page.

"Ugh. Stop talking about your balls, I beg of you."

"Why?" Dad demands. "You are the fruit of my loins. My loin-fruit."

"Okay." I back away. "Definitely just threw up a bit in my mouth. I'm going to bed."

"Night, love," Mum says, reaching her hands up until I come over and kiss her cheek. I squeeze extra hard as thanks for not giving me the Spanish Inquisition.

"Sleep tight, Spew Grant!" Dad calls after me. "Happy end of childhood."

I climb the stairs. Ham's door is open, through which I can see Gran's heeled shoes dangling off the end of his bed. She's cuddling him like a stuffed animal while he snores into her hair. Goldie's asleep in the rocking chair holding eight or nine picture books in her lap.

It's pitch black in my room; I pull clothes off and crawl into bed in my underwear with the fan on full blast.

I'm too full of today to sleep. My chest is a light globe—bulbous and bright. I lie in bed, listening to Mum and Dad downstairs.

They bicker back and forth in soft voices. After a while, I hear Dad clomp across the floorboards and flick the kettle on to make tea. He scrapes mugs out of the cupboard, bumps the tea-bag jar, puffs the fridge open, and then stirs everything too loudly, as usual.

Every sound's as familiar to me as my own breath in the dark.

I wonder, suddenly, if I'll leave it soon. If next year I'll be like, "That yellow house on the street with the café at the end? The one with the leadlight windows? Yeah. That's my parents' place." Who I'd say it to. If there's people I'll know, just out there existing, while I'm lying here, staring at the ceiling.

The door flies open.

I jump and pull the covers up over my chest.

"It's not a ghost," announces Ham blearily, dragging me back to earth. "Can I come in with you? Gran smells funny."

He crawls up on the bed without waiting for an answer, then lies down horizontally and flops onto my legs.

I prod his red head with my knee. "You right there, little man?"

Ham yawns. "Yeah. Was your night good?"

"It was all right."

Pause.

"Did you see Len?"

I sit up a bit, squinting at him. "I did. Why?"

"Because he's your special favorite."

"Uh. Sure." I try not to feel the dark dropping thrill in my stomach when I think about seeing him tomorrow. "We're friends."

Ham yawns again and shakes his head once. "No, not like a friend—like a boyfriend. I heard Mum and Dad talking about it, but I don't understand why it's a sad-feelings thing."

The globe in me flickers and zaps. I squeeze the duvet with my armpits.

"Um. Well. I mean, *yes*—we were that, for a while. But sometimes . . . adults can get . . . and now we're not, anymore."

Ham rolls his face upwards, reading mine. "Oh, that is a sad-feelings thing."

I stare at him with wide eyes. "Mmm."

"You're still my special favorite," he proclaims sloppily, and then his head gets all heavy, and he's asleep.

28

Vince shows up on my doorstep the next day, wearing a lot of hairspray and his game face.

"Where's everyone else?" I'm so keyed up I might pass out.

"They're coming later."

"What—"

"Just get in," he says, shepherding me toward his car. "We're going, and I don't care what you say."

I protest, even as I'm buckling my seat belt. "Are we really sure I should—"

"Not engaging with this."

"But did he *say* . . . "

Vince just keeps his eyes fixed on the road as he drives us through the suburbs.

"He probably just did it to be polite," I say. "It'll be awkward, because he doesn't really want me there."

"Of course he bloody does!" Vince snaps. "Shut up."

I lean back with a sigh, trying not to hyperventilate.

The gallery is in Newstead, down a twisting residential street blanketed by a giant fig tree. It looks as though it used to be a house, in a former life. It's gray and clapboarded, but also very warehouse-y.

There's at least ten cars already lining the street. As always, Vince scrapes the curb slightly while parking.

It's a soft-cloudy day, humidity weighing down the air. We follow the stream of people headed for the light of the doorway.

I pause, pulse hammering. The knowledge that he's here, somewhere, makes it hard to do the walking.

"You right?" Vince asks, with uncharacteristic care.

"I'm fine."

(Potentially about to throw up, but fine.)

"You sure?"

"Yes. Perfectly fine."

(Maybe if I say it enough times, it'll be true.)

I step inside and see several exhibits, each arranged to look like a giant room. I find Len's immediately, off to the right, and steer us over.

The works are arranged in four separate sections, photographs elegantly framed and clustered together.

"Blimey." Vince blows out a breath. "Where do we start?"

I squint around, considering. Then I see: it's a story.

I walk over to the right of the entryway, to the biggest cluster of images. The first section is mostly made up of self-portraits, different images transposed over one another.

The pictures vary, moving from rigid focus to dreamy surrealism. I recognize his parents' faces, chaotically interspersed with his own. They're fighting, smiling, leaving, all captured with ruthless clarity. An extreme close-up of Sarah's face makes me flinch.

In the last picture on this wall, Len's about fourteen. He's alone, bony arm hugging his knees to his chest, camera held up to one eye. I reach out toward it instinctually, but Vince shuffles me along.

Next is a series of cityscapes, mostly as seen from over the top of the Canes' front gate. His lens gives the structures a human quality, their facades like aged faces. The view is panoramic from frame to frame—looking at them is like being inside a glass box.

The third section is a row of stand-alone portraits, black and white, equally spaced apart.

I suck in a breath. Here goes.

Vince's is first—face tipped to the left, halfway between a smile and a glare.

"Huh," he says from behind me, staring intently. "Is that really what my nose looks like? Bit beaky, isn't it?"

I leave him to stare at himself.

Harrison is next. Len's captured him smiling, with teeth—a rarity, but it means you can feel his warmth.

I move on to Ged's portrait. It's blurred slightly, giving the impression that the subject is constantly moving. His mouth is poised mid-word, which almost makes me smile. It must have been tough going getting him to shut up for more than a two-minute stretch at a time.

I dally in front of Ged for a long time, until Vince catches up with me and there's a queue forming behind us.

He steers me by the elbow to the last frame. I shift my gaze up from my feet reluctantly.

It's . . .

Not me.

My first reaction is shock, but what did I expect? Of course I'd be written out of the narrative. I feel stupid for coming here, for thinking it would be any different.

Once I let out the breath I've been holding, I can take time to appreciate it.

It's another self-portrait—color, blown up wide. Len's older, harder, the square line of his jaw more pronounced. His eyes are melted steel—impenetrable. And *sad*.

Vince touches my shoulder. "Shit. I'm sorry, mate. I thought . . ."

I shake him off. "It's fine. Better this way, actually." I turn around to face his concerned grimace. "Really," I say with false cheer. I even manage a nonchalant shrug, despite the hot feeling clogging my chest. "I'm not in his life anymore. It makes sense for me not to be up there."

(It's amazing how if you compartmentalize enough, you can say the words even as they choke you.)

Vince rubs his eyes, smearing eyeliner across one cheek. "I don't get you two. You're just pissing it all away without even putting up a fight."

"There *was* a fight," I say through clenched teeth. "That was the problem."

Vince sighs heavily. He stares off into the distance, looking at something. "If you punch on," he says wearily, "I'm not getting in the middle. I reserve the right to be an innocent bystander until one of you dies."

"What are you talking about?"

Vince gestures behind me.

I look over my shoulder and see Len standing by the last panel.

He looks good. Grown-up and sure, with his shirt tucked in and face unshaven. He pauses to rub a hand through his hair and notices me watching him.

His expression changes, features softening. Before I have a

chance to make a speedy exit, he's excusing himself from his conversation and walking over.

"I mean it," Vince says. "Standing back until it's life or death."

"Shush!"

Lennon Cane is in front of us.

"What do you think?" he asks, no preamble.

"I think it's smashing, mate," Vince pipes up. "Really wonderful. I also think I'm gonna get myself a *beveragini*."

I widen my eyes at him in protest, but he's already moving away.

"So?" Len asks quietly, looking at me as if mine is still the opinion that matters.

"Er." I shift awkwardly under his molten gaze. "It's fantastic. Your best."

His shoulders loosen up, like he's relieved. "You captured them really well," I add.

His brow furrows slightly.

"What?" I ask.

"You didn't see," he accuses.

"See what, exactly?"

He doesn't answer, just grabs me by the forearm and pulls me along, to the last wall by the door.

"It's *fine*, Len, I'm not . . ."

He drops my arm and points.

I look up. There's a cluster of smaller images bunched together, taking up the entirety of a jutting far wall I didn't see when we first came in.

They're all me.

It's a wall of Henrys.

My age varies—snapshots from over the years in no real

organized order. I'm eleven with a mouth full of braces. Eight with a book under each arm. Twelve wearing Coke-bottle glasses. Seventeen and using a wine bag as a pillow. Fifteen and smiling over my shoulder.

I'm stoic, joyous, sympathetic, irritated, laughing, hiding, flung wide open.

The color varies too—some are digitally edited to ethereal pastel, others dark and moody from his film camera. A couple are old enough to have faded a bit and curled at the corners.

"How . . ." I stammer, transfixed. "When did you do this?"

He shrugs. "I've done it forever."

I don't know what to say to that. The room feels very hot, all of a sudden. There's no oxygen when he's this close.

The last panel, the biggest, is the picture he took in September—my portrait. It's black and white like the others, and I'm sitting with one leg folded, glasses loosely gripped in one hand, the other hanging over my knee. I stare down the lens, eyes wide, mouth slightly open. It's so obvious, in that look. I'm so obvious.

I know, on some level, that this is important to him, that I'm reacting badly to something that should be good. It's selfish, but I can't sit through it—this final closing chapter.

"I'm proud of you," I force out, not looking at him. "It's brilliant, it really is, but I just . . . I have to go."

It's not far to the back door. I stride over, push it open hard with both hands, and walk out into a concrete stairwell where I collapse against the wall.

"Henry."

I spin around.

Black denim and paisley, he burns bright as the moon.

"What?"

"Just—wait."

"*Why?*"

"Can we talk for a second?"

Is that why he's here? Honorable Lennon Cane wants to now, after the fact, stage a proper goodbye? Still, I nod.

This is the kind of dark spot Vince always finds at parties, to sit and quietly judge everyone.

I picture an alternate version of this day. Everybody here, us together—*friends*. Nothing ventured and nothing ruined.

I wait for him to kick us off with a platitude. That's how proper goodbyes usually start, isn't it? He knows better than I do.

Len doesn't do that, though. He sits down on the stairs, then almost immediately stands up again and paces.

He doesn't say anything for so long that I start preparing to farewell myself for him.

Then he grabs my hand, so fast I don't see it coming.

"I miss you," he says, his voice a thin thread of sound.

All of my internal organs jump into my throat. I look down at his fingers, those bloody elegant piano-player-looking fingers, holding mine.

"Henry?"

It hurts—the way my name still sounds possessive in his mouth.

"I miss you too," I tell him unwillingly.

He looks relieved again. That can't be right.

"There've been so many times," he says rapidly. "That I wanted to call. To talk. But I didn't know if you'd want me to. I didn't know what to say. I still don't."

It's okay, a part of me wants to say. But I'm starting to wish he'd just cut to the chase.

"I'm bad at this," he apologizes. "Ask anyone."

I raise an eyebrow.

He laughs shortly. "Sorry. Bad joke."

There's a flickering light on the wall next to us. Its beam glances off the side of his worried face, over his collarbones. His eyes are wide and bright. It's an all-out battle, now, not to openly stare—a battle I'm losing.

I feel the familiar heavy longing in the pit of my stomach. Time healing wounds is such crap. All of this hasn't done anything at all to dull how much I want him.

He's still got my hand.

I should pull away, but then slowly, carefully, he moves his other hand to touch my palm. My breath hitches.

His eyes search me—to check if this is okay, I think fleetingly—but he doesn't look unsure.

He starts tracing the veins in my wrist with the tip of his middle and index fingers, feather-lightly. I stop breathing.

He pauses, testing. I don't pull away.

His fingers follow the pattern up my arm, into the crease at my elbow. He keeps doing it, back and forth, mapping, leaving a trail of fire.

"I'm sorry," he repeats.

I gulp. "Sorry for what?"

Len pushes at the front of his hair, so that it sticks up on one side. "I'm sorry I had to figure some stuff out. But you and me . . ."

Everything in me clenches like I'm waiting for gunfire. "If you're about to say you want to be friends again—"

"Shut up for a second," he begs.

I do.

"I—" He takes a breath. "I'm saying I'm in love with you."

(Stop, rewind, replay. There is no way he just said that.)

"I love you," he says it again. "So bad. God—so bad, Henry."

I can't speak.

I'm actually speechless.

He mistakes my silence for trepidation, and plows on. "I want to do this. If you still do."

When I flick my eyes up, he looks like *that's it*. Like *please*.

I step forward, then I kiss him. And kiss him. Until his face loses its surprise and he kisses back, his body opening up and wrapping around mine.

Len sighs into my mouth, and I swallow it. He grips my shoulders, knotting in the fabric of my shirt. He tries to say something else—I swallow that too.

I twist my fingers in his hair, because I can. I push him against the wall. He pushes back, neither of us giving in, lips shaping searching finding.

Len's hands are everywhere, under my clothes and under my skin and I can't—won't—breathe because that would mean letting him go.

His mouth is so serious on mine too. Heavy with everything we wouldn't say before. He bites down on my lower lip, and it takes every ounce of my (rapidly dwindling) self-control not to groan.

Len pulls away first, leaning his head back and breathing hard.

He's staring at me. I stare back. His pupils are blown-out, only a rim of gray visible around the black.

"So," I say.

He smiles slightly. I can see where his pulse is hammering at his neck.

"You literally can't even stay quiet long enough for us to have a moment, can you?"

I like the way he says "us."

"So . . ." he picks up, after a minute. "Wow."

"Oh!" I realize suddenly. "Me too. In case it wasn't obvious."

"I did kind of figure." His tone is sarcastic, but he's glowing.

"I love you too."

Len lets out a long breath.

"*Very* bad," I say without irony. "Even though that's not technically grammatically correc—"

He cuts me off with his mouth, dragging me down onto the stairs and holding my face in his hands.

If he cares that people could come out and find us here, he doesn't let on. I certainly don't care—the entire school could be sitting at our feet right now, and I wouldn't see anything but him. The entire planet. Every twisting and far-flung galaxy, from here to always.

———

"Well," I say later, when I'm pulling him to his feet. "I'm glad that's sorted. Really didn't take long at all."

I thread my fingers through his while he rolls his eyes.

"What now?"

"Everything else, Hamlet."

"Everything?"

"Yeah."

Acknowledgments

The seeds for this book first planted themselves in my mind in 2015, then became corporeal after a cemetery visit in 2018, and were polished into a Proper Thing in 2020 during a worldwide pandemic. My heartfelt thanks to the following people for safeguarding my sanity, and allowing their jokes to be shamelessly mined, over the course of that journey.

To my wonderful publisher, Clair Hume, whose warmth and love for *Henry Hamlet's Heart* shone brightly from her very first read; I'm beyond grateful to have wound up in your hands. My brilliant editor, Felicity "Speedy" "Stunning" Dunning—where to begin? Thank you for thoughtful Zoom check-ins, quality Seth Cohen GIFs, and completely reading my mind every step of the way when it came to these characters and their story. It is immeasurably better because of you. To my US editor, Karen Boss, for "getting" this book and its essence implicitly and making working through text tweaks a joy.

Thank you to the judges in my category of the Queensland Literary Awards for believing in the boys, and in me.

Parental units, Ben and Michelle—thank you for reading all the books to your (quite) precocious eldest child, and encouraging her to imagine all the stories of her own.

My beloved sisters: Caits, first and most enthusiastic reader of everything I write—you never doubted we'd one day be here, and therefore we are; and Mia, who grew up funnier than I am and patiently fielded editing questions prefaced with "as a #youth, what do you think of . . ."

To my loud and hilarious extended family, for their robust support of my big little dreams.

Thank you to Heather "Hector" "The Oracle" Ovens, who was there for every book phase with texts, love, and memes when I needed it most. All the emo Easter eggs in these pages are for you. Thanks also to Izzy Harrison, for being a stalwart life and writing champion across ten years and the seas. Told you it could be a name.

Sophie Morrison, for telling me to fight for this.

Tom "McGraw" O'Shea, for tangential discussions that made 2020 less of a hellscape: thank you, double also, truly.

Rachel Partridge, for accidentally inspiring bits of Willa and your enduring enthusiasm for both Henry and me, despite that time I quit our shared profession.

My own "Boiyss" throughout high school, particularly Emilie, Morgan, and Ashleigh, without whom 2008 wouldn't have been the black-mulleted and glorious ride it was—thanks for the (ridiculous) memories.

Sincere thanks to Will Kostakis for his apt and considered thoughts on an early draft that was, in parts, something of a garbage fire.

To Jess Cruickshank, for creating the AU cover of dreams. And Shannon Molloy, for offering such beautiful words to go on it.

To Vincent Chen for his gorgeous artwork for the US cover,

to Sarah Richards Taylor and Jon Simeon for all their work on its design, and to Shelley Isaacson for her eagle eyes.

Thank you to the entire UQP team, for all their many and varied efforts in launching my debut into the world.

Thanks also to everyone at Charlesbridge, for making this US edition happen and letting my little story that originally contained the phrase "Macca's run" resonate with you so much.

To all the students I've taught over the years for making me laugh and think and for giving me an unshakably high opinion of teenagers (even when they are one hundred percent eating up the back).

James, to whom I dedicate this book because he insisted I could do it; thank you for being my heart.

And to you, dearest reader—thanks so much for picking up my book. And for being you, exactly as you are.

Rhiannon Wilde has been telling stories for as long as she can remember—inside her head as well as during her time as a journalist, a terrible barista, and a high school English teacher in Brisbane, Australia. Rhiannon's interests include caffeine, Elton John–esque outfits, characters both real and imaginary, and the power of well-strung words to challenge and change us. *Henry Hamlet's Heart* is her first novel. Originally published in Australia, it won the Queensland Literary Awards Glendower Award for an Emerging Queensland Writer in 2019.